Blood Country

SEAN BLACK

ISBN: 151758065x
ISBN-13: 978-1517580650

COPYRIGHT

PRAISE FOR SEAN BLACK

'Sean Black writes with the pace of Lee Child, and the heart of Harlan Coben.' Joseph Finder, New York Times Bestseller (Paranoia, Buried Secrets)

'This is a writer, and a hero, to watch.' Daily Mail

'Ace. There are deservedly strong Lee Child comparisons as the author is also a Brit, his novels US-based, his character appealing, and his publisher the same.' Sarah Broadhurst, Bookseller

'Black's style is supremely slick.' Daily Telegraph

Other books by Sean Black

Byron Tibor Series
Post
Blood Country

Ryan Lock Series
Lockdown
Deadlock
Lock & Load (Short)
Gridlock
The Devil's Bounty
The Innocent
Fire Point
Budapest/48 (Short)

Malibu Mystery Series
(with Rebecca Cantrell)
'A' is for Asshat
'B' is for Bad Girls

CHAPTER ONE

CIA Headquarters
Langley, Virginia

They wanted Byron Tibor dead. What they wanted, they usually got. Perhaps not immediately, or in the manner they had first envisaged, but sooner or later.

It was Lauren Stanley's task, along with roughly a dozen other individuals spread out over the Central Intelligence Agency, National Security Agency, and State Department, to make sure it happened.

But before they could kill him, they had to find him. And that was easier said than done. Byron Tibor didn't want to be found.

That morning, Lauren finally had some good news. After months of dead ends and wild-goose chases, there was a solid lead.

She took a sip of juice, and looked away from her screen, then turned back to the man's face on it in front of her. It was a low-resolution frame grab taken two weeks previously from a security camera in a Greyhound bus station at Corpus Christi in the Texas panhandle. Even with high-end image-enhancement software, it was hard to tell whether or not it was Tibor.

She moved back to the video footage, hoping to find something more concrete. Maybe the original data analyst at the NSA had missed a trick. She took a sip of juice (substituting carrot, apple and kale juice for coffee was her slender attempt to retain some sense of being healthy while pulling twelve-hour shifts at her desk), then ran back and forth through the footage.

Twenty minutes later she circled back to the same solitary frame grab. The analyst had been correct. That was the best they had – a partial view of his face in profile. It was as if Tibor was in possession of some kind of supernatural power that allowed him not only to know the location and angle of every security camera he passed but automatically to adjust his movement and posture to minimize his facial exposure.

Lauren supposed that this apparent ability might have, in some way, confirmed that this was their target. She knew from the file that he was (correction: had been) one of their most experienced operatives. You didn't survive in the ultra-hostile environments that Tibor had without the ability to move from point to point while ensuring you popped up on as few surveillance systems as possible.

Most anti-surveillance techniques were nothing more than the rigid application of common sense. Look down, wear a brimmed hat, turn up your collar. Survey where cameras were placed. Assume their placement in certain public areas such as banks and government offices, and act accordingly.

For a man such as Tibor, it was probably second nature. Yes, he was experienced, that would account for it. And, if it didn't, his file alluded to what were cryptically called 'augmented abilities'. When Lauren had questioned her superiors as to what they were they had shut down the conversation pretty quickly. It was only by looking at the people Tibor had killed that she was able to make an educated guess as to what those abilities might be.

Like many in the department, she had heard of the program Tibor had been placed in. And, like everyone else, she had put down the rumors of what it had involved to the Chinese whispers that could take hold in the intelligence community. That view had changed as she had spent more time on the hunt for him.

The incidents he had been involved in since he'd gone

rogue – or, rather, the details of the incidents – were so fantastical that she had begun to wonder if she was dealing with something more outlandish than she had first imagined. Of course she had sought more information. It had not been forthcoming.

She glanced at her watch, a college-graduation gift from her mom. She should have gone home five hours ago. Not that she had anything to go home to. Her life outside work had narrowed as the demands of the job had expanded. Even weekends, which she had vowed would remain sacred, were spent, at least partially, in this windowless office, poring over possible leads, and getting nowhere fast. The man in the Greyhound station might well have been Tibor, but they couldn't be sure.

Remembering a detail from Tibor's file, Lauren tapped again on the video player, and pulled the footage back to the moment that the man entered. She advanced the video frame by frame.

There. She stopped on a frame, dragged it over to the image-enhancement software and zoomed in on the man's neck. Just above his collar there was a small red scar about an inch and a half long. Just like the one Tibor had been left with after he'd cut out the RDF tracking chip that been implanted under his skin.

She cut and pasted the scar into a separate file. She ran it through image-comparison software. The process took less than a second. It was a match.

CHAPTER TWO

Kelsen County, Texas

It was dark by the time they reached the containers. Dark and bitterly cold. If they had arrived in daylight then perhaps they would have offered more resistance. But it was late, and they were exhausted from a full day of walking in the searing desert heat. The day had begun at four in the morning, and the men escorting them had promised them something to eat if they did as they were told.

There were seventeen in their little group. Four men, twelve women and the little girl, Matilde, who had come with her father because there was no one to look after her at home. Her mother had died the previous year while making the same journey, and her mother's family had blamed Matilde's father. He'd had too much pride to ask them to care for Matilde while he was gone. Instead, he had brought her with him, carrying her on his shoulders while she kept a firm grip on the pink bunny rabbit that went everywhere with her.

The tallest of the three white men nodded for the other two to open one of the containers. They did it with ceremony, springing the padlock, wrenching open the door, and ushering the seventeen people inside.

When no one moved, the tall man walked back to the truck. He reappeared a few moments later with some brown-paper lunch sacks. He handed them to an elderly woman standing near the front of the group. She peered into the bag.

'Food,' said the man, waving them towards the open door. 'You go inside, you get fed. *Comprende*?'

The group began to shuffle forward as the brown bags were handed out. The tall man walked back to the truck. This time he returned with two five-gallon plastic containers of water. 'Go on,' he said. 'Inside.'

At the back of the group, Matilde's father hunkered down so he was face to face with his daughter. He brushed a strand of long dark hair away from her eyes, and whispered to her in Spanish. She looked at him, puzzled. He told her it was going to be okay. Did she understand what he was saying? Matilde nodded and clutched her pink rabbit even tighter to her chest.

He straightened up. He could feel a lump forming in his throat. If only he had swallowed his pride and asked his wife's family to take care of his daughter. But it was too late for that now.

He watched the people ahead of him shuffle forward into the darkness of the metal box. He stepped away from his daughter, and began to protest loudly in Spanish. Those around him shouted at him to be quiet.

One of the white men pushed his way towards him. 'What's the problem here?'

Matilde's father noticed that the man's right hand had fallen to his gun. He didn't doubt that he was capable of using it. He quietened down.

'Okay, then,' said the white man, satisfied that the eruption was over. 'And don't you folks worry, y'hear? You came here to work. We got plenty of work for you. Long as you do as we say, everything'll be just fine.'

Matilde and her father followed the others into the container. The doors clanged shut. The darkness was complete.

CHAPTER THREE

At first glance, Byron Tibor had assumed he was looking at a wanted poster. Murder maybe, or rape. Something serious. Something that would make the authorities want to plaster the man's image all over the county.

The face on the poster was that of a man in his early sixties with a tanned complexion. He had dark, beady eyes that were set deep below a sharp overhang of forehead, and framed by eyebrows with no discernible gap. Razor-thin lips parted to reveal a jagged yellow smile that was more predatory than welcoming. His expression was one of cold, calculating hardness that bordered on psychotic.

This was the third poster Byron had seen that morning but the first time he had stopped for a closer look. A moment passed before he registered the words that accompanied the image. He choked back a laugh at his own stupidity. Of course. It all made perfect sense.

The man on the poster wasn't a fugitive from justice. Far from it. His name was John Martin, and he was seeking re-election as the sheriff of Kelsen County, Texas.

The poster was a timely reminder of what Byron had always suspected to be the case. If, overnight, you swapped the people on wanted posters with the ones featured on election flyers, less might change than people assumed. The prison population might have nicer teeth, and access to better drugs, while Congress might feature more neck tattoos and wife beaters (both literal and figurative). Otherwise the world would roll on pretty much the same.

Byron tipped his hat in Sheriff John Martin's direction, and continued along the heat-scorched desert road. As he walked, he reached back to pull a canteen from the rucksack slung over his shoulder, twisted off the cap and took a sip. The water was warm from the midday sun. The landscape that stretched off into the horizon didn't offer much shade. He took one more sip, and put the canteen back in the rucksack. According to the signs he'd passed, it was four miles to the next town, and he had no idea how long it would be before someone stopped to offer him a ride. If they would stop at all.

Over the past ten minutes four vehicles had passed him, including a truck driver who had slowed down to take a better look, then thought better of it. Byron could hardly blame him. If the situation had been reversed, he would have thought twice about picking up a six foot four, 250-pound hitchhiker, who looked like he'd been living on the road for months.

Byron's plan was to walk into town and see if he could find a bus. Airports were out, as was renting a car. Both left too much of an electronic trail. Headed for California, he had stuck to hitching rides or transport that could be arranged with cash and no need for identification. It was a lot tougher than he had anticipated.

Ten minutes later, he heard a vehicle behind him slow to a crawl. It inched forward, the driver's foot barely touching the gas pedal. Byron listened more closely. Another vehicle was coming down the same road behind the first. The driver of the second had braked sharply to avoid running into the back of the one that had slowed down. That they had braked, rather than passing, told its own story.

If you came up fast on a slow-moving vehicle on an open road, you went around it. Usually with a honking horn and a raised middle finger. Unless it was a cop car.

CHAPTER FOUR

Byron kept walking at exactly the same pace. The only adjustment he made was to ensure that his hands were clearly visible by his sides. Then he waited for the low-speed pursuit to catch up with him.

In truth, he was relieved. The heat was relentless. He was soaked in sweat and any half-decent cop car in sunny Texas would have air-conditioning. If he was polite about it, they'd likely take him the rest of the way into town and put him on a bus themselves. Or, when they couldn't figure out who he was, they might even drop him on the other side of the border. That would suit him fine too.

He had already thought about traveling through Mexico, navigating a course parallel to the border until he reached California. But the Mexican side of the border held its own dangers. It was a volatile place where a lone stranger would be even less welcome. And there was the matter of the crossing. If he used an official crossing point to re-enter the United States, he would need identification.

The patrol-car siren whooped a single blast. Byron did his best to feign surprise. He knew better than to turn around so instead shuffled to a halt, and raised his arms slowly in the air.

He heard both the front passenger and the driver's door open, then a man's voice: 'Do not move. Now, I want you lower yourself onto your knees. Keep your hands where I can see them.'

A smartass might have enquired as to how you could simultaneously not move while lowering yourself to your knees. The smartass would have got himself shot. Byron had no intention of being shot. Not because the prospect worried him, but because it would have led to a scenario littered with complications. People in general, and cops especially, tended to react with panic to an individual who didn't die from being shot in the back at close range.

Byron complied with the instructions he had been given. It took a lot of core strength, and balance, but he did it.

'Okay,' said the cop. 'Now I want you to put your hands on top of your head, and lace your fingers together nice and tight.'

Byron did as he had been asked. He could hear the cop's footsteps as he walked towards him. He could feel the heat radiating from the blacktop. If the cop asked him to lie face down on the broiling hot tar they'd both have a problem, and right now Byron couldn't afford to have a problem with law enforcement, if he could avoid it.

Mercifully for both of them, Byron heard the cop close in on him, take the cuffs from his belt, snap them open and start to place them around his wrist. As the cop cuffed him, he ran through the Miranda Rights. He was arresting him on a charge of vagrancy. Except it wasn't called that. It had been wrapped up in some new terminology that seemed to have been invented specifically by the good people of Kelsen County. There was a mention of 'public nuisance'. Byron wasn't sure how walking down the side of a highway made him a nuisance. Maybe they'd been watching him and seen him laughing at the sheriff's election poster.

When he had finished his recitation, the cop asked if he understood. Byron told him that he did, throwing in a 'sir' to let him know that he wasn't going to be a problem. The cuffs snapped closed.

For a man on the run from the might of the entire US government, he felt remarkably calm. He doubted that the cop who was pulling him roughly back onto his feet would have been as calm if he'd known who he'd just arrested. Never mind what he'd done to the last cop who had tried to slap cuffs on him.

CHAPTER FIVE

Byron had been wrong about the air-conditioning. The front of the Crown Vic may have been air-conditioned, but the cooling system in the back seat extended only as far as having one of the rear windows cracked less than an inch. The heat raging through the glass had brought the interior to a simmering boil, threatening to cook him from the inside out.

In under sixty seconds his clothes were soaked in sweat, and he was feeling light-headed. Even if he'd had the desire to escape, he now doubted that he'd have the energy. He raked his tongue over dry, cracked lips as the cop who had slapped the cuffs on him took a sip from a bottle of Evian. Byron was debating whether to ask him for some when the cop reached back, pulled open a slot in the Perspex partition, and pushed the bottle through. Thankfully he'd cuffed Byron's hands in front so that he could reach up and take the water.

Byron made a point of thanking him. He'd seen the man's partner shoot the cop a look, which he'd greeted with a shrug and a 'Poor bastard must be dying back there.' The partner's look and the cop's own defensive response suggested some minor breach of protocol.

They edged towards the outskirts of town. It wasn't what Byron had expected. Not at all. The usual fast-food joints, bars and grimy gas stations were noticeable by their absence. The first proper building he saw was a gleaming white four-story office block. An equally gleaming sign out front read, 'Kelsen County Corporation'.

Beyond the office building lay a golf course. A number of McMansions were dotted around the plush fairways. The other side of the road revealed another golf course with yet more expensive, executive-style housing. The front lawns were as neatly cut as the greens of the golf courses. The housing developments were gated, with manned security booths to ensure that no one entered without first being properly vetted.

Beyond the golf courses, the landscape got a little more urban. There was a strip mall with a dry cleaner's, a bookstore, and a small upmarket grocery. The sidewalks were immaculate but empty. The searing heat might have prevented anyone from walking, but Byron guessed that even when it was cooler, people here tended to use their cars.

The cars were something else that stood out. Aside from a couple of battered old pickups being driven by Hispanic men, and laden with gardening equipment, most of the cars they passed were expensive imports of the Germany variety. The drivers and passengers were exclusively white and mostly middle-aged or elderly, with a few glammed-up soccer moms thrown into the mix for a little variety.

He was starting to see why the local police department might not have taken too kindly to someone who looked like he did hitching a ride on the outskirts of their town. The thought cheered him. If they didn't want someone like him making the police look untidy they'd be happy to see him on his way with the minimum delay.

They turned into what Byron assumed was the town's main street. He counted two banks, a pet store, three or four cafés and restaurants, and a couple of boutiques. If there was anything as vulgar as a Walmart, it was well hidden.

In the middle of the street he saw a modest courthouse and local government building, and next to that was the police headquarters – a large, muscular, two-story red-brick building that dwarfed everything around it. Maybe there was more crime here than he'd have thought possible, though he couldn't imagine what.

There was one more feature that appeared to set the town apart from the other towns he'd passed through so far in this part of the state. Almost every single building he'd seen since he'd arrived, from the Kelsen Corporation offices to the boutiques, had at least two cameras mounted on the outside. The cameras themselves were identical, suggesting that they'd been placed there by some central authority rather by individual business owners. Whoever was running the town sure liked to keep an eye on things.

The police driver swung the wheel hard, and they sped down a narrow alleyway. They hung a sharp left and were met by a vast metal gate that slowly inched open, the eye of a camera watching the patrol car as it drove down a ramp and into an underground car park that held row upon row of fresh-off-the-assembly-line police vehicles.

Whatever the hell kind of a place Byron had stumbled into, they had enough hardware for a medium-sized city, never mind a small Texas border town.

CHAPTER SIX

The cops pulled into a parking spot right next to an elevator. Byron had already counted off over fifty separate vehicles with Kelsen County Sheriff's Department markings. All the vehicles were either new or a year or two old at most. Another hundred or so unmarked vehicles were also parked there. Presumably they belonged to the cops and support staff. There were a lot of trucks and SUVs, again almost all either new or only a few years old. Byron had even glimpsed a valet stand. A couple of Hispanic men were busy buffing a Ford F150 to a gleaming showroom shine while another couple of cars parked behind the pickup waited their turn.

The cops got out. They opened the rear door and stepped back. Byron hustled his way out, glad to get some air. Not that it was cool, far from it, but it was still ten degrees cooler than the sauna he'd been sitting in. They guided him towards the elevator.

They still hadn't asked Byron any questions. Not who he was, or where he was going, why he was traveling across their turf, or if he intended sticking around.

The elevator door slid open as they reached it. No buttons pushed. From the corner of his eye Byron noticed yet another camera, which had possibly signaled their arrival. Out of habit he kept his head down so that it wouldn't capture his face. He was in no doubt that at some point someone in DC would figure out he'd been here, but he planned to be long gone by the time they did.

The scar tissue on his neck itched. As they stepped into the elevator he raised his cuffed hands to scratch it. The smaller of the two cops looked at him. 'What you do to yourself?' he asked, with a nod to the scar.

'Accident,' Byron told him. 'Drill bit snapped and

caught me.'

By now his lies were well rehearsed. People tended to ask the same questions. His responses had become engrained to the point where the truth took him longer to recall than the alternative he had invented.

The elevator door closed. They began to move up. A few seconds later, it stopped. The doors opened. The three men stepped out into a blessedly air-conditioned corridor. The cop who had been behind him for the short elevator ride stepped in front of Byron and they went down the corridor to a dark blue metal door. Another camera. Byron kept his head down again, hoping that neither cop would notice. There was a buzzing sound as the door was remotely unlocked. The cop in front pulled it open.

They stepped into a lobby area. There was a seated section with a half-dozen metal-framed chairs that had been bolted to the floor. A high reception desk ran along the opposite wall. Behind it and to one side were doors that led, Byron assumed, to the cells and the offices.

A middle-aged white man in civilian clothes sat behind the desk. His hair was black with a streak of white running down the middle. It reminded Byron of Pepe Le Pew, the overly amorous skunk smitten with a cat, which always seemed to encounter a tin of white paint that led to a series of romantic confusions.

Behind Pepe was a picture of Sheriff John Martin standing, in full uniform, complete with Stetson, in front of the police headquarters. Apart from his hairstyle, the man behind the counter bore an uncanny resemblance to his boss – a mixture of permanently angry and chronically constipated.

He ignored Byron. Instead he directed his questions to the taller of the two cops. 'What we got here, Arlo?'

'Found him hitching out on the Interstate,' said Arlo.

Pepe looked Byron up and down, as if he was a lab specimen. 'He anything to do with Ms Martinez?'

The cops looked at Byron. He had a feeling that,

whoever Ms Martinez was, she wasn't popular. Even if he'd had some connection, he wouldn't be admitting it.

'Hey,' the other cop said to Pepe. 'Don't mention Thea in front of Arlo. He's still sweet on her.'

'I was just passing through,' Byron told Pepe. 'I don't know anybody called Martinez.'

'Speak when you're spoken to,' Arlo snapped.

Byron had noticed that the centre of Arlo's head pulsed red with anger when he'd been teased by his partner about this woman. Due to a trans-cranial neural implant placed inside his brain, Byron could sometimes read people's emotional states just by looking at them. If they were scared, their skull looked yellow, and if they were angry it turned red.

Pepe jabbed a couple of beefy fingers at the computer's keyboard. 'Okay, name.'

'Davis. John Davis,' Byron said.

Pepe punched the name into his computer. 'You have any ID?' he asked.

'You're going to have to take my word for it,' Byron told him.

'What kind of a person wanders around the country without ID?' Pepe asked.

'I didn't realize it was mandatory, and in any case, I know who I am,' said Byron.

'You search him?' Pepe asked the two cops.

'When we arrested him.'

Pepe Le Pew sighed. 'Date of birth?'

Byron gave them a date that was one day and one month off his own. Pepe tapped it into his computer. His pockets were emptied and his rucksack placed on the counter. He watched as they went through everything. There was nothing that confirmed or contradicted what he had told them. Byron's meagre belongings were placed in a large clear bag and sealed.

'Okay, put him in Holding,' Pepe instructed the two

cops.

They each grabbed an arm. Byron got the feeling that they would have been happy to let him walk unassisted but that the guy behind the desk demanded some show of force from them. The cop who had arrested him had grown irritated from the moment they had stepped out of the elevator.

They pushed him through the door at the far end of the waiting room. There was a large, open pen with a couple of benches. In the far corner there was a toilet and a sink. If you had to use the toilet you'd be doing it in full view of the pen's other occupants. Right now there were two. A couple of Hispanic men sat on the benches, staring into space. They made a point of avoiding the cop's gaze.

The door leading into the holding pen buzzed open. The arresting cop took his cuffs off and clipped them back onto his belt. Byron stepped inside. The door closed behind him.

'Don't I get a phone call?' Byron asked, not that he had anyone in the world to call. But he wanted to get an idea of how far they'd observe the basic Constitutional niceties.

His question went unanswered. 'What about an attorney?' he asked.

That question was met with a drawn-out sigh. 'This your first time in Kelsen County?'

The cops walked back to the door leading to the lobby. The last one out stopped just before he left. 'Enjoy your time here,' he said to Byron. 'This is about as good as it gets.'

Byron sat down on the bench opposite the two men as the cops left. He looked up to see yet another picture of Sheriff Martin. He wore the same scowl he'd had for the election poster. He wasn't asking anyone in here for their vote. Quite the opposite. The slogan emblazoned beneath the picture read: *Criminals Have No Rights.*

An hour later, two people wearing mud-brown uniforms with Kelsen County Jail badges sewn onto their shirts walked in. They had no guns, but they did have pepper spray and a Taser — the weapons of choice for prison guards, something to stun and subdue, but nothing that could be taken off them and used to facilitate an escape. The first guard was a man in his early twenties with a scraggy mustache and bad skin. Behind him waddled a middle-aged woman with brassy blonde hair and an expression that suggested a life full of low-rent disappointment. They had the muscle tone of people better suited to slinging burgers than escorting prisoners.

'Up on your feet, *amigos*,' barked the woman.

Byron's two companions jumped up. Byron took his time. Even though they hadn't yet opened the door into the pen, both guards took a step back as he stood up.

CHAPTER SEVEN

'You!' the male guard barked at him. 'Turn to face the wall. Hands behind your back.'

Byron did as he was told. He wasn't about to cause trouble. He had no reason to. He was hoping that he was about to be taken in front of a judge. He planned on making a guilty plea in return for accepting a small fine and a ride to the county line. He'd have lost the best part of the day and a few bucks, but that was no great hardship.

There was something else too. He had been mulling it over as he'd been sitting in the holding pen. He'd had his picture taken, but not his fingerprints. Given the amount of money and personnel available, it didn't strike Byron as a clerical error. Everything else had seemed well organized. The staff had been blunt but efficient, which made them typical. But not taking his fingerprints? It seemed an odd omission.

The cuffs snapped around his wrists. He turned and felt a hand in his back push him towards the open pen door. They snaked their way out through the lobby and into the elevator, all the way down to the parking lot.

An old yellow school bus with Kelsen County Sheriff Department markings was waiting for them. The door opened with a pneumatic hiss and they got on. The two guards sat behind the three prisoners. The driver gave the guards a piece of paper on a clipboard to sign. The bus door closed. The engine started up. The vehicle pulled forward.

No sooner had it started moving than it stopped again. The doors hissed open. The two guards sitting behind Byron and the two other prisoners rose from their seats. 'Okay, we're here,' they announced. 'On your feet.'

Byron looked at them. The bus hadn't travelled much more than fifty feet.

Byron and the other prisoners' puzzlement was met by two granite stares. One guard grabbed the back of Byron's shirt and yanked. 'Get up.'

Byron did so and shuffled forward, still wondering why a fifty-yard journey had involved a bus trip. He stepped down. The bus driver handed the guards the clipboard. They signed for a second time and gave it back to the driver.

Directly in front of them was another blue metal door. One of the guards moved in front of Byron and pressed a buzzer located at the side of the frame. The lock clicked. The guard grabbed the handle and pulled the door open. They stepped back into the self-same corridor they had exited a minute or so ago. It wasn't even a separate section of the building. They could see the same grey walls, the same posters they had passed before.

Byron was facing a stairwell. The two guards herded them towards it. They took two sets of stairs up to a second floor. There were more buzzers, and more doors, more short stretches of identical corridor.

Finally the little party reached a set of double dark-stained oak doors. A row of chairs ran along the wall opposite. The guards motioned for them to sit down. They sat.

Byron was starting to wonder if the implant in the center of his brain had suffered some kind of malfunction. It was as if he was caught up in a dream in which nothing made any sense but everyone carried on as if it did.

He caught sight of a sign on the right-hand side of the double oak doors. It read: 'Kelsen County Court. Judge William Kelsen presiding.' As if the bus ride hadn't been strange enough, he'd found a place where everyone seemed to share a surname. He knew that was how small towns were, but Kelsen didn't appear to be that small a town.

The doors opened. A mousy woman with her hair in a bun appeared. She pointed at the Hispanic man sitting next to Byron, and said simply, 'Him.'

One of the guards hoisted him upright, and pushed him forwards though the doors. Byron caught a glimpse of a barely populated courtroom – wooden-bench seating, tables at the front, a court stenographer, and a raised dais with a Kelsen County seal hanging over an empty leather-backed seat – before the doors closed again.

He settled back into the hard plastic seat and shut his eyes. Barely two seconds had passed before he felt an elbow nudge hard into his side. He opened his eyes and turned his head to look at the guard sitting next to him. 'Don't get too comfortable,' the guard said. 'This shouldn't take long.'

The guard hadn't been kidding. Less than thirty seconds later, the doors opened again. A courtroom guard led the young Hispanic prisoner back out. His eyes darted everywhere. He looked ready to burst into tears. He started to say something in Spanish but was cut off by the guard next to Byron with a curt 'No talking!'

CHAPTER EIGHT

Judge William Kelsen smiled warmly as Byron took a seat behind a desk near the front of the courtroom. He picked up a piece of paper and studied it for a moment, peering at it through wire-rimmed, half-moon glasses. Taking them off and putting them on the desk in front of him, he smiled again at Byron.

'Mr Davis?' said the judge.

Byron got to his feet. He allowed his shoulders to slump. He bent a little at the knees to minimize his height. He wanted his body language to reinforce the idea that he wasn't a threat. 'Yes, sir.'

'Do you understand what you were arrested for?' the judge asked him.

The question brought him to a crossroads. By saying no he risked antagonizing the man who would decide immediate his fate. By saying yes he'd be admitting that he understood something he really didn't, which was rarely a good idea in a court of law.

'Not really, Your Honor.' He hoped that the switch up from plain old 'sir' might win him some points and take the edge off his display of ignorance.

This time Byron got a smile that was a little less benevolent. 'The arresting officer did tell you why you were being arrested, didn't he?'

It was another crossroads, another moment of decision. To say, 'Yes, he did,' but that Byron didn't understand the charge would be to irritate Judge Kelsen. To say that he hadn't would be a lie, and one that could be easily disproved. Byron decided upon a middle road. One that risked annoyance but might also bring some measure of clarity.

'I'd like to exercise my constitutional right to an attorney.'

The judge met his request with a weary sigh. 'You weren't already offered counsel, Mr Davis?'

'No, sir,' Byron told him.

'Do you have an attorney in mind or would you like the court to appoint one for you?' Judge Kelsen asked him. This was a polite way of asking whether he had the money for a lawyer or whether he needed a public defender. Asking for an attorney from the public defender's office undermined any defense against a charge of vagrancy, but he wasn't about to start throwing money away either. His funds were adequate but low.

Judge Kelsen glanced across at the court bailiff. 'Can you make the call? And while you're at it, could you also make a call and tell the booking sergeant I'd like to speak with him later today?'

With a degree of relief Byron sensed that the judge wasn't irritated with him as much as annoyed that someone downstairs had dropped the ball. 'Mr Davis, it may take us a little while to find you someone. In the meantime I'm afraid you'll have to return to your cell. I apologize on behalf of the court for any inconvenience caused. But don't worry, as soon as we find someone I'll try to make sure that you're on your way as quickly as possible.'

A little taken aback by the judge's sincerity, Byron mumbled, 'Thank you, Your Honor.'

For the first time that day he started to feel that this might be nothing more than a minor diversion. A strange detour into a strange small town at the ass end of Texas.

He was half right.

CHAPTER NINE

A half-hour later, Byron was woken by the sound of the holding pen being unlocked. He opened his eyes, swung his feet back onto the bare concrete and stood up. Behind the guard opening the pen's door he saw a young woman with long black hair tied into a ponytail. She smiled warmly at Byron as he rubbed the last vestiges of sleep from his eyes.

The guard turned back to her. 'You want him cuffed?'

'No, thank you,' she said.

'Come on out,' the guard said to Byron.

The woman put out her hand towards him. 'Thea Martinez.'

He hadn't registered how attractive she was until he almost said his real name. It had been on the very tip of his tongue. He recovered quickly, covering his near-slip by clearing his throat. 'John Davis. Good to meet you.'

She held his gaze for a split second longer than seemed natural. Or that may have been Byron reading something that wasn't there. He tended not to notice women, these days. But Thea Martinez was impossible to ignore. Especially up close. She had large brown eyes that seemed to take everything in, and a wide, sensuous smile. Byron pegged her as early, maybe late thirties. Whatever her age she had a figure that suggested she kept herself in shape.

Together, they followed the guard down the corridor. The man opened the door and ushered them into a small interview room that held a couple of whiteboards, a table, a water-cooler and four fold-out metal chairs. 'Holler if you need anything,' he said.

The guard left. Byron waited for Thea to sit down before he did. Old-fashioned manners.

He watched as she placed a soft leather briefcase on the

table, and took out a bundle of papers. 'How are they treating you, Mr Davis?'

'Fine,' he told her. 'The back of their patrol cars could use some air-conditioning, but I don't have any real complaints.'

She lifted her eyes from the sheaf of papers she had been leafing through. 'I hear you,' she said. 'They tend not to spend any money on home comforts for anyone they arrest. Not if they can avoid it anyway.'

Byron glanced around the room. 'They do spend money, though. At least, that's the impression I have so far.'

'No expense spared on themselves.' Thea made eye contact with him again. 'Encourages loyalty, according to the sheriff.'

'I get that,' Byron said. He could feel his throat starting to dry. He had just spoken more complete sentences in the past few hours than he had in the entire last week, which he had spent on the road. 'Do you mind if I get some water?'

'Go right ahead,' she said.

He got up, crossed to the water-cooler and filled a small paper cup. 'You want some?' he asked.

'No, I'm good. But thank you,' she said.

He drank the water and refilled the cup. He sat back down opposite her. She ran through the false details he'd given when he'd been arrested. He confirmed them. For some reason that he didn't understand he felt bad for lying to her.

Guilt.

'So you were walking into town when you were arrested?' she asked him.

He had the feeling that this was the second time she'd asked the question. The first time, it must not have registered with him. This time, it sounded like an echo.

'That's correct,' he said. 'Sorry, I'm feeling a little

light-headed. Or something.'

She shot him the same smile that had made him notice her in the first place. 'The heat down here can get to people if they're not used to it.' She took a breath. 'Where was it you're from, Mr Davis?'

He wasn't from anywhere. He'd been from New York, or that was where he had lived with his wife. Even back then he had spent weeks and months at a time out of the country. Mostly in the Middle East. That was where the action had been and, to a lesser degree, still was.

Before he'd been married, his life had been even more itinerant. When he was back home in America he was mostly in DC, but Washington wasn't a city he considered to be home. Thinking about it now, everything had been dictated by his work, to the point at which his life and his work had become next to inseparable. Little wonder that he had suffered some kind of a breakdown.

He realized that Thea Martinez was waiting for an answer. Her smile had begun to wane. It had been replaced by a look of concern. 'I'm not really from anywhere, really. I move about,' he said.

'That may not help us when we go back before Judge Kelsen,' she said.

'I guess not.' Byron could see her point. Claiming he had no fixed abode when faced with a charge of vagrancy probably wouldn't help his cause.

'Where was the last place you lived?' she asked.

'It's been a while since I've lived anywhere,' he said truthfully.

She was growing exasperated, he could tell.

'I suppose the last place I called home was New York,' he said. 'Look, I'm happy to put my hands up here. Take a guilty plea, pay the fine, and get out of the county. I'll even promise the judge never to set foot here again, if that will help. I was just passing through anyway,' he said.

Thea scribbled a note on a piece of paper. 'You've

really never been in Kelsen County before, have you?'

The way she said it seemed to suggest that there was something different about it, a vibe he had picked up already. 'No, ma'am, first time.'

'Okay, then,' Thea said. 'Well, let me give you some advice. As far as we can, let's try and establish that you have some kind of settled life somewhere. People who will miss you. Or, more pertinently, people who might start asking questions if you don't come home.'

The words hit Byron hard. What Thea was describing was the polar opposite of his life. He had no home. He had no family or friends waiting for his safe return. He was alone. A man cast adrift in his own country. Worse still, an enemy of the state.

He looked across at the table at her. 'I can't help you.'

She sighed. 'I'm not asking you to help me. I'm asking you to help yourself.'

He looked away, breaking eye contact. The conversation was stirring things up inside him that he had believed had been cauterized long ago. Feelings. Emotions. Things that simply shouldn't have been there. 'I can't help either of us,' he said. 'I'd like to plead guilty.'

She looked as if she was about to say more, but stopped herself. 'Fine.'

He had let her down. Perhaps in some way he didn't fully realize. She must have had clients who wanted to plead guilty before. Every lawyer did. 'Perhaps you can speak to the judge on my behalf. See if he'll reduce the fine, as how I've been co-operative,' he said.

She gave him a tight little smile that was all professional. 'Sure. I'll see what I can do. But you have to understand that the judge usually prefers the custodial option to a fine. Probably the only way I could persuade him to levy a fine is if it's an amount that makes it worth his while.'

Byron wasn't sure what that meant, but he had a vague

idea. 'You mean like a bribe?'

Thea laughed. 'No, Mr Davis, not like a bribe. No one ever takes a kickback in the county. No kickbacks. No bribes. Nothing like that.'

Byron said nothing. From Thea's tone, he guessed he had insulted her or at least stumbled into sensitive territory.

'You don't want to ask me how I know that?' she said.

She clearly wanted him to ask. He decided to play along. 'How do you know that?' he said.

'No one would take a bribe here because they don't have to.' She started to gather her papers together and put them back into her leather briefcase. 'I'll see you back upstairs.'

CHAPTER TEN

Thea was already in court when he arrived. She leaned over and asked if he had reconsidered his guilty plea. He informed her that he hadn't. She had seemed as disappointed as she had been the first time.

Byron did his best to tune her out. She was a distraction, nothing more. He would either pay the fine or be given a short stint in the county jail. Either way he would be walking or riding out of Kelsen County with no prospect of seeing her again. He'd have plenty of time later to reflect on what had passed between them, and what it might mean.

When Judge Kelsen had made his appearance back in court, Thea had asked permission to approach the bench. Permission was granted. Byron watched her as she walked over and spoke to the judge. Whatever case Thea was making for leniency, she appeared to be making it with some passion. The judge didn't appear to be moved.

She stepped back to the table and sat down. 'I wouldn't get your hopes up,' she told Byron. 'He's pretty steamed that you asked for an attorney.'

'Steamed that I exercised my Constitutional right as a citizen?' Byron said.

Thea shrugged. 'His thinking doesn't go that deep. It's more along the lines of him missing his tee time at the Kelsen Country Club.'

The court bailiff swiped some post-lunch crumbs from his shirt and stood up. He asked everyone to stand.

Byron and Thea got to their feet. Judge Kelsen peered at Byron over the top of his glasses. From the red dot pulsing in the middle of his skull, Byron figured that he must enjoy his afternoon golf a whole lot.

'Mr Davis, before I pass sentence I'm going to ask if

you have anything to say,' the judge said.

'No, sir,' Byron said, eager not to delay the man's tee time any more than he already had and risk annoying him any further.

'In that case I sentence you to either a fine in the amount of ten thousand dollars or ninety days in the county jail. Mr Davis, do you have ten thousand dollars?' the judge asked, a hint of a smirk settling at the edge of his lips.

'No, sir,' said Byron.

'In that case, I sentence you to ninety days in the county jail,' the judge said, banging his gavel to indicate an end to the court's proceedings.

Glancing back over his shoulder, Byron saw the door open and the two guards walk in. He guessed that this time his bus journey would be a little longer. He looked back to Thea.

'I'm sorry,' she said.

Byron managed a smile as he put out his hand. 'You did your best. That's all I could ask.'

She shook his hand and held it a second longer than necessary. 'Is there anyone I can contact for you? If you know someone who can stand you the money then I'm sure I can come back to the court and persuade them to take the cash instead.'

'Thanks, but I'll be fine,' he said.

'You seem pretty relaxed for a man who just got ninety days for walking along a highway,' Thea said.

'Would getting upset change anything?' he said.

'You always this chilled?' she asked.

'Who said I am?' he said.

Thea began to gather her papers from the table. She ripped off a strip of paper, scribbled her number on it and handed it to Byron. 'This is my cell. If you need me while you're in County just give me a ring. Day or night.'

He took the piece of paper and glanced at the digits.

'Thanks,' he said.

'I give all of my clients who are sentenced to jail time my number. Things can get a little out of hand once you're in the system here.'

'Out of hand?' he said.

She didn't say anything more, just looked at him. 'I'm sure a man like you will be fine.'

He wondered what the hell that was supposed to mean. 'Can I ask you something?' he said. 'It's been niggling at me. It might sound stupid but …'

She folded her arms across her chest. 'I had a law professor who said that the only stupid question was the one you never asked.'

'The bus trip from the holding area to the court. Wouldn't it be easier, faster even, to walk?' he asked.

'Yes, it would,' she said.

'So what's with the bus?' he said.

She held up her hand and rubbed the tip of her index finger and thumb together. 'Court security is operated by a private company. Every prisoner who's transferred by bus, regardless of the distance, earns the company a flat fee of fifty dollars.'

The guards were either side of him now. Byron sensed that Thea had more to tell him, but that she wasn't about to say it in front of them. 'Come on, buddy, let's go,' the smaller guard said.

'Good luck, Mr Davis,' Thea said.

CHAPTER ELEVEN

Byron was guided onto a long silver bus by the two guards. A belly chain linked the cuffs around his wrists to the shackles around his ankles. The guards deposited him in a window seat about halfway back. They walked back down to the front, the driver opened the door and they got off.

The driver sat there in the broiling heat. Minutes passed. The driver dug out a bottle of water from a bag by his feet and took a swig.

More time passed. The driver made no sign of starting the engine. Byron wondered what he was waiting for as the heat began to build. The front half of the bus was shaded by the court building. The rear was in direct sunlight. Byron was sitting in the first seat that caught some serious rays. He had no idea if the guards had put him there for that reason. He didn't want to think about it. Whether they had or hadn't made no difference.

Byron pulled his hands apart, testing the strength of his handcuffs. Broadly speaking, handcuffs came in three types, chain, hinge, or bar, depending upon how the cuffs themselves were linked. Because the most popular method for getting out of cuffs was to pick the lock, chained cuffs were the easiest to escape. The chain gave the hands more flexibility and range of movement. Bar cuffs were tougher to pick, though not impossible. Hinge cuffs were way more difficult. These were hinge cuffs.

The side door he had come through half an hour before opened. Three more shackled prisoners were escorted onto the bus by the same two guards. Mercifully, the guards took their seats. The driver started the engine. The bus pulled forward.

Byron closed his eyes for a moment and savored the

very faintest breeze as the bus made its way down a long alley towards a gatehouse. Wall-high metal gates opened slowly. The bus moved forward and to the left.

The turn seemed to detour them round the super-neat sidewalks, McMansions and lush golf course that Byron had seen on the way there. Within minutes they were on an open highway heading out of town.

The landscape was one of scrub desert, harsh and unrelenting. It made what they had left behind seem all the more surreal. It was as if someone had lifted an upscale, west-coast college town, like Santa Barbara, and dumped it just   inside   the   Texas   border   with   Mexico.

CHAPTER TWELVE

In the distance, Byron could make out a long stretch of chain-link fence topped with curved razor wire. Within the outside perimeter fence there was another fence. Guard towers were placed every thousand yards between the two fences. A patrol road ran parallel to them all the way round.

They drove closer. He could make out a series of single-story buildings. He counted off four, each divided by more fencing and with a yard in front. There might have been more. He would find out soon enough.

The bus made one last turn and stopped at a gatehouse. The driver opened his window and exchanged a few words with the shotgun-toting guard manning the station. A barrier swung up. The driver pushed on through. The bus came to a stop. The driver killed the engine. The two guards got out and disappeared through a doorway.

They sat there for a few minutes, quietly baking in the mid-afternoon sun. The three other prisoners, all male, and all Hispanic, whispered to each other in Spanish. Byron made out a few words but not enough to piece together what they were saying. He didn't miss the tone, though. They were scared.

The guards returned. The larger one clambered back onto the bus. 'Okay, *muchachos*, on your feet.'

When the three other prisoners didn't move, he barreled his way down the bus, sighed and hauled them upright, one by one. Standing behind them, he gave the man closest to him a hard shove in the back. They moved along the bus, down the steps and towards the doorway.

Byron decided to save the guy the trouble. He got to his feet and shuffled, as fast as the leg shackles allowed, towards the front. He had to concentrate hard as he took the steps. The chain linking the cuffs around his ankles had barely enough length to allow him to navigate them. With his hands cuffed, he knew that if he lost his footing, he would fall face first, with no way to save himself.

The door opened and he followed the other prisoners through it in single file. A short stretch of corridor opened up into a reception area. A prison guard sat behind a Perspex screen. He was in his late forties, with washed-out grey-white skin and a drooping grey mustache that gave him the appearance of a refugee from the set of some 1970s San Fernando Valley porn movie.

The prisoners were directed towards a bench. They sat down, awaiting their next instructions. The guard behind the screen didn't look up from the book he was reading. From time to time he would reach over and dip his hand into a bag of candy, take a fistful of multi-colored button-shaped chocolates and pop them into his mouth. Byron figured that if he wasn't already diabetic then he was likely well on the way.

A door at the other end of the waiting room-processing area opened. Two prison guards walked through it. Standing in between them was a middle-aged Hispanic man wearing a suit and a bad hairpiece that looked like it belonged halfway up a eucalyptus tree in a zoo's small-marsupials exhibit. From the way he carried himself, chest puffed out, hands dug into his pants pockets, it was clear that he thought himself pretty special.

Byron noticed that the desk-jockey pushed his family-sized bag of candy to one side. He picked up a clipboard and slid it through a slot at the bottom of the Perspex barrier. One of the guards picked it up and handed it to the man in the suit, who studied it with some degree of intensity. He looked at each of the prisoners in turn. Finally his gaze settled on Byron.

Byron looked down at the floor, avoiding eye contact. His general rule for dealing with people who thought they were pretty special was not to disabuse them of the notion until he absolutely had to. There was rarely anything to be gained from a pissing contest. That went double when you were in handcuffs and leg irons, with a belly chain setting off the ensemble.

'Couldn't come up with ten grand?' the guy in the suit said to the guard on his right.

The guard's reply came in the form of a shrug.

The man in the suit drew himself up to his full five feet six inches. 'My name is Warden Castro.' He paused for a moment to allow the guard on his left to translate what he had just said into Spanish. 'Let no one be in any doubt that I am in charge of this facility.' Another pause for the translation. The other three prisoners were also staring at the grey-tiled floor. They were probably hoping, like Byron, that the speech would be short.

'My word is law,' said Warden Castro. 'If it makes it any easier for you men, you can just assume that, when it comes to this facility, my word is the same as the word of God Himself.'

The head of one of the prisoners, a man wearing a small brass cross on a chain around his neck, snapped up.

The warden didn't miss the man's reaction. He jabbed a stubby finger at the prisoner. 'Start him off in secure housing. Three days. If he gives anyone any trouble he can stay there.'

The guard glared at the offender as the man's eyes slid slowly back to the floor. Some things obviously didn't need an accompanying translation to be understood.

'As for the rest of you,' Warden Castro said, 'while you're here, you'll be expected to pay your way. You'll work. Work hard. From sun-up until sun-down and then some. That's how we do things in Kelsen County. Don't like it? Well, that's too bad. You should have thought about that before you broke the law.' He whipped round and disappeared back through the door, leaving his translator to deliver the good news in Spanish. When the translation of Warden Castro's welcome speech was completed, the prisoners' processing began.

One by one, they were uncuffed and unshackled. They were ordered to strip off their clothes in front of the other prisoners and guards. The man with the crucifix on a chain around his neck was reluctant to take it off. It took one of the guards pulling his baton to ensure compliance. The message was clear: do as you were told or they'd do it for you.

All four men were ordered to stand facing the wall, spread their legs and then their ass cheeks, while one of the guards checked their rectal cavity with a flashlight. When the guard reached Byron, his hand slid slowly up the inside of Byron's thigh.

'You're not my type,' Byron said.

The guard withdrew his hand without finishing the examination. 'He's clear,' the guard said, his voice jumping a half-octave.

'Eyes front,' one of the other guards shouted at Byron.

His point made, Byron complied.

Next they were marched through a door at the far end of the room into an open shower area. There were six shower heads built into either side of the tiled wet room. The prisoners spread out. A guard came through and sprayed them down with what Byron guessed was some kind of disinfectant. Whatever it was it stung like hell.

The showers were turned on remotely. The water was hot to the point of scalding. Byron rubbed at his wrists and ankles as he rinsed off.

Without warning the water temperature went from boiling to freezing. The guards watching them smirked as the men jumped back, startled. Byron heard one make a lame crack about 'Mexican jumping beaners'. He made a mental note of the wisecracking guard's face for future reference. It was one thing to humiliate grown men who had no power to fight back, quite another to revel in their humiliation. Calling three Mexicans 'beaners' in a bar was one thing. You risked getting your ass kicked. Doing it here was the mark of a coward.

The guard, a skinny-fat white guy, who managed to be even shorter than the warden, caught Byron staring at him. 'Got a problem, inmate?'

Byron didn't say anything. But he didn't look away either. If the guard wanted to make something of it, well, that was fine by him.

They were both in no man's land. The guard had challenged Byron's facing him down. Byron hadn't escalated things by answering back, but neither had he backed off. It would come down, possibly literally, to who blinked first.

Staring at the guard's face, Byron saw the red pulse of anger in the middle of the man's head give way to the yellow shade of fear. The air seemed to clear from the room. Byron could feel the eyes of the other men on him and the guard.

Byron held the guard's gaze. When the yellow had crowded out the red, Byron's eyes snapped to the floor. He had made his point with no blood spilled. Only pride had been injured. Not that injured pride hurt some men any less than physical pain. If he didn't catch up with the guard, whose nameplate read 'Lieutenant Mills', he had a feeling that Mills might just try to catch up with him. He hoped for Mills's sake that neither came to pass. It could only end badly.

After drying off with towels that had the absorbent quality of industrial-strength sandpaper, they were given prison blues to wear, along with a welcome pack that consisted of a bar of grainy yellow soap, a toothbrush, a small tube of toothpaste, two towels, a fresh pair of prison blues for when the first set was in the laundry, a blanket, a foam pillow, and a pair of canvas shoes. Suitably attired, they were split up, with Byron separated from the other three. They were led out while he was told to stand where he was. He wondered if Mills was about to take his revenge: Byron had challenged his authority in front of other guards.

Mills snuck dirty looks at him as he stood in the reception area but made no move towards him. 'You ready, Davis?' the other guard asked him.

Byron nodded.

'Come on,' said the guard, walking back into the shower room, then through a door and out into a large open dirt yard, Byron behind him.

The yard was one of four that Byron could see. Each was separated by the same type of chain-link, razor-wire-topped fencing that ran round the perimeter. The yards were empty. The only other inmate Byron could see was an older man who was busy sweeping dirt from a concrete walkway with a long wooden-handled broom.

'You got lucky,' the guard said to Byron, nodding in the direction of a low, white-washed single-story building at the far end of the yard. 'D Block is probably the best of the bunch round here. It's where we put the Anglos, Asians and assorted others. 'Less, of course, you'd rather mix it up with the Mexicans.'

Byron didn't reply. The guard had obviously picked up on his earlier reaction and was probing a little further.

'Silent type, huh?' the guard said. 'Fine by me. Just do your work, keep your head down and you'll be out of here by Christmas. Of course, I can't guarantee which Christmas. Not that it matters much to a guy like you. No family able to raise the money. You were up in front of Billy Kelsen, right? What'd he try and hit you for? Five grand?'

'Ten,' Byron said, throwing the guard a bone.

The guard burst out laughing. 'Ten big ones? What you do? Get caught trying to screw his wife?'

'I was just passing through,' Byron said.

The guard stopped to survey the yards and the cavernous prison buildings. 'Yeah, we get a lot of that around here.'

They reached the entrance to D Block. A camera mounted high on the outside wall swiveled round. A second later there was a click and the door swung open. Byron followed the guard inside.

There was a rectangular waiting area with two doors off it. The guard motioned for Byron to step through the one on the right, then followed him into a long room crammed with what looked like green metal-framed military-issue bunk beds. Each was neatly made, the corners squared, any personal belongings stowed away in matching green-metal lockers. The room was around forty feet wide and 120 feet long. There must have been at least forty running along each side with another column down the middle.

Byron flashed back almost immediately to the many army camps he had spent time in over the years. Strangely, he felt more at home than he had in some time. It was a world he knew well, and with this rush of familiarity came a sense of comfort.

The guard pointed out a bunk near the door. 'The top one there should be free.' He walked over to it, and nudged open the top locker with the butt of his baton. It was empty. 'Yup, it's all yours. You can throw your shit in here.'

Byron carefully placed his gear on the two shelves and closed the locker door. The guard tilted his wrist, glancing at his watch. 'Dinner's in the mess hall at seven. Until then your time's your own. Enjoy it while it lasts. Your little vacation finishes tomorrow.'

The guard turned on his heel and walked back towards the door. Byron watched him leave, listening as the sound of his boots on the bare concrete floor died away to a distant   echo.

CHAPTER THIRTEEN

Since leaving New York for the last time, Byron had led a solitary existence. Now he stood in the middle of the bunkhouse and listened to the silence. From the rows of lockers filled with meagre belongings, he knew it wouldn't last.

He climbed up onto his bunk, stretched out and closed his eyes. He ran through what he had gathered so far about the Kelsen County Jail.

Security was medium grade and focused almost exclusively on the perimeter. Two fences running parallel with coils of razor wire at the top. They didn't look juiced. Electrifying one or both would have demanded warning notices and he hadn't seen any. No doubt movement sensors were buried at the fence in case anyone tried to tunnel their way under it. Other than the fences and a few locked doors, that was it.

Once you were inside the unit you were free to move around at will. Two cameras, one mounted at each end of the bunkhouse, monitored the prisoners, but Byron would bet that the guards in the control room didn't watch things closely. Unless there was a fight or some other disturbance.

Reassured that escape would be difficult but far from impossible, Byron slowed his breathing. Within five minutes he was asleep.

He was woken by the sound of inmates walking back into the unit. Peering down, he watched an exhausted procession of men in prison blues make their way wearily towards their bunks. Each man carried a pair of heavy work boots, dusted with red desert dirt.

Some flopped immediately onto their bunks. Others undressed, grabbed a towel from their locker and headed for the showers. A few of the men were Caucasian, the rest Hispanic. They were lean to the point of skeletal but with ridges of muscle on their arms and backs that suggested hours of heavy labor.

A white man with close-cropped ginger hair and a ragged red beard sat on the edge of the bunk directly beneath Byron. He looked to be in his early forties, although Byron might have been out by ten years either side. He let out a low groan as his head fell into his hands. 'Goddamn, but it's hotter than a son of a bitch out there,' he said.

Byron didn't offer a response. He wasn't looking to make friends. He didn't plan on being around much longer than a few days. If, as he suspected, the prisoners were sent out on a daily work detail, he figured that the razor wire and fences wouldn't be a factor. He could simply pick his moment and slip quietly away.

His bunk mate stood up again. He dug his thumbs into his lower back. He looked up towards Byron. 'Not much of a talker, huh?' he said.

Byron swung his legs over the side of his bunk and jumped down. Instinctively the man took a couple of steps back. Byron towered over him.

'Didn't mean anything by it,' the man said. 'Just making conversation.'

Byron stared at him, holding his gaze, not blinking. He was aware of other prisoners throwing sideways glances, curious to see how this encounter would turn out. The man took one more step back.

Assured that he had established his dominance, Byron reached out his hand. 'John Davis.'

Tentatively the man shook it. 'Clayton Rice, but everyone calls me Red.'

Byron dropped the man's calloused hand without

saying anything further.

'So, what they get you for?' Red said. 'No, wait, let me guess. Speeding?'

Speeding, thought Byron. Speeding was a ticket. It didn't involve the county jail. Not unless you racked up a bunch of tickets and didn't pay them. 'People are in here for speeding?' he asked Red, curiosity getting the better of him.

Red smiled. 'Speeding. Dropping litter. Spitting on the sidewalk. Round here they have what they call a policy of zero tolerance. If you're not from here, of course. The locals can pretty much do as they please but that's a whole other story.'

'I wasn't caught speeding,' Byron said. 'You?'

'Found me hitching a ride on a freight train. That was enough for 'em. It was five thousand bucks or thirty days in County. I didn't have no five grand but I do have all the time in the world. Least, I figured so at the time. That was six months ago,' Red said.

Red's answer begged an obvious next question. Byron didn't get to ask it before Red offered up the explanation.

'Bet you're wondering how come thirty days became six months,' he said.

Byron nodded.

Red tugged at the corner of his blanket, pulling it out from where it had been tucked under the mattress. 'That there,' Red said, holding up the edge of the blanket, 'that's a violation. Three violations is an extra week. Half of the time guys don't know they've broken a rule until they're standing in front of Castro.'

Out of the corner of his eye, Byron saw another inmate heading towards them. He was naked bar a towel wrapped around his waist. The route from his bunk to the showers wouldn't have taken him that way so Byron knew it had to be a deliberate detour. The guy was big, close to Byron's height and almost as heavy.

As he walked through the bunkhouse the other men either made sure to get out of his way or suddenly took an intense interest in something else.

'Well, I'd better get a shower before all the hot water's gone,' said Red, hurriedly reaching into his locker.

He was already too late. The big guy stepped in front of him as Red tried to step away from their bunk area. 'You got those smokes for me?' the big guy said to Red.

Red's body language shifted. His shoulders dropped. So did his head. He couldn't bring himself to look at the guy. 'Kinda light this week, Franco,' Red said.

'That's too bad,' Franco said. He glanced across to Byron. 'Bunk rent is two smokes a day.'

Byron's body tensed. He stared at Franco. There was no blush of yellow. No smear of red. Franco was neither scared nor angry. He was simply conducting business and obviously didn't perceive Byron as a newcomer who presented any threat to him or his bunk-rental scheme.

Although he didn't plan on an extended stay, Byron didn't take well to being shaken down. Not by a judge, and certainly not by a convict whose neck measurement was larger than his IQ.

At the same time, Byron had already seen a fellow prisoner sent to the hole for a minor show of dissent. He guessed that beating a fellow prisoner within an inch of his life would earn him a stint there too. He could handle solitary but it would almost certainly make escape more difficult.

There was something else. If he got into it with the cell-block bully, Byron wasn't sure how it would go. He wasn't worried about beating the man in front of him. But it would take an effort that could easily get out of control. Murder was murder, whether it happened on the outside or inside prison walls. And while he doubted the guards caught everything on the live camera feed, they wouldn't miss him beating another inmate to death.

'Two smokes?' Byron said. 'Not a problem.'

Franco's expression suggested he'd been hoping for more of a reaction from the newcomer but also that part of him was relieved it had gone so easily. 'Okay. Good,' he said. 'Now, Red, you got until tomorrow. You don't have what you owe by then, well, you and me are going to have a problem.'

'Don't worry,' said Red. 'I'll have them.'

Franco lumbered off. Red put his towel back in the locker. A shower could wait.

Byron watched Franco continue his bunk tour, making threats and picking up rent as he went. He had zero intention of being extorted by a wall-puncher like Franco. In any case, he assumed it would be academic. By the time Franco started pushing him for cigarettes, Byron planned on being long gone.

CHAPTER FOURTEEN

Byron sat at a table in the cavernous mess hall with his bunk mate, Red. Going by the chatter of Spanish, the jail's population was mostly Mexican. The prisoners appeared to self-segregate along racial lines. Despite his mixed parentage, Byron appeared to have been accorded honorary white status: he was sitting with the jail's minority Caucasian population.

The food was slopped onto metal trays. A gristly stew, two slices of white bread, rice, beans, chocolate cake that had the consistency of a house brick, and a moldy orange. It was a grim offering. Byron didn't mind. He was hungry. He had spent so much time in far-flung parts of the world with bizarre local cuisines that he had come to regard any meal that didn't give him food poisoning as adequate. To maintain his spirits he made a promise to himself to hit a diner for steak and eggs as soon as he was clear of Kelsen County Jail.

Red jabbed at a lone piece of meat in the pool of gravy. 'Didn't figure you as a guy who'd let Franco push you around so easy,' he said to Byron.

Byron continued eating. He looked beyond to the sea of inmates hunched over their trays. Their primary state seemed to be one of exhaustion. 'Everyone works during the day?' he asked Red.

His question earned a few smiles from the other inmates at the table. 'Twelve hours. Six until six. Hard labor. Six days. They give us Sundays off. 'Less you're lucky enough to get yourself a job cleaning or in the kitchen. But those jobs tend to be kept for the locals, or people with families that send in extra cash.'

Byron guessed that hard labor served two functions.

For one thing it acted as a deterrent, demonstrating that the sheriff was tough on people who broke the law. More importantly, though, an inmate exhausted by backbreaking manual work was far less likely to cause any disciplinary problems. Or, for that matter, to have the energy to plot an escape. Work was a good way of controlling a population and ensuring compliance.

'What do you mean, "the locals"?' Byron asked. 'Aren't most of you from around here?'

The questions elicited some wider smiles. Red threw back his head and laughed. The sound caused a guard standing by the mess-hall door to look over. The smiles evaporated. Red made like he was having a coughing fit. 'You don't get it, do you? I had you figured as a smart guy too,' he said.

'Most county jails are full of people who live in the county,' Byron said.

'Not here they ain't,' said Red. 'Kelsen's like one of those Venus flytraps – they take their time eating you.'

Byron watched as Mills swaggered towards them, his hand falling to his baton. Byron gave Red a warning nod. Red clammed up, and buried his head in his meal. The guard switched course, distracted by another table where a small knot of Latino prisoners seemed about to have a fight over some minor infraction of prison etiquette.

The rest of the meal passed in silence. There was no lingering. Once a meal was finished, or abandoned, the inmates got up from their table, scraped off any leftovers, and dumped their trays in a pile next to the serving hatch. Some went straight back to the bunkhouse. A few hardier souls headed out to the yard. Here, too, the groups seemed to be broken down along racial lines.

Byron took a walk around the perimeter with Red. 'You're the second person who's said to me that Kelsen County is different,' Byron said to him.

Red reached down and picked up a pebble. He tossed it from hand to hand. 'I don't know if it's all that different.

They're just another grade of asshole.'

'So what did you mean about it being like a Venus flytrap?' Byron asked him. He was interested in the answer, but only to a degree. He wanted to give the impression of being occupied by the conversation while he got closer to the inside fence so that he could scope it out better. He could have asked Red about security but he didn't yet trust him. It would only take Red making a casual mention of Byron's interest in it for him to find himself in solitary, facing an extra level of escape challenges.

Red shook his head. 'Like I said, you're a smart guy, you'll figure it out. Everyone does, eventually.'

CHAPTER FIFTEEN

An hour later a klaxon sounded from one of the guard towers to announce the end of yard time. The inmates filtered slowly back into the bunkhouses. Byron couldn't tell whether it was reluctance to leave the yard or sheer fatigue that had reduced many of them to a zombie-like walking pace. He guessed it was a mixture of both.

Inside the bunkhouse some men hit the showers. Others, who had already washed, lay on their bunks. A few played dominoes or cards or sat around bullshitting about the usual staples of male conversation: sport and women.

Franco sat across the bunkhouse. He was surrounded by a little posse of thick-necked buddies who looked like the left-hand side of a poster showing human evolution. Byron was aware of him peering now and then towards his and Red's bunks. He would glance at them, say something to his buddies and they would snicker among themselves. Byron stripped down to his underwear, left his clothes folded with razor sharp creases on top of his bunk, grabbed a towel and headed for the showers.

Once he had dried off, he walked back to his bunk. He climbed onto the top bunk, laced his fingers behind his head, and stared up at the ceiling. For the past few weeks he had been sleeping outside. He would dig in under a juniper tree, with his boots hanging up on a branch to prevent scorpions climbing into them, and watch the stars until his campfire died to the embers.

This was a very different experience, and not in a good way. Byron did not crave the company of others. He never had. His preference, even when working for the government, was to operate on his own. He enjoyed solitude. If anything, his need to be alone was even more pronounced now than it had been before. There was an additional tension underlying it. Byron needed to be apart from others because he no longer trusted himself not to hurt people.

That was what he was thinking about as he lay awake, craving the blue-black dome of a vast sky. He thought back to New York, Las Vegas, and the facility. To the people he had hurt. To the people he had killed. Some, it could be argued, had deserved to die. Others had not.

As soon as he could, he had to get out of here. To move on. To separate himself from people.

Byron's eyes snapped open from a deep sleep. It took a moment for his conscious mind to tell him where he was. In that moment he felt a sudden acceleration of his heart rate. He remembered. His heart rate stilled to a normal level.

It was dark in the bunkhouse. Quiet. But not silent. Beyond the low-level snoring from every corner, Byron heard something else. It was a man's voice. He couldn't pick out the words. He could only get a sense of tone. Whoever it was, and whatever words he was using, he appeared to be pleading.

He listened more intently. He heard someone else speak. By contrast this person sounded calm and in control.

None of my business, Byron reminded himself. He closed his eyes again. Tried to conjure up an image of the stars he should have been looking at.

It was no use. He would struggle to sleep now. In any case, he needed to pee.

The nearby talk was louder now. He did his best to filter it out. It was no use. More voices joined the two he had already heard.

Byron leaned over the edge of his bunk, making sure that Red was still there. He was. He looked up at Byron, eyes open.

'None of our business,' Red whispered.

'What's going on?' Byron asked.

'Go back to sleep,' Red said.

Byron sat up. He swung his legs over the side of the bunk and jumped down, then started slowly towards the showers. Red reached out a hand to stop him. Byron shrugged him off.

'It's your funeral,' Red said.

Byron reached the doorway to the showers. Now he could hear what was being said and suddenly wished he had taken Red's advice.

A man's voice, the slow, calm one he had heard before, said, 'Let it happen and it won't hurt so much.'

Byron took another step. His bare feet found wet tiles. Two of Franco's buddies each had the arm of a young inmate. His face was pressed against the wall, his pants pulled down. Franco was kneading the young man's ass cheeks.

'I said, relax,' Franco told his victim.

Franco's head turned slowly as he realized they were no longer alone. That Byron was standing there watching them.

Franco's tight expression gave way to a smile. 'Hey, Davis. This is a private party.'

'Party's over,' Byron said, taking another step towards the three men.

CHAPTER SIXTEEN

Franco's hand pressed against Byron's chest.

'You can either party with us,' Franco said, 'or you can go on back to your bunk.'

Franco's two buddies had loosened their grip on their young victim. They still had hold of his arms, but he wasn't pressed up against the wall. He wrenched his head round and stared at Byron, his eyes pleading for someone to save him.

Byron's eyes flicked back to Franco. He met his gaze. Franco was as big as Byron. His two buddies were about the same size. All three men had bodies hardened by weeks and months of manual labor. They were three and Byron was one. Their intended victim looked too petrified to be of any assistance.

'I told you. The party's over,' Byron said.

'And I told you to run along,' Franco said.

Three to one. Not great odds. Assuming he had to fight all three.

They wouldn't wait their turn. Prison fights tended not to go like that. They wouldn't take a number and wait for him to deal with Franco before they stepped up. They would wild-dog him. Punches and kicks would come from all sides. They would swarm.

The shower room was wet. If he slipped and went down, he'd likely be kicked and stomped to a pulp. Possibly to death.

If he fought back, he could lose control of himself entirely, switch into a mode where he was no longer really human. If that happened, it was entirely possible he could kill all three.

Neither option was good. Both would all but obliterate any chance he had of escaping. At best it would complicate matters beyond a point where he had any control.

He should have stayed in his bunk. He should have taken Red's advice. Shoulda. Woulda. Coulda.

He had allowed curiosity to get the better of him. And now he couldn't stand by and surrender the boy to his fate.

Franco's eyes narrowed. 'You're still here. Thought I told you to run along.'

Byron allowed his body to relax. His shoulders slumped, his feet inched apart. He stared into Franco's eyes. Slowly he brought both his arms up from his sides. He smiled, moving his hands up slowly until the tips of his fingers touched Franco's cheekbones.

Franco didn't move. He seemed transfixed. A punch. A kick. A lunge. That was what a man like Franco might have expected. What the hell was this guy doing?

Franco raised his hands to push Byron away. 'I ain't no faggot,' he said.

Without warning, Byron spread the fingers of both hands wide, digging his thumbs into Franco's temples and his little fingers into the mandibular nerve under the hinge of his jaw. Then he opened his mouth and bit down hard on Franco's nose, biting straight through the cartilage. Blood spurted out.

Franco tried to push him away. To prise him off. Byron's grip held fast.

The pain in Franco's temples, mandibular nerve, and from his near amputated nose would have been overwhelming. Individually each offered a rich harvest of pain. Together, the shock and trauma to the central nervous system would have been catastrophic.

Byron kept biting down. Finally, he felt the last stand of cartilage and flesh give way. He let go, shoving Franco hard in the chest. The man was screaming with pain. His high-pitched keening seemed completely at odds with his size.

Byron spat the bulbous chunk of Franco's nose onto the shower-room floor. Franco's two compadres had let go of their victim. They stood there, arms raised, fists clenched, but ultimately frozen.

There was a white plastic bottle of disinfectant sitting on the floor. Byron picked it up. He reached over and turned on one of the shower heads.

He took a mouthful of disinfectant. It burned as he sluiced it around his mouth. Better a mild chemical burn than Hep-C, HIV or whatever the hell else was coursing through Franco's veins.

Franco was lying on the floor. His legs were tucked up under his chin. He was still screaming.

Byron spat out his improvised mouthwash and stepped under the torrent of water, quickly washing off the blood that had dribbled down his chin and onto his chest. An alarm had started to sound. It was deafening. But not deafening enough to drown out Franco's screaming.

Franco's two sidekicks stared at Byron. They didn't know whether to call or fold. They ended up doing neither. Their victim had wriggled free. He squeezed past Byron. One of the other two began to go after him. Byron took a single step to the right, the warning implicit.

He turned on his heel and walked out of the showers. By the time the first guard came rushing into the bunkhouse, still hastily pulling on pieces of riot gear, Byron was already on his bunk, staring at the ceiling. The only clue that he'd moved was the damp blanket covering his body.

CHAPTER SEVENTEEN

Prison law dictated that no one was going to offer up Byron as the man who had bitten off Franco's nose. Partly that was down to the code that dictated a snitch was the lowest of the low. But there was another factor at play. Put simply, what penalty might a man pay for informing on someone who had demonstrated such extreme violence in a situation that, again according to prison rules, had been (strictly speaking) none of his business?

Besides, Franco had terrorized the unit for months. He had taxed every inmate outside his very small circle. He'd had it coming. The Darwinian law of survival of the fittest dictated that, sooner or later, someone would to knock him off his perch. No one had guessed that he'd lose his beak at the same time, and there was a secret delight among the inmates that even the most regimented of jails could offer up a rare surprise.

After the lights had gone on and the guards had arrived, after Franco had been carted off to the prison infirmary, claiming, between shrieks, that he had slipped and fallen, after his nose had been bagged up in a Ziplock full of ice, Warden Castro had appeared, red-faced from being woken at home, his hairline at a jaunty angle

'I want to know who the hell did this,' he fumed, pacing up and down the length of the bunkhouse.

The inmates stood by their bunks. Eyes forward. Backs straight. Saying nothing. Byron had witnessed this scene back in the military. The rules were the same. You didn't rat anyone out and you took your lumps. If someone kept screwing up they got dealt with by the group. Somehow he didn't see that happening under these circumstances. Everything else was noise and fury.

Castro stopped in front of Red and Byron's bunk. 'What about you two assholes? You know anything about who bit off the man's nose?'

Byron stared straight ahead, his face set like granite.

Castro prodded his chest. 'Answer me.'

Byron could smell cilantro and gut-rot whisky on the warden's breath. 'No, sir,' he said. 'I was sleeping. Didn't see nothing.'

'You slept through that?' the warden bellowed.

'Guess I woke up for the screaming part,' Byron said, unable to rein in a childish desire to yank the warden's chain just a little.

The warden stepped behind him. He reached up and ran a hand across Byron's bunk. 'Why is your blanket wet, inmate?'

Byron didn't answer.

The warden stepped back so that he was standing in front of Byron. 'I asked you a question, inmate.'

'Guess I must have had a nightmare, Warden. I get night sweats sometimes,' Byron said.

'Night sweats? You expect me to believe that bunch of bullshit?'

'Or I pissed the bed,' Byron offered.

The inmates' snickers ran the length of the bunkhouse in a wave. They were snuffed out by the guards shouting for silence, telescopic steel batons smacking into their open palms for emphasis.

Byron waited for the warden to explode. He was pretty sure that his smart mouth had earned him a week or more in solitary. He had just dug his own grave. He would sit in the hole and when the door opened someone from Washington would be there and it would be over, once and for ever.

He closed his eyes. He cursed his own stupidity. He had ridden right up to the line, then gleefully skipped over it. Now he would pay the price. When Byron finally opened his eyes the warden was still staring at him. 'See me in my office tomorrow morning, before you head off on work detail.' He turned around to face the body of men standing by their bunks. 'I see any more trouble from any of you and you'll all be sorry. Real sorry.'

CHAPTER EIGHTEEN

The mess hall buzzed as Byron stood in line. One of the servers, a short, muscular Mexican whom Byron recognized from his own unit, slopped a double portion of rehydrated eggs onto his tray with the glimmer of a smile. Byron wasn't sure whether an extra serving of eggs that had likely never been near a chicken was a good thing, but he appreciated the gesture.

He took his tray to a seat at what was already his regular spot at the table next to Red. Red hadn't yet said anything to him this morning about the previous night's events. A four-fifteen alarm call tended to put a dampener on conversation. Most inmates navigated their morning routine with little more than the odd grunt.

It was not yet five a.m., and all the inmates were showered, dressed and having breakfast. Byron had already worked out that the dawn call wasn't in place so that they could sit around doing needlepoint or watching TV. He dug into the food in front of him. Years of military issue MREs (meals ready to eat) had conditioned him, in certain circumstances, to switch off his taste buds. Sometimes food was nothing more than fuel. This was one of those times. He ate mechanically and kept his head down.

He sensed other inmates sneaking glances at him from every corner of the mess hall. It was not a good feeling. Byron's working life had been predicated on being a 'grey man', someone with a particular set of skills who managed to blend into the background to the point of anonymity, and he'd had to work to develop the ability. His height and build had made it more of a challenge than it was for other operators. Contrary to popular mythology, men who did this work tended to be shorter and more compact than a regular special-forces soldier. Now, having done what he had to Franco, he could have been five feet zero and a hundred pounds and he would still have been the center of attention.

Perhaps he should have stayed in his bunk and let the law of the jungle run its course. After all, everyone else had. Last night probably hadn't been the first time that Franco and his two buddies had attempted to rape another inmate. Byron guessed that Franco used violent sexual assault as an instrument of control. The threat of being beaten or shanked was one thing. Rape was violence of a different order. It was as close as one human being could come to taking another's soul. That was its power, and also its horror.

One of the other inmates at Byron's table finished his meal. He pushed away his tray, reached into the top pocket of his prison blues, took out two cigarettes and palmed them across the table to Byron. Glancing up, Byron said, 'Keep them. I don't smoke.'

The man seemed puzzled. 'Franco didn't either.'

'Tell you what,' Byron said, 'if I need a favor, I'll expect you to oblige. But until then ...'

The inmate seemed discomforted by this new regime. 'What kind of a favor we talking?' he asked.

'One that won't involve anyone putting something in their mouth they don't want to.'

Red laughed. The other inmates sniggered. Whatever tension had lain like a thick blanket of smog over the mess hall seemed to evaporate. The chatter at the other tables turned from whispers to the usual level of conversation.

Normal service had resumed.

Byron was dumping his tray when Mills walked over to him, thumbs dug into the belt loops of his khaki pants. 'Davis, warden wants to see you in his office now.'

The tray clattered onto the stack, and Byron followed the guard out of the mess hall and across the yard.

CHAPTER NINETEEN

Mills led Byron into the main administration building. They passed offices occupied by a mix of guards and civilian workers. Left-turning down a long stretch of corridor, they emerged into a small reception area. Byron was told to take a seat.

Mills fell into a conversation with the warden's secretary, a woman in her mid-forties with auburn hair cut into bob. Byron tuned into their conversation just long enough to work out that the topic was their kids' little league baseball teams.

A few moments later, the warden's office door opened and Castro's head appeared round the frame. 'Come on in, Davis. This won't take long.'

Byron stood up and started towards the office. Mills threw an arm over his chest, barring his way. 'You want me too, Warden?'

The warden smiled. 'No, I don't think that will be necessary, Billy. Will it, Mr Davis?'

Byron shook his head. 'No.'

Castro held the door open. Mills stepped back. He sat down in the seat that Byron had occupied. 'I'll be here if you need me, Warden,' he said.

'Appreciate that,' Castro said.

Byron walked past Castro into the office. Castro motioned him to a seat in front of the desk, then closed the door.

The warden's office was about two hundred square feet of grey carpet and plain grey walls. Besides the desk and chairs, there was a small couch with a coffee-table covered in magazines about sport fishing and hunting. A credenza was topped with family pictures. A wife, two daughters as kids, then grown-up, grandchildren . . .

Castro followed Byron's gaze. 'You have any family, Davis?'

Byron looked back across the desk to him. 'No,' he said flatly.

'Not much of a man for small-talk?' Castro asked.

Byron shrugged his broad shoulders. 'All depends on the company.'

Castro got up from his seat and stood, knuckles on his desk. 'You don't like me? That's okay. I don't much like lawbreakers. But seeing as we're both here . . .'

Byron stared at him. 'I don't think of myself as a lawbreaker, Warden.'

That earned a smile from Castro. 'Sure. Sure. This is all one big misunderstanding. Hell, the jails in this country are full of innocent people. Anyway, I guess we'll both find out which side of the line we've fallen on when we go to meet our maker.'

'I expect we will,' Byron said. He was careful not to make any claims as to where he'd end up. Heaven and Hell held little promise or threat for a man who had already been condemned to a living form of purgatory. As for other people, Byron didn't presume to judge, though he suspected that the warden's heavenly seat might not be quite as secure as the man's apparent smugness seemed to suggest. Unless they guarded against it, high rank could have that effect on people.

'Should we talk about last night, Davis?' Castro said.

Byron smiled inwardly at the warden's choice of words. It sounded like the opening line of a romantic comedy. 'Yes, sir,' he said.

Castro sat down. He let out a sigh. Byron could sense a speech coming down the track. He wasn't to be disappointed.

'What happened last night has been coming for a while

now. Long before you ever set foot in Kelsen County,' Castro began. His eyes narrowed. 'Not that I can condone it, you understand?'

Byron gave a solemn nod, which, he hoped, communicated that he regarded the event with equal gravity.

'Violence of any kind is not something I like to see here,' Castro continued. 'Unfortunately, with so many men living in such close proximity, separated from the calming influence of their families, it's almost inevitable. But I like to keep a lid on it. Minimize it, if you will.'

Byron said nothing. There was nothing to say.

'I know it was you, Davis,' Castro said. 'I'm not asking you to admit it. I don't need you to. But I want you to understand that I know you're guilty. There's nothing that goes on inside these walls that I don't know about. I make it my business. So don't think you got one over on me.' He coughed into his hand.

Byron braced himself. He assumed this was Castro's lead in to telling him that there was no alternative bar a week in solitary for such a brazen infringement of the rules.

Castro went on, 'I guess old Franco had outlived his usefulness. It was always going to happen. But it kind of leaves me with a dilemma. You see, I like to have one man inside every unit to make sure I don't have any problems.'

Of course, thought Byron. He should have seen this coming. Punishment would have been swift and sudden. It wouldn't have required a trip to the warden's office for the metaphorical equivalent of coffee and cake. Castro wanted Byron to pick up where Franco had left off. 'What kind of problems are we talking about, Warden?'

Castro positively beamed. He stood up again. 'See?' he said, jabbing a sausage-shaped finger at Byron. 'Franco would never have thought to ask me. I had to pretty much tell him exactly what I needed from him.'

Byron wondered if the warden's instructions to Franco had extended to the attempted rape of young inmates in the showers after lights out. Probably not, but if they had, Castro wasn't about to admit it in front of another inmate. Byron allowed the question to go unasked. There was no need to spoil the warden's good mood.

'Let's not think of them as problems, Davis. Let's just say that I like things to be orderly. To run smoothly. For there to be as few interruptions to the smooth running of this facility as possible,' Castro added.

Byron allowed a smile to cross his face. He chose his words with care. 'Franco has a couple of buddies still in the unit. I don't think they were too happy about what happened last night.'

'They give you any trouble, you can deal with them. I doubt they will, though. One of the men you're talking about was the shot caller before Franco. They know how this place operates,' Castro said.

Byron wasn't sure he shared the warden's optimism. A former shot caller was more than likely to see Franco being deposed as an opportunity to assume his former position. 'Why didn't you ask him to take over?' he asked.

'Pretty simple, ain't it? Franco kicked his ass. You kicked Franco's ass. That leaves you in the catbird seat,' Castro said. 'Anyway, like I said, that's all up to you.'

'Anything else I should know, Warden?' Byron asked.

Castro studied the corners of his office, as if trying to conjure up something important that he had forgotten. As a piece of acting, Byron wasn't buying it.

'Oh, yeah,' Castro said, when he was done ruminating. 'Matter of fact, there is.'

Byron waited.

'There's a Mexican gentleman who's currently thinking about things in our secure housing unit.'

The secure housing unit, or SHU, was solitary.

'Goes by the name of Romero. He's what you might

call an agitator. Communist agitator would be more precise. He'll be back in your unit in a few days. If he starts any more trouble, stirring things up with the beaners, well, I'd like you to ...' Castro trailed off. 'I'd like you to speak with him. Perhaps persuade him to keep his views to himself. Save them for back home where his kind of talk might be better received. Remind him, if you need to, that this is America.'

CHAPTER TWENTY

With Red and a dozen other inmates from the unit, Byron clambered into the back of a pickup truck driven by one of the guards. His head was still reeling from the meeting with the warden. He had gone in expecting to face further sanctions but had come out as the unit's shot caller. The only conclusion he could draw was that, sadly, Kelsen County Jail, like so many other places on earth, prized violence more than kindness, brutality more than compassion.

Two long metal benches holding work tools ran along either side of the truck's flatbed. Byron took a seat next to Red and grabbed at the lip of the truck to steady himself as it pulled out of a side yard where they had assembled after breakfast.

'You're the shot caller now, huh?' Red said to him.

Byron glanced at his bunk mate.

'It's okay. You don't have to tell me if you don't want to,' Red told him.

'That's good,' Byron said.

A few more moments passed. They were reaching a main gate. Beyond it lay the wide-open scrub desert of southern Texas. It was just a shame that all of the men had been issued with longer-chained cuffs and shackles, which would allow them to swing a pick or dig, before they had left the jail. Byron had watched the guards hauling out the irons with a slow, sinking feeling in his stomach.

The truck joined a long line of others on a service road leading from the jail complex. Heavy-duty Ford SUVs, with Kelsen County Jail markings, led and brought up the rear of the convoy. The SUVs each held two guards armed with pump-action shotguns. If the shackles didn't slow down a fleeing prisoner then a solidly aimed shotgun blast would do the trick.

They headed south, towards the city of Kelsen. A golf course appeared to their left. Byron glimpsed a mixed foursome, made up of two elderly white couples, lining up their putts. None of them so much as looked at the prisoners as they drove past. The chain-gang convoy was a familiar sight, not worthy of notice.

To Byron's surprise, the convoy slowed. The lead SUV peeled off with two of the trucks and turned down a road that led into the golf course. Byron nudged Red. He'd been trying to avoid conversation but curiosity had finally gotten the better of him. 'They use us to maintain the golf course?' Byron said. He caught himself. Why had he said 'us'? It had slipped out. It was a reminder of the danger, if one was needed, of how easy it was to become institutionalized. He would have to guard against it and keep at the front of his mind that his task was to escape, not to settle into the routine of jail life.

Red put up a hand to shield his eyes from the blazing Texas sun. 'Golf courses. Roads. Sewers. If there's a shitty job that the locals won't do, you can pretty much guarantee that we'll catch it.' He began to regale Byron and the rest of the prisoners with an elaborate story about a sewage blockage. Byron tuned out. Slowly, piece by piece, he was beginning to work out how, and more crucially why, Kelsen County was starting to make sense.

As the other prisoners howled with laughter at Red's tale, Byron watched the rear SUV close up, then overtake the rear of the convoy and slot into the middle. Another half-mile down the road, the work trucks that were left began to slow. The lead truck turned off the road.

There were four trucks left now. They drove on. After a further quarter-mile they, too, slowed and turned off, heading down a dirt road towards a row of low farm buildings. They stopped outside a large barn. The guard drivers clambered up, dropped the tail gates and ushered the prisoners down.

It was no easy task getting off the back of a truck with leg irons. Byron watched the others' technique, which involved clasping the rear edge of the truck until the last moment and then jumping. Byron took his turn, stumbling slightly. He had yet to do a lick of work but already the oppressive heat had begun to sap his energy. The guards ordered the men into a line while they climbed onto the back of the trucks and collected the tools, which they laid on the ground. The guards stepped back. The men were ordered to step forward and collect the spade, pick or hoe in front of them.

Depending upon what they had picked up, they were ordered into gangs of four, then led in single file beyond the farm buildings. More guards followed them, each holding a pump-action shotgun.

The prisoners were set to work on a large open expanse of rough ground. Byron's new rank as bunkhouse shot caller hadn't saved him from drawing a gig on the pickaxe gang. He and the other three men were told to begin breaking ground.

Unlike golf-course maintenance, Byron couldn't see the purpose of breaking the hard, dry ground. It didn't look like land that would bear any kind of a crop. He worked anyway, finding a steady rhythm with the pick, pacing himself as best he could in the suffocating heat. He watched the other men. He made sure to match his pace to a little above the slowest man. He would need all the energy he could conserve if he was ever going to get the hell out of here.

CHAPTER TWENTY-ONE

Every half-hour the men were allowed a five-minute break and given water. A half-hour at a desk, doing a job you didn't much care for, might seem to some like a long time. A half-hour swinging a pickaxe was an eternity.

When they stopped working and took their break, there was no talking. They caught their breath, massaged burning muscle with their fingers, and drank as much as they could.

They went on for three hours, then Mills called lunch. Brown bags were produced from the front of the trucks and handed out, along with fresh water.

Byron looked around. 'How long do we get now?' he asked the man standing next to him.

The man shrugged.

The man on his other side said, 'He doesn't speak English. We get forty minutes.'

'Be good if we could get some shade. Maybe in one of those barns over there,' said Byron.

Mills was passing and Byron called to him. 'Hey!'

Mills turned, a sour expression on his face. Byron was way too hot and exhausted to care. 'Couldn't we have our lunch over by the barns? Get some shade.'

Mills's response was to rack the shotgun, dropping a round into the chamber. He brought the weapon up to his shoulder, pointing it straight at Byron.

Byron didn't flinch. He'd had guns pointed at him before. Many times. Sometimes by people who actually planned on pulling the trigger. This was not one of those times. Not that Byron wanted to push the point. 'I guess that was a bad idea,' he said.

Mills lowered the barrel. His glare was replaced by a smirk. 'You guessed right. Now finish eating and get back to work. All of you.'

As Mills wandered out of earshot, one of the other men turned to Byron. 'You got lucky there. The last time a man on a work crew spoke to Mills like that they got pistol-whipped and thrown into the hole.'

Byron thought back to his morning meeting with the warden. 'The guy's name wasn't Romero by any chance, was it?' asked Byron.

The inmate's eyes fell to the ground. He looked over to the guards and back to Byron. 'Don't say that name round here either. Not unless you really want to see them lose their shit.'

CHAPTER TWENTY-TWO

Prison blues soaked through with sweat, Byron lowered his pickaxe as Mills called time on the day's work. He rested on the handle for a moment as he caught his breath.

He stared down at his hands, bloodied from the pressure blisters that had burst sometime in the late afternoon. Blood and sweat had made the handle of the pickaxe slippery. Tightening his grip to retain control of it had completed a loop of pain and discomfort.

He'd tried to comfort himself with the knowledge that the first day of any heavy labor was always the worst, then remembered that the second day, with muscles aching, was probably going to be worse. Whoever had coined the phrase 'the dignity of labor' had clearly never spent a full day under the unforgiving Texas sun, breaking bone-dry ground with a rock-like crust.

At least he knew now why, according to Red and other inmates, escape attempts from the Kelsen County's penitentiary were all but unheard of. The prisoners were likely too exhausted to plan, never mind execute, a successful escape.

Looking around, Byron saw other men frozen in place, without the energy to move. A stranger passing by might, at first glance, have taken the chain gang for a living-statue performance group. It was only when the guards began to urge them back towards the truck that they moved.

Not completely heartless, a couple of the guards helped one or two of the older convicts up onto the flatbed for the return journey. Byron managed to climb up without assistance but it was a closer run thing than he would have imagined that morning.

He stood as the guards gathered the shovels, pickaxes and hoes from the inmates, one guard keeping his shotgun trained on them in case they found the energy to try to embed the business end of an implement into a guard's skull. The guard running shotgun needn't have worried.

The inmates shuffled along the benches and, to an accompanying soundtrack of moans and groans, finally sat down.

The ride back passed in silence. The men stared with vacant eyes as they drove through the lush greenery of Kelsen. Even when they pulled up alongside an attractive blonde soccer mom driving a red convertible at one of the town's few stop lights, they could barely raise their heads, never mind pucker their lips to wolf-whistle.

They were spent, every last ounce of energy wrung out of them.

Byron thought back to how common this kind of life must have been for the generations that had come before him. A time before air-conditioned spaces, and office jobs in which the most physically demanding part of the day was changing the container on the office water-cooler. His experience today had been unexpected, and largely unwelcome, but also salutary.

Thanks to generations who had come before him, Byron had inherited a life that was free of manual labor. His decision to risk his body had been just that: a decision made of his own free will. A decision made after 9/11 when he had wanted to do something to safeguard the country he loved. None of it changed the fact that many people, most of them poor and brown, lived by hard labor.

The sun began to sink. The air cooled a few degrees. The truck left behind the perfectly manicured golf courses and spotlessly clean sidewalks of Kelsen City and settled back into the barren hinterland beyond. In the back, chins sank onto chests that slowly rose and fell. No one spoke.

Byron looked up as another truck fell in behind them. Then another. In a few minutes the morning convoy had reassembled, complete with front and rear security details.

Through the fog of tiredness clouding his mind, Byron

felt a sudden breath of clarity. They had security now. But for the past few miles it had been the inmates on the truck and the guards driving.

They turned down a service road and through the outer gate of the prison. The work day was done. They were home.

The truck came to a stop in the same yard it had left from. The inmates clambered down. The guards removed their cuffs and leg irons. They snaked their way in line through the yards and into the bunkhouse.

They had an hour until dinner. An hour of what, according to Red, the warden termed 'recreation and leisure'. Most of the men spent it lying on their bunks. A few took a shower. There was little leisure and even less recreation.

Byron lay on his bunk and did his best to run through the day. He conjured the details he had noted. Details that alone signified nothing but put together might allow him the barest skeleton of an escape plan. He didn't yet have a plan. That would take a little longer. Right now, he had what he needed. He had a start. A start was sufficient to keep a man going, even in the darkest of places.

CHAPTER TWENTY-THREE

Franco's two buddies stared at Byron from across the mess hall. When Byron stared back, they put their heads down and got back to their meal. Prison etiquette dictated that staring at another prisoner was an invitation to violence. The only thing worse, apart from trash talk or actual physical engagement, was pointing a finger at someone.

Red tossed his meal tray onto the table and sat diagonally across from Byron. He glanced over his shoulder at Franco's two enforcers. Ever since Byron had taken the role of unit shot caller, Red had found new confidence.

Byron would have to talk to him about it. Tell him to dial it back. Byron wouldn't be around much longer to keep the other inmates in check. They would be out for revenge and Red would be walking the yard with a big old target on his back. A few days in and already he was caught up in an unwelcome web of hierarchies.

Byron picked up his plastic spork and began to eat. It was amazing how a full day's manual labor could so vastly improve the food in the mess hall. He had to slow down his eating to avoid a post-dinner flush of indigestion.

Something else was different. Despite a day spent working in the hot sun, the men's mood in the mess hall had lightened. He doubted it could all be put down to his deposition of Franco and his taking up the mantle as a more benevolent dictator. For one thing the prisoners who seemed most happy weren't from his unit. The excitement seemed contained almost exclusively to the Mexicans.

He tried to tune into their conversations, which still took place at a discreet volume. After a few minutes, he began to pick up snatches. His Spanish was good enough for him to pick up the overall idea that change of some kind was coming . . . He heard Romero's name.

Byron would wait until he was back in the bunkhouse and ask Red. There were too many people to overhear, and too many people prepared to offer an opinion in the mess hall.

He mopped up the last of his gravy with a final hunk of plastic bread. He picked up the green, unripe apple he had been given, took a bite and ate it in record time. Then he sat back, listening to more fragments of conversation about Romero.

Suddenly the entire mess hall fell silent. Byron looked across at the serving area. The cooks had stopped mid-serve. The line of prisoners still waiting to be fed had frozen. Romero must have appeared, he thought.

Glancing over Red's shoulder, he saw the warden standing at the entrance, flanked on either side by the jail's meaner-looking guards. They were slapping the business end of their batons into their open palm, like riot cops itching to have an excuse to go to work.

'Prisoner Davis,' the warden said, plenty loud. 'Come with me.'

CHAPTER TWENTY-FOUR

Palms planted on the table, Byron got to his feet. He stepped out of the bench seat. He picked up his meal tray and walked over to the garbage area. Every inmate in the hall tracked his progress, most of them watching his feet.

He laid his tray on top of the stack, turned and walked slowly, hands loose by his sides, towards Warden Castro and the two guards. He was waiting for the two guards to swing their clubs. Or to order him onto the linoleum floor so that he could be safely cuffed and shackled. Perhaps they would dish out a beating in full view of the others. Maybe they would wait until they were clear of witnesses.

As far as Byron could figure it, there could be only two reasons for the warden arriving to escort him personally out of a busy mess hall. Neither was good.

First, someone had arrived from Washington to collect him. He wasn't on any official lists, such as the FBI's top ten most wanted. There was no way that the CIA, NSA or State Department would have sanctioned it. It would have invited way too many questions. Questions that all the main government agencies would have been terrified to be asked, never mind to answer.

There was, however, no doubt that he was near the top of any number of private watch lists. He had seen them when he'd been an operator. Those lists immediately triggered an alarm, usually deep within the bowels of the NSA. The person reporting, whether a local, state or federal worker, would never have any idea that what they had fed into the system was significant. Not until the Black Hawk helicopters and blacked out Escalades appeared to investigate further.

The second reason held less of an immediate threat to

Byron's life but it held a threat nonetheless. For the warden to call him out in public was dangerous in any prison population. Cozy chats between an inmate and a warden were usually kept on the down-low. No inmate wanted to be seen as close to the authorities. You'd be labeled a snitch, and that would get you hurt. Maybe not straight away, but eventually.

Maybe the warden had experienced a change of heart about Byron's shot-caller suitability. He could deal with that quite simply by getting out as soon as the opportunity presented itself. What really scared him, in as much as he was capable of feeling fear, was the first option. If he walked into the warden's office to find two men in suits, it was game over. Byron was a loose end, and the government didn't like loose ends. Especially loose ends who knew where the rest of the bodies were buried.

His heart sinking into his boots, Byron followed the warden and the two guards out of the mess hall. No one said a word. Behind him he heard the chatter resume. This time Romero was not the name on everyone's lips. Now the name was Davis.

Byron stepped into the warden's office. Castro looked at the two guards. They were still clutching their batons.

They looked crestfallen. They weren't going to reduce Byron to a shredded pulp of blood and bone. Not just yet, anyway.

'Sit down, Davis,' Castro said.

Byron sat. At least there didn't seem to be anyone waiting for him. That didn't mean they weren't, of course. But he doubted he would have been left alone in an office with one man if he was being picked up on his way to a grey site.

Warden Castro let out a long sigh. 'Davis, I put you in charge to keep things even, not to go stirring them up.'

His mind still filled with thoughts of being whisked

away, Byron didn't immediately follow. He looked at Castro. 'How have I stirred things up exactly, Warden?'

'The guards here don't like being questioned. Not by an inmate. Not by any inmate.'

He'd asked the guard if the work party could eat their lunch in the shade of the barn. Mills hadn't taken it too well. No doubt he'd expressed his displeasure to the warden. Marching Byron out of the hall seemed like an overreaction. He guessed that there was more to it than a disgruntled guard.

In the meantime there was nothing more for Byron to do than apologize. 'It won't happen again,' he said. 'I guess I didn't think before I opened my mouth.'

The warden was still irritated. 'You're damn right you didn't. Anyway, I have a few other things to talk over with you.'

Byron waited. He was still taken aback by how quickly his act of violence had earned him a regular place in the warden's office.

'Maybe,' the warden began, 'a man with your responsibilities might be better off with a job that's a little less physically taxing.'

Byron didn't like where this was going.

'Perhaps I could find you something in the kitchen. Or one of the cleaning crews. Something inside.'

That was the last thing Byron wanted. His chance of escape hinged on being outside. Not that he couldn't escape from inside, but it would be a hell of a lot more challenging.

While he had lain on his bunk, he had already begun to formulate an escape plan. He had started by examining the resources that the guards who went out with the work details had at their disposal. First, they had firearms, in the form of a handgun on their hip and a pump-action shotgun. They had communication tools in the form of cell phones and a radio. Finally, they had transport.

Byron had concluded that all he needed to do to forge a successful escape was to transfer the second and the last of these resources from one or more of the guards to himself. If he could get their cell phones and radio at the same time, all the better. But for the most part he was sure that a truck and a shotgun would serve his purpose pretty well.

If he was stuck inside the perimeter he would find getting his hands on either or both much more difficult. As was standard practice in every prison, the only guards who had guns were the ones in the watchtower. Guards on the yard or within the units didn't have them, for the very reason that someone like Byron could easily turn the tables by a fast transfer of possession.

'I appreciate the offer, Warden. I really do,' Byron said.

Castro glared at him. First Byron had questioned one of the guards, now he appeared to be questioning him. 'Maybe this whole thing was a big mistake. I'm trying to help you out here, Davis. Make your time here go easier. But it seems like all you want to do is complain.'

For a man running a jail, Castro seemed as touchy as his staff. Maybe that was where they got it from. 'You want me to keep things quiet in the unit?' Byron asked.

The question seemed to ramp Castro's agitation level up another notch. 'That was the idea, Davis.'

'Well, Warden, men tend to be led better from the front. By my setting an example and showing that I can do the same work they do. I take a job in the kitchen and I might lose some of that respect. Lose their respect and I lose my authority to keep them in check.'

Castro eyeballed him. He seemed be searching Byron's features for some measure of disrespect. He found none. Byron kept his face expressionless. He believed what he'd just said. Leaders who led from the back weren't really leaders. Not in Byron's experience.

'You sound like you have some experience, Davis,' the

warden replied.

Byron had unwittingly opened an avenue of discussion that he'd prefer stayed closed. At least for the time being. 'Not really, Warden,' he said. 'It's just common sense.'

'Hmm,' the warden said, clearly not convinced. 'I kind of had you tagged as military first time I saw you. You carry yourself a little differently. Men who've served usually do.'

Decision time. Did Byron lie and raise further suspicion or did he admit to his background and risk further investigation, even if what he told the warden was partially fabricated? He had no intention of giving the man sitting across from him the details of his actual career. That would be asking for trouble.

'I was National Guard for a few years when I was younger,' he told Castro.

Castro slammed a hand on his desk. 'I knew it. I can always tell. I was ROTC at college myself. Never got the chance to serve.' He reached up and massaged his left shoulder with his right hand. 'Football injury. Kind of ruled me out for what I'd have wanted to do. SEALs. Rangers. That kind of stuff.'

Byron had to choke back a laugh at the idea of a man like Castro being a Ranger or a SEAL. The guy had already gone way past his natural level to get to his current job. He nodded.

'National Guard, huh?' the warden said. 'Where were you based? Which state?'

Goddamn. Byron should have lied. Now that he had offered up a detail of his life, and a false detail at that, Castro would pick at it like a fresh scab. It had been a rookie mistake. More than anyone, Byron should have known better.

Warden Castro was staring at him, waiting for an answer.

'California,' Byron said.

'California National Guard,' the warden repeated. 'I had a cousin who served with the California National Guard. Eighteenth Cav. What was your unit, Davis?'

Byron had to think fast. 'I was in the 160th. Infantry. Nothing too exciting.'

'Huh,' said the warden. 'Guess I finally know something about you.'

Byron looked at him. What did he mean? It seemed kind of a loaded statement. Like Castro was hinting at something more.

'You see,' the warden continued, 'when we ran a check on a John Davis with the birth date you gave us, we came up with nothing. 'Cepting of course a couple of guys who weren't even close to your age. Kind of strange. Don't you think?'

The warden had been holding a trump card all along. Byron's blood ran cold. He tried to play it off. 'Maybe someone wrote it down wrong.'

That earned him a smirk. 'Maybe, Davis. Maybe. I mean, we're all country bumpkins this far south. Barely know how to switch on a computer.'

Where was this leading? 'I could have given the wrong date.'

'You could have, huh?' Castro said. 'Or maybe you have outstanding warrants somewhere else. Maybe that was it.'

Byron said nothing. Anything he did say could only make his situation worse. Deny it, and he'd come off like he was a guilty man protesting too much. Agree, and that opened another can of worms. The warden might just go looking for where 'John Davis' was wanted, which might involve a set of fingerprints being fed into the national system, the last thing Byron could afford to happen.

'You pleading the fifth, Davis?' Castro growled. 'Well, you might just be the luckiest son of a bitch in here because I'm going to need you to help me out with some things. So your secret, whatever it is, is safe with me. At least for now. And as long as you don't give me any more trouble.'

The warden stood, indicating that the meeting was coming to a close. Byron got to his feet.

'We understand each other, Davis?' the warden asked.

'Yes, sir,' Byron said.

CHAPTER TWENTY-FIVE

Byron wasn't sure what he'd expected Victor Romero to look like, but it wasn't like this. The Mexican inmates, who had spoken about him with such reverence, were crowded around a stooped, elderly man standing by one of the work trucks. Like everyone else, Romero was in the standard-issue shackles and cuffs. He was short, no more than five feet five. At one time he must have been physically powerful. Now there was a curve to his spine and he moved in a slow shuffle that, Byron guessed, had more to do with age than the restriction of the leg irons.

Standing next to Byron, Red nudged him with his elbow. 'Beaners are gonna be beside themselves with excitement now that the old man is out.'

Ignoring the racist epithet, Byron decided to gather some additional intel. The way he saw this new development, anything that kept the prison authorities preoccupied would run in his favour. If the guards had their their ass cheeks clenched over Romero stirring up trouble among the Mexicans, they were less likely to be looking at him.

'What's the story with Romero?' he asked Red, as the trucks sat in the yard, engines rumbling.

Red spat a wad of chewing tobacco that he had collected the previous evening onto the ground. 'I don't know. Think he was some kind of union guy in Mexico. You know, going into the *maquiladoras* and getting people to join the union.'

'*Maquiladoras*?' Byron asked.

'The assembly plants, the factories,' Red said, apparently surprised that Byron wasn't familiar with the term, with them being so close to the border.

'How come he ended up here?' Byron asked.

Red shrugged. 'No idea. Maybe he wanted his piece of the American Dream like everyone else. Maybe he had family over here. Came for a visit. Got picked up in Kelsen. I mean, that's enough. Walking through Kelsen must be why most of us are here.'

Mills strode onto the yard. 'Okay, you shitbirds, I see a lot of jawing and not much else. Get up on those trucks and let's move.' To emphasize his point, he jabbed the business end of his pump-action shotgun hard into an inmate's back.

The warden's words still ringing in his ears, Byron put his head down and made a point of mustering the guys in his work party onto the bed of their truck. A sudden commotion to his left drew his gaze.

Two of the Mexican inmates stood either side of Romero. Each man took his arm, ready to boost him up onto the back of the truck. Mills marched over to them. 'Leave him.'

They didn't move.

The sound of the guard's shotgun being racked silenced the yard. 'I said, let him get up there on his own.'

Romero lowered his head, and whispered something to the two men standing either side of him. Reluctantly they stepped away from him. Mills lowered his shotgun.

No one else spoke. It seemed to Byron that every inmate in the yard was watching Romero as he slowly reached out, grasped the inside of the truck's side panel and began to haul himself up.

Byron could feel electricity crackle around the yard. He studied the heads of the Mexican inmates. Their eyes flicked between Romero and the guards who had prevented them helping him. The middle of their foreheads blazed red with anger. Outwardly, to the guards' eyes, their expressions were flat.

The guards were looking at a herd of dairy cattle, while Byron could see a bunch of raging bulls. All it would take was the slightest spark and then, shotguns or not, they could be caught in the middle of a riot. Mills might have thought he was establishing his dominance over Romero. From where Byron stood, he couldn't have been more wrong.

Romero found some purchase. He began to pull himself up. There was a flash of his previous strength as he clambered onto the truck bed. One of the Mexican inmates, who was already sitting on the bench near the back of the truck, got to his feet to help Romero. Mills waved him off with his shotgun. The inmate sat down.

The old man grunted with the effort as he pushed himself up from the bed. He swayed slightly as the chain linking his leg irons reached its limit, the tension threatening to send him sprawling backwards.

The yard, guards and convicts alike, held its breath. Romero found his balance again. He shuffled backwards and sat down with a thud next to the inmate who had stood to help him. He closed his eyes. A smile spread across his face. Byron's abilities didn't extend as far as telepathy but he had a hunch that the two words forming in Romero's cerebral cortex, the part of the brain that processed language, were some variation of 'Screw you.'

The other inmates began to move again. Within a few minutes the trucks were loaded and ready to go.

Their morning commute took them on the same route through Kelsen and out the other side. It was striking to Byron how quickly it all seemed so routine. What had been grotesque and otherworldly — being part of a chain gang driving through a prosperous American town — seemed suddenly normal to the point of being banal. He understood now why the good citizens of Kelsen looked straight through the prison trucks transporting the chain gangs. Familiarity didn't breed contempt. It bred indifference.

The truck pulled down the same dirt road it had

yesterday. It came to a stop just past the barn. Another work truck pulled up alongside. Byron narrowed his eyes against the burning Texas sun and saw that it was the one that held Romero.

His heart sank a little. Putting a man of Romero's age to work in conditions that Byron had struggled with was crazy. Unless they planned on finishing him off.

Romero coming to harm, suffering a heart attack or a heat-induced stroke, would cause mayhem. Perhaps not out here, but almost certainly back in the jail when word got round. Just making the man climb up onto the back of truck had been a stretch. There was no way he would make it to lunch while doing manual labor in the fierce heat.

Byron neither knew nor cared about the warden's beef with Romero. But he did know that a riot, and the lockdown that would follow, would seal his chances of a quick escape. He couldn't let that happen.

As the inmates climbed down from the trucks and began to line up in rows, Byron made sure that he was next to Red. The guards busied themselves handing out the work tools. Byron leaned closer to Red. 'How much did you collect last night?' he muttered.

Red ran through an inventory that ranged from cigarettes and candy to tinned goods and cash. He seemed excited that Byron was taking an interest in the bottom line of their newly inherited extortion racket.

When Red had finished reeling off the bounty, Byron asked, 'How much money do the guards take home?'

As the men set to work, Byron kept an eye on Romero. Common sense must have prevailed because he had been given a hoe and set to work on the ground that had been broken the previous day. It was still hard, but not at the same level as breaking new ground with a pickaxe or shovel.

Byron hefted his pickaxe, arcing it high into the air and letting gravity do the work on the way back down. He tried to find a rhythm that he could maintain for a decent stretch at a time. Take too many breaks and the guard would be on top of him.

From time to time, he sneaked a glance at Romero. What he lacked in strength, the old man was making up for in technique. Union organizer or not, he had clearly spent some part of his life doing this kind of work. The muscle memory was still there.

After a half-hour, the guards called the first break. The men passed a plastic jug of water between them. One of the older guards walked down to where Byron was standing with Red.

The guard took off his hat and swiped the sweat from his brow. Byron offered him the jug of water. He waved it away. 'No offense, but I ain't swapping spit.'

'None taken,' Byron said. He looked over the guard's shoulder to Romero. 'Guy looks like he should be playing canasta in a retirement home.' His comment was directed at Red but made for the guard's benefit.

The guard took the bait, and glanced over his shoulder. Romero was doubled over, catching his breath. He had made it this far, but it was still only mid-morning. There was a long way to go and this was only his first day on work detail. 'Don't let him fool you,' the guard said. 'That old bastard is a lot tougher than he looks.'

Byron knew better than to challenge his opinion directly. 'Mexicans seem to look up to him.'

'No surprise.' The guard shrugged. 'They're dumber than dirt.'

Byron caught Red looking at him, puzzled and more than a little concerned. Like most of the other inmates, he held to the belief that the less interaction you had with the guards, the better it was for your health.

'No argument from me,' Byron said. 'But they all get pissy and there's more of them than there are of us.' He felt bad appealing to the guard's casual racism, but it was the only way of building common ground that he could think of right now.

'No kidding,' the older guard said. 'They breed like goddamn cockroaches.'

It was a sad insight into the way the man had come to think that he saw the Mexicans as insects.

Byron kicked the toe of his boot into the dust. 'The old guy, what's his name? Romero?'

The guard nodded.

'He's loving this. Getting to play the martyr in front of the others.'

'Hadn't thought of it like that,' the guard said.

No kidding, thought Byron. 'Hey,' he said, with a shrug, 'I just want a quiet life.'

'I hear you,' the guard said, and strode away, back towards the Mexican prisoners who were huddled around Romero. 'Break it up,' he shouted. They began to scatter. Romero hobbled off, using his hoe as a walking stick. He was suffering but he had too much pride to show his weakness to a guard.

The older guard reached over and grabbed for Romero's hoe. Romero let it go, but he didn't flinch. 'Go take a rest over there,' the guard barked at him, nodding towards the barn. 'I don't want anyone collapsing on my watch. Too much goddamn paperwork to fill in if that happens.'

Byron smiled as he lifted his pickaxe high above his head and brought it crashing down into the bone-dry earth. Red shuffled back along the line until he was next to Byron, who did his best to ignore him. Red wasn't prepared to be ignored.

'What the hell you doing giving away our shit to help out that goddamn Commie beaner?' Red hissed.

Byron wrenched his pickaxe from the ground. He held it chest-high. 'You want to repeat that?'

Red shrank back. 'I was only saying that—'

Byron cut him off. 'Listen, there is no "our" shit. There's *my* shit. That's all. And when shit's mine, I get to say what happens with it.'

'Okay,' said Red. 'But I still don't get why you're helping that Commie.'

Byron's expression softened a notch. 'Give me another week out here and I might just be a Commie too.'

CHAPTER TWENTY-SIX

Byron's eyes snapped open at four fifteen on the button. He sat up and rubbed his eyes, then swung his legs over the side of his bunk and jumped down onto the bare concrete floor. He kneaded at a knot in his shoulder, then grabbed soap and a towel from his locker and headed for the washroom.

Inmates moved out of his way as he walked in. A few of the Mexicans even smiled. In the context of standing naked in a shower, he found their new regard for him a little unsettling.

He washed, dried off, went back to his bunk, dressed and headed to the mess hall with Red. More nods of acknowledgement from the Mexicans. Obviously news of his kindness towards Romero had spread. Byron could only hope that the guards, watching the men eat, didn't notice. Fear or respect was one thing for an inmate to attract. Popularity, Byron imagined, might bring its own set of problems.

Back on the work truck, the day was taking its usual rhythm until just before they were about to depart. A side gate opened and an inmate, dressed in work clothes, stepped through. The man kept his head down. It took Byron a moment to recognize him.

It was Franco. Released from the prison hospital. There was a snicker among some of the other inmates as he lifted his head to reveal the flattened scar tissue where his nose had been before he'd tangled with Byron. As deformities went, it provoked a treble take. A man with missing teeth, one eye or a scar on his face was almost run-of-the-mill in a prison. Barely worthy of note. A man missing a good part of his nose still held a certain novelty value.

Like a whipped dog, Franco kept his head down. In

contrast to Romero, who had a retinue of Mexican inmates tending him, Franco's two buddies kept their distance from their former leader. Weakness, it seemed, was viewed as a disease that no one wanted to catch.

Byron got up onto the back of the truck next to Red. That morning the guards allowed Romero to be helped by two other inmates. The truck was full by the time Franco was ready to get on.

A guard screamed at him, 'Go get on the other truck, asshole.' Franco's reign was well and truly over.

CHAPTER TWENTY-SEVEN

The next day, Byron woke to a bunkhouse buzzing with life. Men who usually shuffled to the showers, stretching aching muscles as they went, walked past with a spring in their step. Where there was normally silence, or at most the occasional grunt, there was now a low hum of excited chatter. Byron was fairly sure he detected the smell of cologne among the usual rancid odor of stale sweat and dirty laundry.

He leaned over the edge of his bunk. 'What's up?' he asked Red.

Red was lying back on his bunk, hands behind his head. 'Sunday's visiting day.'

'Sunday?' Byron asked.

Red smiled. 'I know. Easy to lose track of the days here. Kinda nice when it creeps up on you, though, ain't it?'

Byron's heart sank. Sunday meant no work detail. No work detail meant no time outside the prison. No time outside the prison meant no chance of escape. Another day of never knowing when the CIA or State Department or the NSA would descend upon the prison to take him into custody.

How could he have been so dumb? Botching an escape in some way was one thing. Forgetting the days of the week was a whole other magnitude of stupidity.

Red was oblivious to Byron's distress. 'Well, enjoy it. Monday'll roll round soon enough,' he said, his voice filled with weary acceptance.

'Hey, Red?'

'What?'

'How long are you in for?' Byron hadn't asked this most obvious of questions before. Or, if he had, he had forgotten the answer.

Red folded his hands over his chest. 'How long's a piece of string? You go down in Kelsen for six months, you can end up spending a year. They catch you on some minor bullshit inside and tack on a few extra weeks. Or, they let you out on parole, but as soon as you're outside, the Sheriff's Department picks you up again on another vagrancy charge, which is a straight-up PV.'

PV was shorthand for 'parole violation'. Usually PVs covered things like failing a drugs test, being caught with a gun, or plain old committing another crime. Rarely did they involve walking down a public highway. Then again, not many people ended up in jail for doing that in the first place. Byron knew of men who had gone inside for something minor, killed someone in jail, sometimes in self-defense, and ended up catching a life-without sentence.

'Come on,' Red said, getting up from his bunk. 'Don't want to miss breakfast. It's usually pretty good on a Sunday.'

The carnival atmosphere continued all the way into the mess hall. The workday tension seemed to have gone. The seating arrangements still ran along racial lines but there was none of the constant vigilance between groups that Byron had noticed before.

He dug a plastic spork into a greasy hash brown, took a bite and had a sip of coffee. Something was gnawing away at him. It formed into a thought. He glanced at Red.

'Something I don't understand,' he said, with a nod to one of the tables of Mexicans.

'What's that, boss?' Red asked, egg yolk dribbling down his unshaven chin.

'All these guys are illegals. They were picked up crossing the border.'

'Yup,' said Red.

'So how come they're having visits from family? I

know border control isn't what it might be but people from the other side can't just waltz over any time they like, can they?'

Red looked blank. He didn't seem to understand the question. Finally, he said, 'They don't have to waltz. They're in the women's prison across from here.'

CHAPTER TWENTY-EIGHT

Byron had caught fragments of conversation between prisoners about wives and children. He had never connected them to another facility just next door. There had been no reason to. The other prison was down the road a ways, Red explained. It was in the opposite direction from the road they took to go to work. It held almost three times the number of people that the men's facility did, though many of them were children.

The women inmates, many, though not all, of whom had relatives inside the men's facility, worked in a factory that had been built next to their prison. It manufactured electrical goods for a Chinese company.

More questions buzzed around Byron's head than Red could possibly have answers for. Just as soon as he felt like he had a handle on Kelsen County and the people who ran it, the place threw up a fresh surprise.

'So they pick up illegals, or vagrants, and the men go to work here and the women go to work making TVs,' Byron said.

'Yup,' said Red. 'That's pretty much the size of it.'

'And everybody gets paid just enough to buy a pack of cigarettes or some candy at the end of the week, no more?' Byron said, thinking, And even the candy and smokes are taken back by the bunkhouse shot callers in return for keeping a lid on any trouble.

'Kind of genius, if you ask me,' said Red.

That wouldn't have been the word Byron would have chosen to describe what was happening. 'But people do get out, right?' Byron asked.

'Oh, sure,' Red said. 'It's not like they can keep people here for ever. We're still in America.'

Byron saw an opportunity to take the conversation in a direction that would normally raise suspicions. He trusted

Red, but only so far. He didn't doubt that his bunk mate, lieutenant and new best friend would happily rat him out to Castro if he thought the reward would be worth it. 'What about escapes? Anyone get tired of waiting to get out and jump the fence? Or just take off?'

'What?' said Red. 'And leave their family behind?'

Visiting with family seemed to be a phenomenon restricted to the Mexicans. Apart from a few individuals, the other prisoners didn't have visitors. To reduce the sting of not being able to spend time with loved ones, the authorities laid on some extras for them. Two old TVs were rolled into the mess hall and placed at either end. One showed sports and the other showed movies. Those inmates who didn't want to watch TV were free either to get some rest in their bunkhouse or hang out on one of the yards. The guards handed out a couple of basketballs and footballs. Red had also told Byron that lunch, while bagged like the rest of the week, was usually better on Sunday.

Byron elected to go outside, hang in the yard, and watch some of the inmates play basketball. As he left the mess hall he saw Franco, sitting on his own, getting ready to watch a movie. Byron gave him a wide berth. No good would come from an apology. The other prisoners would see it as weakness. That might lead to another challenge and Byron didn't want to have to hurt anyone else, or get hurt himself for that matter. Franco was best left to his own devices. With luck the warden would show some mercy and let him go.

Red wandered onto the yard and immediately headed over to where Byron was standing. It was like having a shadow.

'What's up?' Red asked him.

Byron took the question as rhetorical and kept watching the basketball game. All he could do was wait for Sunday to be over. On Monday he would make his move.

Delay had already cost him.

'You have family somewhere, Davis?' Red said.

'Nope,' said Byron. 'You?'

'Old lady and a couple of kids back in Arkansas. Haven't seen them since I walked out six years ago next month.'

Red was obviously waiting for some kind of follow-up questions. Like why he had walked out, or how old the kids were, if he missed them. Byron gave him none of that. Partly he wasn't all that interested. But mostly he didn't ask because it wasn't a subject he liked to dwell on. It was too painful.

Two guards walked onto the yard and headed in Byron and Red's direction. Glancing up, Byron saw the guard in the watchtower raise his rifle, tracking their progress, ready to fire if any of the inmates made a move on them. Not that such a thing seemed likely. From what Byron could see the inmates were too wrapped up in their Sunday treats to want to do anyone harm.

Byron had to hand it to whoever had designed the system. During the week, long hours of laboring out in the sun drained the prisoners of the energy they'd need to cause any trouble. On Sunday they got the good stuff, and they didn't want trouble to interrupt that. Not many dogs bit their owner when they'd just been thrown a juicy bone.

To Byron it was just an engineered way of ensuring the passivity than went on outside. The principles were the same. Keep people busy, or distracted, or fearful, or some combination of all three, set them up against each other as a way of allowing them a pressure valve, and you could pretty much do what the hell you wanted.

The guards stopped about ten yards from where Byron was standing with Red. 'Davis,' one guard shouted, 'you have a visitor.'

Byron looked at the man, his heart sinking. Maybe he had misheard. 'Warden wants to see me?' he asked.

'No. Visitor.'

As Byron looked up at the watchtower, he saw the guard was aiming his rifle straight at him.

CHAPTER TWENTY-NINE

Byron followed the guards back across the yard and towards the gate that would lead him into the main administration building. The guard in the tower tracked his every step, the center of Byron's back never leaving the cross-hairs.

This was it.

The moment Byron had been dreading.

Capture.

He didn't know what would follow, but he knew that it wasn't likely to be pleasant. He doubted that it would be as simple as losing his life. There would be stages that came before death. Interrogation. Torture. A search for what had gone wrong that, he imagined, might well involve surgical procedures. If the problem lay in his brain, who knew what they might do to render him compliant?

More than fear, he felt dread. He had already lost part of his humanity. He didn't want to lose any more. He had pondered one question during his time on the run. If they took what was left of his humanity from him, how would he know?

As he followed the guards down a corridor, Byron considered his options. Given that he was handcuff- and shackle-free, he was in a good position to overpower the guards right here and now. There were two of them but neither was in great shape. Nor would they be a match for his close-quarters combat skills. But what lay beyond them?

There would be additional security measures between the corridor and the entrance. Those didn't faze him either. If need be, he could take the guards hostage and use the immediate threat of harming them to force whoever controlled the gate to open it. If it came down to it, and he had to, one dead guard would do the trick.

But what about whoever had come to see him? If it was a person or persons from back east they would have plans in place that anticipated him trying to escape. He could end up injuring or even killing one of the guards only to be captured. Needless death or injury was not something he wanted to inflict upon anyone.

He would surrender. Go along with whatever they had planned. Then, as soon as an opportunity arose, he would make his move.

The guards stopped outside a wooden door marked 'Interview Room'. Byron hadn't asked them who his visitor was. He had taken his cue from their stoic expressions. He got the impression that whoever was on the other side of the door was important.

'Should we cuff him?' one asked the other.

'Too late now. Should have done it already,' his partner answered.

The guard on the handle side opened the door. He stuck his head round. 'Prisoner Davis for you. He's all yours,' he said.

The guard opened the door wider. Byron stepped inside the room.

CHAPTER THIRTY

Thea Martinez got up from behind a table in the center. She walked around it and extended her hand. For a moment all Byron could do was stand just inside the doorway and look at her. He had been primed for fight or flight.

Finally, he recovered his composure. Her hand felt impossibly soft against his blistered and calloused skin.

'Did the guards not tell you who your visitor was?' Thea said.

He shook his head.

She shot an irritated glance towards the door. 'I'm sorry,' she said. 'I ask the guards to inform an inmate that I'm their visitor but it always seems to slip their minds.' She smiled. 'I'm not exactly popular around here.'

'You don't seem to be popular anywhere,' Byron said.

She frowned.

'I didn't mean it like that,' he added.

She picked up her soft leather briefcase, took out some papers and put them on the table. 'No, you're quite correct. I'm not very popular around here. People like me rarely are.'

'People like you?'

'People who ask questions that the people in power would prefer weren't asked.'

Silence fell between them.

'Ms Martinez, why are you here?'

'It's a welfare visit. I try to check in with all my clients after their first week. Make sure they're okay.'

Byron wasn't sure he believed her. Unless there was an appeal pending, attorneys tended to lose interest in a client once sentence had been passed. There were exceptions.

But those exceptions tended not to be public defenders. 'From what I can recall, the last time I saw you, you didn't seem very happy with me.'

'I'm still interested in your welfare.'

'Well, I'm fine,' said Byron.

She looked up from her papers. She seemed to be studying him. He found it unnerving. He wasn't used to people looking at him with such intensity.

'You're quite sure about that?' she asked.

Byron leaned forward. 'Why don't you ask me what you really came here to ask me?'

She straightened up in her chair. 'Okay, then. I'm concerned about the conditions here. How the inmates are treated. Working conditions. Violence among inmates and whether incidents are properly controlled, monitored and reported.'

'I'm sorry, Ms Martinez, I can't help you.'

'Can't or won't?' she asked.

'I don't think it's the conditions that are the real issue here, and I doubt you think they are either,' Byron said. 'I assume you know about the women's prison down the track and how it's filled with wives and children of the men in here. The authorities are building golf courses and making television screens for the Chinese with illegal slave labor masquerading as prisoners. But you know all that already so I'm not sure how I can help.'

Thea dug out a blank piece of paper. She reached into her pocket and produced a pen. She handed it to Byron and slid the paper across to him. 'Write me a statement about what you've seen. About how you were picked up and charged for nothing. Tell your story.'

'And what good will that do?'

'On its own, probably not very much. But as one piece in the bigger picture, maybe it will make a difference. And if it doesn't, at least I can say I tried.'

'Who do you plan on sending your complaint to?'

Byron already knew the answer but he wanted to hear it from Thea.

'The Department of Justice. State senators. If they won't listen, I'll try to get a reporter or two interested.'

Byron looked down at the blank piece of paper on the table in front of him. Writing down what he knew would be getting involved in something that wasn't his concern. He'd only meant to be passing through. At the same time, he wanted to help Thea. No, it was more than that. He wanted her to like him. To think well of him. It was a strange feeling, but it wasn't new. He'd wanted his wife, Julia, to like him when he'd met her. The connection startled him.

The tips of his fingers rested on the paper. He stared at it. He knew that once he started writing, it would be a long time before he stopped.

Slowly he slid the piece of paper back across the desk. 'I'm sorry. I just want to do my time and get out of here. If anyone knows I've done this . . . Let's just say I can't afford any more complications in my life.'

Thea took the blank piece of paper and put it back at the bottom of the pile. 'Maybe it's for the best,' she said. 'The DOJ would want to be able to check any witness statements against names'

His gaze met hers. 'Why would that be a problem?'

'Well, I did a little digging around. You don't actually exist, do you, Mr Davis? Not officially, anyway.'

CHAPTER THIRTY-ONE

Byron pulled the blank piece of paper back across the desk. 'What do you want me to say?' he asked.

'I want you to tell the truth,' Thea said, adding, 'As you see it.'

'Starting when?' he asked.

She shot him an exasperated look. 'Whenever you like.'

'I'll start with my arrest. How about that?' he said.

'You really don't want to do this, do you?'

'It's not like you've left me much say in the matter. All I'm doing is defining the parameters of what you want me to write.'

It was clear to Byron that Thea thought he was either stonewalling or being difficult because he resented her having blackmailed him. In truth, he had written many reports in his previous life, and those reports always had preset start and end points. If you controlled where a story began and ended, you could control how it would be read. An air strike on an Afghan wedding party told one story. An air strike after a prolonged battle in which Marines had been killed and in which, less than four hours later, the Taliban had been replaced by a bunch of villagers having a wedding was a different story. Parameters could be decisive.

'Okay. Start with your arrest and what you were doing just before. You were walking into town to get a bus, correct?' Thea said.

Byron nodded.

'Go from there.'

Byron took the pen from her. He began to write. It took a lot of concentration. For one thing it was a long time since he had used a pen to do more than sign for something. For another he was used to writing reports in the kind of quasi-jargon beloved of government: adopting that style would be a red flag. Last, there were parts of his story that wouldn't paint him in the best of lights. Like biting off another prisoner's nose.

'You want me to get you some coffee?' Thea asked.

'Sure,' said Byron.

He watched her as she got up and walked to the door. He enjoyed the sway of her hips, the subtle curve from there all the way up to her neck. It wasn't just that he hadn't seen a woman in a while. He hadn't seen a woman as attractive as Thea Martinez in a very long time.

She closed the door. He could hear the clack of her heels as she walked down the corridor. He reached over to the pile of papers she had left on the table and rifled through them quickly but efficiently. He found his name on a piece of torn-off yellow legal pad that had been paper-clipped to his arrest report. On the piece of yellow paper she had written the name and date of birth he had given and below that the word 'alias'. Then she had scrawled another name, 'Bradley Stang', and a Washington DC number. His heart raced a little at the DC area code.

He moved on, looking for anything else. A minute later he could hear high heels clacking down the corridor towards him. He put the papers back, and hunched over his own piece of paper. It was still blank.

She came in with two Styrofoam cups of coffee, some small packets of sugar and plastic tubs of milk. She set it all down on the table. She glanced at her papers and back at Byron. 'Find anything interesting?' she asked.

Byron took his cup of coffee and raised it to his lips. It wasn't bad. They served something they called coffee in the mess hall, but Byron wasn't sure it bore any resemblance to what most people considered coffee to be.

He took another sip, and put down the cup. Thea was looking at him, waiting for an admission of guilt.

He went back to writing his report. More time passed.

He glanced up at her. 'Who's Bradley Stang and why were you calling him to ask about me?'

'So you did look at my papers,' said Thea.

'Shall I rephrase the question?'

'Try answering mine first. Did you go through my papers?' Thea repeated.

'You leave private papers on a table with an inmate, what do you think will happen? Who's Bradley Stang?'

'A friend of mine,' said Thea.

Byron knew that a single phone call might sign his death warrant. His next visitor might be someone way more threatening than an attorney on some kind of civil-rights crusade. He got to his feet. He took a step around the table. To her credit, Thea stood her ground. She was either very brave, very reckless, or a combination of both.

He took another step, forcing her to move back. He was close enough to smell her perfume. 'Who is Bradley Stang and what did you tell him about me?'

Thea put her hand up to Byron's chest. Rather than shove him back, she let it stay there, her palm pressed against the slab of muscle. Energy crackled between them. Neither broke the other's gaze. Byron could as easily have kissed her as struck her. In the end, he did neither. He took a step back. Her hand dropped.

'Take a seat, John,' she said. 'I'll tell you.'

Byron walked back round the table and sat down. She sat opposite him.

'Bradley was at law school with me. He works in the DOJ. I wasn't calling him specifically about you. In fact, I never even mentioned your name. The reason I never mentioned you to him was because I already knew that John Davis wasn't your real name and I didn't want to cause you any more problems than you already have. Bradley has offered to help me compile evidence and then he'll take it someone at the DOJ.'

'So it was just coincidence that his name was next to

mine?' Byron asked.

'I was looking at your file when I called him so that's why I jotted it down there, yes.'

Either she was a very good liar or she was telling the truth. She showed absolutely no fear or uncertainty. If she had, Byron would have picked up on it.

'You're right,' said Byron. 'I'm not who I say I am.' All he was doing was confirming what she already knew. 'I can't tell you who I am, and I'd ask that you don't go trying to find out. For everyone's sake.'

She didn't say anything to that.

'Can you do that for me?' he said.

'I don't know. I could lie and say I could, but I don't want to lie. So ...'

They had reached an impasse. Or seemed to have. Byron had thought of a workaround. 'Could you hold off for a week? After that you can do as much digging as you like.'

She seemed to be studying him even more intently. 'Why a week? You planning on going somewhere? I mean, even if I entered an appeal for you ...' She hesitated, then corrected herself: 'An appeal for John Davis, on Monday, it would take at least a week at best to be heard before Judge Kelsen.'

'Can you hold off three days?' said Byron. 'Yes or no?'

'I think I can rein in my curiosity for three days. Just about. Though every time I see you, you make it just a little harder.'

Byron didn't ask whether she was still referring to her curiosity. He didn't want to know. He was finding it hard enough to focus as it was. 'Thank you,' he said. 'There's one final thing, since you know I'm not who I told people I am. Do you know if checks have been run on me by anyone in Kelsen County?'

'You mean anything that might ping on the radar

somewhere else?' said Thea.

'Exactly,' Byron said.

'I can't say for sure, but I will tell you one thing. If you want to get lost, this is as good a place as any to do it. Kelsen doesn't feed into any of the national law-enforcement databases. They like to stay under the radar down here.'

Byron tapped the nib of his pen against the paper. 'Hence you want this.'

'Someone has to do it.'

'So why haven't they?' he asked.

'They're scared. Or they like the benefits that the way things are run here have brought. You drive through the town to go to work, right?'

Byron nodded. 'Looks like a pretty nice place to live.'

Thea smiled. 'Oh, it is. Three golf courses. Free to play. They've built a large solar facility that means power is all but free. Of course, the men here did all the heavy labor. You probably haven't even seen the new recreational center. Outdoor and indoor swimming pools. Basketball courts. Gymnasium. Running track. Football field. Soccer pitch. Tennis courts. Again, all free to use for residents.'

'Let me guess,' said Byron. 'All built by the inmates.'

'A lot of it, yes.' Thea said. 'You can really keep the costs down if you don't have to pay for anything apart from materials.'

Byron didn't quite follow. The inmates could do manual labor, the heavy lifting, but there was a lot more to building what Thea had talked about than that. 'What about architects? Engineers? Someone to oversee the work?' he asked.

'Lot of professional retired people down here. They pitch in. When they can't find the skills they need, they hire in people from Houston or San Antonio.'

Something was nagging at Byron as Thea spoke. He didn't doubt the righteousness of her indignation. It was clear that in Kelsen County due process wasn't being followed properly and the fundamentals of the Constitution were being ignored, but making prisoners work, rather than sit watching TV all day, lift weights so they were better prepared for future crime, or jack off in their cells? Personally he didn't think that prison should be an easy ride. 'How come this bugs you so much?' he asked.

'It's not so much that it annoys me. It's more that no one else seems to care. They pay low tax. They get everything laid out on a plate for them. They couldn't care less that the sheriff is scooping up illegals, the courts are putting them in here, and they're being used as slave labor.'

It was Byron's turn to smile. Welcome to the real world, he thought, but didn't say. What Thea had described was a sizable minority of the population. Even kids in bad US neighborhoods, who were considered deprived, bounced around on brand new sneakers, and used cell phones that could operate a satellite. They never gave a thought to the conditions or pay for people on the other side of the world who made it all possible. Whatever your view of human nature, of whether people were good or bad, there was no denying that when life was sweet people were tempted not to dig too deep to find out why. They just might find the answer was that their good fortune was built upon someone else's bad luck.

'You think I'm a naive do-gooder?' Thea said.

'Doesn't matter what I think. But I do wonder why no one else has gotten upset about all this before now. I mean, they must have pulled over the wrong guy at some point. Traffic offense. Something. It can't just be drifters and illegals that they stop.'

'Correct,' Thea said. 'That's their fail-safe system.'

'Fail-safe?' Byron asked, genuinely puzzled.

'Well,' said Thea, 'say you had been able to pay the

fine. Or say you'd refused to pay but phoned some big city attorney, or a family member who was connected in some way. In other words, say you'd had some muscle behind you.'

'Exactly. They can't be shaking down those people,' Byron said.

'No, they can't. They get any kind of pushback or a hint that someone might want to take it further and they back straight off. All your troubles magically disappear. Usually by that time the person is glad to get the hell out of here and not look back.'

'And if they get really mad?' Byron asked, guessing that he already knew the answer.

'City cuts them a check. With a non-disclosure agreement attached at the end so they don't go talking to any reporters,' said Thea. 'They're few and far between, though. The cops can usually sniff out anyone who's likely to be a problem before they get as far as arresting them. Most of the time they just give them a hundred-dollar ticket for whatever it was they pulled them over for and that's it.'

'The locals don't get tetchy about any of this? I mean, free golf is great, but not if you're getting tickets all the time,' said Byron.

'Cops all know who the locals are. They don't get pulled over. Even something like a DUI is dealt with quietly. You ask any of the locals about the sheriff? They love the guy.'

'Because he only locks up real criminals?' Byron said.

'Got it in one.'

CHAPTER THIRTY-TWO

Thea gathered up her papers, including six pages in Byron's handwriting. They stood, a little awkwardly. Thea put out her hand again. 'Thanks for your help, Mr Davis.'

Byron shook it. 'You're welcome. I think.'

Neither of them wanted to let go. It was only when their clasping hands moved into the awkward zone that Byron finally let hers drop.

'Be careful,' Thea said. 'They won't like the fact you've talked to me.'

'Don't worry about me. I can take care of myself.'

'All the same.' she said, reaching into her briefcase and handing him a business card.

He watched her walk to the door, open it and go out into the corridor. It closed behind her. He heard her say something to a guard in the corridor. A few seconds later the door opened again.

'Back out on the yard, Davis,' said the guard.

The guard walked with him down the corridor. Thea was already out of sight.

'She's some piece of ass,' the guard said.

Byron didn't respond.

The guard smirked as he gave Byron another sideways glance. 'Don't get lips like hers from sucking oranges. Know what I mean?'

Byron kept walking. Putting one foot in front of the other. Suppressing the urge to pick up the guard by the throat and smash him into the wall. The guard laughed. He was enjoying what he obviously read as Byron's discomfort. 'Bet she loves it rough,' he continued. 'She's got that look about her. All prim and proper on the outside. But I can tell.'

Byron stopped and half turned towards him. The

guard's hand fell to his canister of pepper spray. 'Like you'd have a shot,' Byron said. 'A man like you wouldn't to know what to do with a woman like her. All you can do is talk shit about her, then go home and jerk off.'

The guard's face flared red. 'Watch your mouth, inmate. That's insubordination.'

Byron pushed through the end door and out into the sunshine. The guard stood where he was, glaring at him. Byron went to join Red, who was watching a small crowd of Mexican prisoners around Romero. The old man seemed to be giving some kind of an impromptu speech. He spoke fast, jabbing his finger in the air to emphasize a point. Byron listened. Romero was giving his followers some old time religion. Hot and heavy. Big on Jesus, and the meek inheriting the earth. Byron could see in Romero's eyes the spark of the younger man he'd been. It wasn't quite extinguished yet. He still had some fight in him.

Something else drew Byron's attention. He glanced skywards. Up in the watchtower, a guard was standing with Warden Castro. Both of them were studying Romero.

CHAPTER THIRTY-THREE

'How can I help you, Warden?' Byron said, sitting down.

'You can start by telling me what Thea Martinez wanted,' said Castro.

'There's such a thing as attorney-client privile—'

Castro cut him off. 'I know what it is. I don't need you to tell me. I could take a guess. She wanted you to tell her how terrible everything is here. How badly y'all are treated. How I'm some kind of a monster.'

Byron stared across the desk at him. He figured he'd let Castro vent. He doubted very much that Castro would punish him and lose a unit shot caller. Franco was a busted flush. There was no way he would be able to resume his previous position, even with Byron transferred out to another unit or in solitary. Castro needed Byron to keep a lid on things.

'She can run her mouth all she wants,' said Castro. He already seemed to be tiring of the subject of Thea Martinez, civil-rights crusader. 'Nobody listens anyway.'

If only Castro had known that Byron had the same opinion of the attorney's efficacy. He didn't think she'd make a difference. And neither did she. Byron would have added a caveat. So far. If she did managed to snag some interest from the DOJ there was plenty for them to get their teeth into down here. A federal prosecutor who wanted to make a name for themselves could, from the little Byron had seen, do a lot worse than Kelsen County.

'You know who Miguel Romero is?' Castro said.

'Sure. Old Mexican guy. Just got out of solitary,' said Byron, deliberately playing it two shades dumber than giving an honest answer. When dealing with authority a little bit of dumb could take you a long way. As long as you didn't overplay it.

Castro hunched over the desk. 'He's a labor organizer. He came across the border and got himself arrested in Kelsen deliberately. Can you believe that?'

'Nothing about what people choose to do surprises me much, Warden,' Byron said.

'Anyway, he's back starting trouble.' Castro took a deep breath. 'I heard from one of my men that you got him taken off work detail. Persuaded the guards with the work party to let him take it easy in the shade. Have himself a little siesta.'

Byron wasn't about to cop to that either. The question would only arise as to how he had persuaded a guard. He guessed that the warden already knew. He also guessed that there was lots more bribery of guards than either of them was aware of.

'I want you to talk to Romero for me, Davis. See if you can't point out how you doing him a solid is going to end up with everyone being punished. I would say you should tell him he's going to be punished. But we tried that already. He's begging me to make him some kind of a martyr. Ain't gonna happen. But if he thinks other people are going to be affected, he might think things over,' said Castro.

'Punished how?' Byron asked.

'I'll think of something. I can get pretty creative.'

Byron didn't doubt it. None of the people running the county could be faulted for a lack of imagination. 'If he won't play ball?'

'Do whatever you have to do. You persuaded Franco into retirement. How tough can it be to convince an old man?'

From what he'd seen so far, Byron had a feeling that Romero was a much tougher character than schoolyard-bully Franco. Romero had something else too. He had belief in a cause. No matter whether it was just or not. From years spent traveling the world, Byron had grown to understand that a man with a cause he held deeply was a powerful entity. Brute force rarely worked. If the warden was going to get through to Romero, negotiation would be the better approach.

In any case, none of this was Byron's concern. Sunday would be over soon enough. Monday would bring an opportunity to get out of here. The last thing Byron needed was to become distracted by a local power struggle. Not that he could let Castro know that.

'I'll find a way,' Byron said. 'Somehow.'

Castro smiled. 'Knew I could count on a man like you.'

'Oh, don't worry, Warden. You can.'

CHAPTER THIRTY-FOUR

'The warden wanted me to speak with you,' Byron said, sitting side by side with Romero as the truck filled with men.

'He can't speak with me himself?'

Byron didn't respond.

'He must be a very busy man,' Romero said.

The driver guard started the engine. Another rode shotgun beside him.

'For a man who wants to speak with me you don't say very much,' Romero said.

'He asked me to speak with you. I never said I wanted to,' said Byron.

Romero was staring at Byron now, his gaze even and unrelenting. 'What are you doing here?'

Byron looked away. 'I could ask you the same thing.'

Romero gave a little shrug. 'My sister's son died here. I came to find out what happened.'

The stark honesty of his answer took Byron by surprise. 'He died in the prison?'

Romero nodded. The amusement was gone, replaced by something more somber. And beneath the sadness Byron could detect a flinty determination.

'He was a labor organizer like me. He had heard about what was happening here. He came to investigate. To see what was really going on and to see if he could help our people.'

Byron had a hunch where this was going. 'They found out who he was?'

'Yes,' said Romero.

'What happened to him?' Byron asked.

'I don't know. They said he was released but no one's

seen or heard from him since. I thought that if I came here I might be able to discover what happened.'

'You getting anywhere?'

Romero sighed. 'I think they are telling the truth about letting him go. But after that . . . it's like he disappeared into thin air.'

Byron reached out to steady him as the truck hit a bump in the road.

Romero looked at him. 'That's my story. And you? Why are you here?'

Byron's hand fell away from the old man's arm. 'Arrested for vagrancy. Didn't have the money to pay the fine, so . . .' He shrugged his broad shoulders. 'Here I am.'

'Here we both are,' said Romero, rattling the cuffs securing his wrists. 'And now Castro wants you to tell me to stop causing him trouble.'

'Something like that,' said Byron.

'There's usually an "or" at the end of that sort of message,' Romero said.

'Yeah,' said Byron. 'There usually is. But you don't strike me as someone who'd respond well to being threatened.'

'This is why I don't understand why you're here. You're smart enough to know I can't be threatened, but not smart enough to find a friend who can bail you out or an attorney who can get you out.'

The truck rolled to a temporary stop. They were passing one of the town's lush golf courses. A couple of overweight white guys stood on a putting green and watched the prison convoy roll slowly past. One said something to his playing partner and they laughed.

'Castro asked me to talk to you and that's what I've done. I'm not going to threaten or harm you. But if I don't they'll find someone who will,' said Byron.

'I'm sure you're right,' said Romero.

'You don't care?' Byron asked.

'You do what I do in Mexico and you get used to death threats. The way I look at it, I can only die once.'

'What do you mean?'

'Well,' said Romero, 'a man who worries about the end of his life, about when it will come, how it will come, he dies many times. But a man who lives his life as the sun rises every morning without thinking whether he'll see it set? He can have only one death.'

The truck didn't make its usual turn. It kept moving down the road until it reached a series of single-story grey warehouses surrounded by chain-link fencing topped with spools of razor wire. The vehicle at the head of the convoy stopped at an unmanned gatehouse. One of the guards walked over to a keypad and punched in the access code. Metal gates swung open. The convoy moved through and inside the warehouse complex.

Byron watched the gates close. Two of the Mexican inmates were busy nudging each other like a couple of school kids, no doubt excited at the prospect of working inside, free from the glare of the scorching sun. Next to him, Romero remained quiet.

'You know what this place is?' Byron asked the old man.

'Never seen it before.'

Romero leaned over and asked the prisoners opposite, in Spanish, if they had been there before. None of them had.

The convoy drew to a halt next to the largest of the four warehouses. Byron guessed that they would all find out soon enough what lay ahead. One of the guards prodded two inmates towards a pair of roller-mounted dock doors. The inmates hauled them back to reveal a dark, cavernous space, filled from floor to ceiling with heavy wooden shipping pallets stacked thirty high in rows of twenty. The rows went all the way back into the very rear of the warehouse.

The inmates gathered in a semi-circle on a raised platform just inside the doors. It was hotter inside the warehouse than it had been outside. The air was stale and heavy with humidity. The guards peeled four inmates away from the main group. They reappeared a few minutes later with each man holding one end of two extendable metal ladders.

Mills strode to the front of the group. 'Romero, can you translate for the *amigos*?'

Byron watched Romero carefully, waiting for a reaction. Romero's answer came in the form of a diffident nod and a simple 'Yes.' This was a man who didn't dodge a battle, but who was also careful about which ones he chose to fight.

'Okay, assholes, here's the deal. We need this warehouse cleared out. So you are going to work in two teams. Each team has a ladder. You climb to the top, pass the pallets down, then take them outside to the waste ground.'

As Mills spoke, his colleagues moved among the men, unlocking handcuffs and removing leg irons. Byron was almost the last to be freed. The guard who took off his cuffs was on edge, his mind yellow with fear until he had put some space between himself and Byron. Byron made a note of his caution.

Mills paused to allow Romero's Spanish translation to catch up. From Byron's very limited Spanish, he noted that Romero had edited out the asshole comment. The inmates probably hadn't required a translation of that.

'Arrange the pallets into a bonfire. When that's done we're going to burn them. Any questions?' the guard said.

Before Romero could finish translating the instructions, the guard marched back towards the pickup's air-conditioned cab. His colleagues moved outside and watched the men set to work in the steaming heat.

CHAPTER THIRTY-FIVE

Byron looked at the rows of wooden pallets stacked floor to ceiling. He looked at the ladders. He looked at Romero.

Romero was shaking his head. He was probably thinking the same thing as Byron. This was a job that only a group of men being held against their will, at gunpoint, would be asked to do. Any regular group of workers would have taken one look at it, turned on their heel and walked away.

'Davis!' Mills called. 'Are you going to get these guys moving or are you going to stand around with your thumb up your ass all morning?'

If he'd had the choice, Byron would have selected the second option over the first. He decided not to share his preference.

Byron walked over to where Romero was standing, flanked by a praetorian guard of the larger Mexican inmates. If he hadn't known better, Byron would have assumed Romero was a high-ranking narco trafficker or *buchone* rather than a semi-retired labor organizer on a fool's errand to find his nephew. He carried the same authority as a *buchone*. It was a rare quality to be able to command the respect of other men by your presence. Anyone with muscle or a gun could do it. Someone with neither had to bring something a little deeper to the situation.

'My Spanish is a rusty,' Byron said to him, 'and I don't think I can afford to have instructions that aren't completely clear for this to work. Can you translate for me?'

Romero looked past Byron to the ladders that the men had propped against the first row of pallets. 'We need a crane. Harnesses. Hard hats.'

'You want to go ask? Because I'm all out of goodwill with the powers that be.'

Romero followed Byron's gaze to Mills, who was standing with the other guards, arms folded, glaring at them. 'They're not very happy with you,' he said.

'No kidding,' said Byron. 'I was supposed to put you in your place, remember, but we're standing around like best buds. We finish talking and you go over asking for extra equipment, it doesn't look good. Know what I'm saying?'

'I do,' said Romero. 'But that doesn't change my mind. I can't put the men here in danger so that you can save face with the warden.'

Knowing that Romero wasn't going to be persuaded, Byron stepped back. Romero walked to the small cadre of guards. Byron tuned into the conversation but Romero spoke so quietly he had to strain to catch even some of what was being said. Romero's voice was another demonstration of power and command. The weak shouted. The powerful spoke softly.

Mills listened to what Romero had to say, arms folded. When Romero had finished, Mills didn't say anything. Instead he called to Byron, 'Davis, get over here.'

Byron walked over to the two men. Mills dismissed Romero – 'Get out of here.'

Romero walked away slowly, his hands tucked into his pockets. Mills glared at Byron. 'You got sixty seconds to get these beaners organized and working.' He nodded towards the retreating figure of Romero. 'One second longer and I'm going to drop a round in his back and tell the warden he made a run for it.'

From the way the veins were popping on Mills's forehead, Byron didn't doubt the sincerity of the threat. A cynic might have assumed that dangerous work like this was the prison regime's way of forcing a confrontation with Romero.

Byron made the walk back to Romero. He stopped in front of him. 'I think we can do this safely with what we have.'

'Forget it,' said Romero.

How the hell had his life come to this? Byron wondered. He was trapped between an immovable object and, in the case of a shotgun shell being deployed, an unstoppable force.

'How about I go up the ladder first?' said Byron. 'If it's not safe, I'll be the one who takes the fall.'

'You go up the ladder?' said Romero. 'With these men here holding it?'

Byron nodded. 'That's right.'

Mills was still glaring in their direction. To emphasize that he was serious about his threat of what would occur if they didn't start working, he hefted his shotgun, and racked a shell into the chamber. As sounds that concentrated a man's mind, it was on Byron's all-time top ten list.

'Deal?' Byron asked Romero.

CHAPTER THIRTY-SIX

With two of the Mexicans holding the ladder and a third ready to move in once he began the climb, Byron put his foot on the second rung and hauled himself up. He tested his weight, feeling for any kind of give, but the ladder was pretty solid. He kept climbing, placing his feet and hands with care. The climb was about sixteen feet. Not crazy high, but enough to make things interesting if you lost your footing or the ladder gave way when you were at the top.

The ladder had been placed so that once he reached the top, he could lean over, tie off a pallet from the adjoining stack and lower it down. He was confident he could have thrown them with enough force to clear the men holding the ladder. The problem was that the guys at the bottom might not have been as confident. If they panicked while holding the ladder, he'd be coming down a hell of a lot faster than he'd gone up.

His plan was to move along, removing the top third of each stack. Once the height was reduced, the other inmates would be able to remove the rest and he could take a break.

He reached the penultimate rung. He leaned over with the rope he had slung over his shoulder and tied off the pallet. When it was secure, he eased the pallet off the top of the stack and began to lower it to the ground. A group of three inmates rushed in to grab it. They untied the rope. He pulled it back, tied off the next and repeated the process. Gradually he inched back down the rungs of the ladder.

With half the pallets lowered, he climbed down to the floor. He rested as the ladder was moved along a row.

Romero organized the removal of the lowered pallets. Outside, a group of inmates had begun to build the first of the eventual bonfires.

Byron climbed back up the ladder. Sweat was already trickling down his back, pooling in the crack of his ass. There was no doubt about it. The heat and humidity would be their greatest enemy.

At the top of the ladder, he got to work and settled into a rhythm. He planned on doing one full row. Then he would hand off to someone else.

The next man up was the tallest of the Mexican inmates in the group. Even so, he was only five ten. His lack of reach made the task harder. Byron watched him carefully. He wobbled a little as he tied off the first pallet. Romero, who had wandered inside to observe the transition, coached the man from the ground. The first pallet lowered safely, the man found his feet. Byron stepped outside to see if he could catch something resembling a breeze.

Like a bunch of weekend dads, the guards were busy directing the construction of the bonfire, ignoring the work inside. Any minute now Byron expected them to crack open a sixer of Bud and start swapping barbecue tips. He registered their relaxed attitude and smiled. Maybe the day would turn out more as he had hoped it would when he had woken that morning.

Two more men took a turn on the ladder. People could say what the hell they liked about those who made the journey from south to north across the border, but one thing they weren't afraid of was hard work. Byron believed in border enforcement, and he wasn't a big fan of handing out a general amnesty to people who had ignored the rules. At the same time he didn't doubt that the majority of Mexicans who entered the US illegally came because they were prepared to work hard in order to secure a better life.

Despite the heat, the Mexicans had begun to tease one another as they worked. One of the younger, smaller men was being joshed fairly relentlessly. As he carried the pallets outside, they were catching on the ground. Byron could see that the teasing was getting him riled. Finally, he turned round and pointed at the ladder. He was volunteering. The laughter grew even louder.

The small man pushed his way to the bottom of the ladder. There was no one on it. He started to climb. One of the men tried to grab his pants leg as he began to climb. The short man kicked out. The ladder holder had to duck to avoid catching a boot in the face. The other men cheered the small man's machismo.

He kept climbing, scrambling up at speed, powered by the cheers and jeers of the men below. Byron watched him make it to the top faster than anyone else had so far. What he might have lacked in height and reach, he more than made up for in sheer determination.

Byron turned to see Romero, arms folded across his chest, trying to hush the other men. They were too busy enjoying the fun to pay heed to him.

The small man reached out to the next row to grab the top pallet. He had to lean over, lifting his left leg off the rung. The catcalls fell away. There was a collective holding of breath.

With the rope in his hand, he grabbed the edge of the pallet, looping the rope around it and pulling the end back towards him. He tied a slip knot and yanked the rope to tighten it. In comparison to a couple of the guys who had spent minutes fumbling with the rope, the small man had done it all in a series of fluid motions. The rope secure around the pallet, he edged back so that both feet were on the ladder rung. Byron felt a sigh of relief run through the men below.

The hard part was done.

The small man pulled the rope, and the top pallet began to move. He gave it another yank and it slid further. A third pull and it was free. Halfway down, he lowered the pallet the rest of the way. It was collected below, to cheers from the other men.

The rope unhitched, the small man pulled it back up. He set himself to retrieve the next pallet. He lifted his left foot from the rung he was standing on and leaned over. He reached, the rope in his hand, for the next pallet.

His right foot slipped out from under him. His arms windmilled. The rope slipped from his hand. He grabbed for the ladder. He missed. Gravity and his own weight ripped his right hand from the upper rung.

Byron and the other men could only watch as he fell backwards and tumbled to the floor. He made a noise that was somewhere between a grunt and a scream.

He came to rest face down, the top of his skull pointing towards the sunlight streaming in through the open doors.

He didn't move.

CHAPTER THIRTY-SEVEN

It was the worst kind of fall. A slip. From height. With no time to adjust the body's position relative to the ground. And a hard, unrelenting surface waiting at the bottom.

The men crowded round him. No one tried to move him. Byron wasn't sure if they knew better or whether they worried that this kind of bad fortune might be infectious. An inmate knelt next to the small man. 'Arturo?'

He didn't respond.

Two guards pushed through the small group of inmates. 'Shit,' one said. They at least had the decency to look shocked. The blood had drained from the face of the younger guard. He hunkered next to Arturo, laid down his shotgun and reached out a hand to check for a pulse.

The shotgun was less than a foot away from Byron. He could bend down, pretend to be helping, and come back up with it before the guard knew what had happened. As opportunities went they didn't get much better.

And yet …

Byron's gaze flicked from the shotgun to the injured man and back again. His mind raced as he ran through his options, breaking them down at the fork in each branch to a workable sequence.

Grab the shotgun from the floor. Rack it, pivot and step back. Point it at the guard's head. If he reaches for it, pull the trigger. If he doesn't, hustle him outside. Keep his body between yours and the other guards.

Find the nearest truck and get the guards to throw the hostage the keys. Go in via the passenger door. Move him into the driver's seat. Stay low to use the engine block as cover and make sure they can't fire through the windshield.

Drive out. Ram the gates if he had to. Stay on the road, ride his luck. If a roadblock showed, or a cop, go off road. The truck was more than capable of eating up miles of bleak, but flat, Texas desert-scrub landscape. Once they were well clear of a highway he could ditch the guard and take over the driving. He could likewise ditch the truck as he neared the border and make the crossing on foot.

Afterwards, assuming he got that far, it would be a simple matter of covering as much distance in as short a time as possible. Every escape followed the same basic formula. The more ground you covered from the point of escape, the greater your chance of avoiding recapture.

But …

'I found a pulse,' the guard said, looking up at his colleague.

Byron reprimanded himself for the disappointment that flashed into his mind at those words. A dead Arturo would have closed the deal.

'Turn him over,' said the other guard.

'No. Don't move him just yet,' Byron said, getting down onto his knees next to the guard and taking a closer look at the injured man. He lowered himself further so that his cheek was pressed against the concrete.

There was no bleeding from Arturo's ears, nose or mouth that Byron could see. No spatters of blood on the floor. Arturo let out a low moan. Another good sign under the circumstances. His eyes flickered open. He started to turn his head. Byron reached out a hand and placed it gently on Arturo's shoulder. 'Stay still.' He glanced at the guard next to him, the shotgun between them. 'We need an ambulance.'

'Ambulances cost money.' Mills was standing in the doorway, hands on hips, silhouetted by the blazing sun.

'If we don't get him to a hospital he could die,' Byron told him.

Mills spat a wad of chewing tobacco onto the floor. 'You can use one of the trucks. Put him in back.'

Byron knew that a truck wouldn't cut it. It wasn't just that they needed something with an engine and a set of wheels: they needed the specialist knowledge and expertise inside the ambulance. They needed paramedics with the correct equipment. People who knew how to transport someone with a spinal injury. Even then there was no guarantee that Arturo would make it. It had been a bad fall. All kinds of bad.

There were times to save money. This wasn't one of them.

Byron opened his mouth to explain some of this. Not that he believed the guards didn't know it. It was more that they didn't care. Especially once they had got past the initial shock.

Someone stepped between Byron and the guard. It was Romero. He reached over to place his open palm on Arturo's back, then grabbed the shotgun from the floor. The guard attending to Arturo went to snatch it back. Romero straightened up, and slammed the butt of the gun into the guard's face, breaking his nose. He racked a round into the chamber, spun round and pointed at the other guard's chest.

'Even an old man like me can't miss from seven feet,' he said.

Two inmates grabbed the guard with the broken nose and hauled him to his feet. They took his cuffs from his utility belt and locked his hands behind his back. Other inmates swarmed around his partner and stripped him of the handgun tucked into his holster.

In the doorway, Mills shouldered his shotgun. It was too late. He couldn't risk taking a shot now. Not without killing one of his own men. Even if he could take the shot, the inmates had two guns. Plus numbers. 'Put down the guns, and release the officers. Right now,' he said.

He managed to squeeze more authority into his voice than Byron would have guessed he'd be able to muster.

Romero handed the shotgun to one of the younger inmates. His movements were smooth. One thing was for sure, that wasn't the first time he'd handled a shotgun. Maybe the impression he gave of being a frail old man had been an act all along. Or maybe watching a man about to die in front of him had given him a burst of energy.

Whatever the reason, when Byron had been imagining an escape, this wasn't the scenario he would have picked.

'Okay,' said Romero. 'They can go and you can have your guns back. But first I want an ambulance for Arturo. If he dies before it gets here, or before he gets to hospital, it will be bad for your men here.'

Mills turned to the other guards. They were holding at gunpoint the inmates who'd been building the fire. 'Order an ambulance. Tell 'em one of the guards has been hurt.'

'Thank you,' said Romero.

CHAPTER THIRTY-EIGHT

The most dangerous moments of a stand-off are at the start. Fingers drop to triggers. Muscles tense. Adrenalin surges. Someone can fire a round without making a conscious decision to do so.

At the other end of the gun barrel, fight or flight can kick in. Even if the person under threat doesn't run, or try to resist, they can get twitchy. Sudden movement can draw a bullet. Byron had once seen a Swedish NGO worker in Kabul shot by a Talib because she'd suddenly decided to power down her cell phone without having been asked to do so. The tips of her fingers had slid into her jeans pocket as her cell trilled with an incoming text and the nervy Talib had taken her out with a three-round burst to her chest.

It had taught Byron an important lesson. If you were going to make a move, be decisive and commit to it. If you weren't, and that was almost always the best option available to you, it was best to stay where you were.

Thankfully, they were now past the tense initial stage. Ten minutes had passed. Fingers had straightened along trigger guards. Barrels had been lowered. Cigarette smoke filled the air. Pockets of whispered conversation had sprung up. Gunpoint had become the new normal.

Byron was still kneeling next to Arturo. He was doing the only thing he could: he was trying to keep the injured man calm and still. It was not an easy task. As the first shards of shock and concussion cleared, pain moved in. Sharp and searing. Arturo's instinct was to move, to find a position that offered some relief.

Romero was pacing back and forth in front of the injured man. Byron suspected that he had no plan beyond getting Arturo to hospital. He hoped he was wrong. What Romero needed was an exit strategy. There was no way that what he had done would go unanswered either by Mills or Castro. You could challenge authority. You might even win the battle. Winning the war was a whole other matter.

Byron motioned Romero over. The old man walked across and squatted next to him.

'How is he?' Romero asked Byron.

'Alive. Breathing. But that might not mean much if there's internal bleeding.'

Romero sighed. 'This is my fault.'

'How'd you figure that?' Byron asked.

'I should have refused to work like this. It wasn't safe. An accident was certain to happen.'

'It wasn't like Mills gave you much of a choice in the matter.'

'I had a choice,' Romero said flatly.

Byron looked up. Mills wasn't paying much attention to their conversation. Neither were the other guards. 'What about now? You have a plan here or not?'

'Get Arturo to hospital,' said Romero.

'I got that part,' Byron said. 'I meant after he's gone to hospital.'

The twinkle came back into Romero's eyes. 'If Mills keeps his word, so will I. He can have his guns back and it'll be over.'

There was a fine line between idealism and reality. For a man who must have endured his fair share of defeats, Romero acted like doing the right thing trumped everything else. The level of his naivety took Byron by surprise. He couldn't tell if it was an act. He hoped it was. 'As soon as you hand those guns back, they'll kill you,' he said. 'Maybe not right away, not in front of witnesses, but it'll happen. Mills might have been bluffing before, but now … You humiliated him in front of everyone. That pretty much guarantees payback.'

'What do you suggest?' said Romero.

'The border's . . . what? Fifty miles? Sixty?'

'About that. But I can't leave the others behind. If they don't have me to punish for this, they'll punish them. What kind of man would that make me, Mr Davis?'

One who's still breathing, thought Byron.

CHAPTER THIRTY-NINE

The ambulance driver slammed the rear doors. He walked round, got into the cab, started the engine and took a wide turn. The inmates and guards watched him go.

Byron's eyes were on Romero. The old man gave a signal and the two inmates who'd had their guns trained on the two guards pointed them at the floor. Ten yards away Mills stood with the other guards. Their guns remained trained on the inmates.

The inmates laid the shotgun and the handgun on the floor. The two captive guards walked sheepishly back to join their fellow officers. Romero had surrendered his advantage. Whatever chance he'd had of escape was gone. So, for that matter, was Byron's.

Not that Byron could complain. He'd made his choice. Flee or stay and help Arturo. No one had twisted his arm. He had stayed of his own free will.

The thought stopped him in his tracks. He had stayed as a matter of conscience. He had placed the wellbeing of a man he barely knew above his own need to escape.

But was it that straightforward? That noble? Or was he simply ascribing to himself a motive that made him feel good?

Perhaps he'd stayed because he was scared of being on his own again. Of being back out there and hunted, if not by the state, by the sheriff and prison guards.

There was something about incarceration, being told what to do and when, that he'd found comforting. The last few months of his existence had been feral. He'd lived on the road. He had been in perpetual motion. Never stopping more than two nights in any one place. Distrustful of everyone he encountered. Constantly questioning people's motives, even – no, particularly –

when they'd shown him kindness.

The idea that on some subconscious level he had chosen to stay was more frightening than having lost the best chance he'd had to make his escape.

The inmates, and the guards, were waiting to see what Mills's next move would be. The Mexican inmates clustered around Romero. Byron was hoping for everyone's sake, the guards included, that Mills wouldn't dish out immediate retribution. Romero getting a beating would spark a fresh confrontation, and this time Byron doubted that every single shotgun shell would stay chambered. The guards might have the firepower but the prisoners had the numbers.

Mills could take his revenge behind closed doors. With no one there to stop him, and plausible deniability as a cover, an 'accident' with no witnesses was a hard thing to disprove. With a compliant police force and judiciary, it would be a slam dunk.

Sadly, Mills wasn't that bright. Anger had clouded whatever judgement he had.

'Romero! Get over here,' he shouted.

The group of Mexican prisoners moved closer to the old man. If Mills wanted Romero he would have to go through them first.

Mills had obviously anticipated such an eventuality. He raised his shotgun to his shoulder and pointed it at one of the younger Mexicans, who was standing on the fringe of the crowd. 'Either you get your ass over here, or I'm gonna shoot this wetback. I'm going to count to three.'

Apart from the young man in Mills's sights, who nervously shifted his weight from one leg to the other and back again, no one moved.

'One,' said Mills, his finger closing around the shotgun trigger.

A couple of the men flanking Romero moved forward, placing their bodies more directly in front of their leader.

'Two!'

Romero said something in Spanish that Byron didn't catch. The men standing next to Romero looked at him. Romero clapped his hand on their shoulders, a paternal gesture designed to reassure, then stepped to the front and began to walk slowly towards Mills. He kept his head high, and his shoulders back. Mills pivoted and swung round, shifting his aim. Romero's gaze ran all the way down the barrel of the shotgun until he met Mills's eyes.

When Romero got within fifteen feet of him, Mills lowered the shotgun. He handed it to the guard standing next to him and pulled out his baton. He slapped the business end into the open palm of his left hand. The message was clear. Romero was about to get a beating in front of the inmates.

Byron watched the faces of the other guards. They weren't going to intervene on a prisoner's behalf. Especially not a prisoner like Romero. But, from the tight yellow balls of fear that Byron could see pulsing in the middle of their heads, they were worried about what might happen next. A couple of them had drawn their weapons and leveled them at the inmates standing just outside the warehouse dock.

The Mexican inmates looked equally set. Glancing around, Byron didn't see any fear. He saw anger. In Byron's mind's eye the red was deep and rich, shading into scarlet. It wasn't going to take much to tip them into a blind rage. Mills raising his baton to Romero would be plenty.

If someone didn't do something they were less than sixty seconds away from a major shit show. There would be blood in the Texas dirt. That much was certain.

Byron stepped forward from the pack of inmates. A shotgun swiveled in his direction.

'Stay where you are, Davis,' Mills barked.

Byron kept walking.

CHAPTER FORTY

Byron had rediscovered his conscience, and his ability to switch off a fear response seemed to have remained intact. He kept walking towards Romero. Mills was shouting at him to back off. He had two more guns on him. That made three in total, all pointing at his chest.

Romero half turned to him. 'This isn't your fight.'

Byron had to hand it to the old man. He had some set of *cojones*.

Two more strides and Byron had caught up with him. He placed a hand on Romero's shoulder. 'This isn't a fight. A fight takes two people.' As he said it, Byron was staring at Mills. Mills didn't like the suggestion of cowardice, although it was plain to see in him, even by his fellow prison guards. An unarmed old man versus a guard with a baton. It wasn't even close to a fair contest.

'Why don't we make this more of a contest, Mills?' said Byron. 'I'll even let you keep that little stick you like waving around to compensate for your lack of balls.'

Mills flushed. He was getting angrier. Fury was overwhelming whatever misgivings he had about going toe to toe with Byron. He was big, but he was out of shape from a job that mostly involved sitting on his ass and barking orders. From the thick spare tire of fat around his abdomen, Byron figured he was no stranger to a Big Mac either.

'Okay,' Mills said. 'But once I'm done with you, Davis, Romero's going to have to take what's coming to him.'

Somehow Byron doubted that.

CHAPTER FORTY-ONE

The end of Mills's baton slashed across the sun in a high arc. Byron ducked, planting his feet and launching himself forward.

As opening salvos went it was about predictable as they came. Why throw a punch when you had a baton? Especially when you were facing someone who was, at a minimum, your physical equal. The only surprising thing about Mills's first move was that he hadn't asked the other guards for his shotgun.

The baton slammed into his lower back. Painful, but not as damaging as it would have been to the intended target: his skull. Wrapping his arms around Mills's waist, he used his existing forward momentum to take Mills to the ground. Rather than letting gravity do the work and think about his position on the ground, Mills fought it. Byron slammed his shoulder into Mills's chin. His jaw clicked. He fell back. Byron was on top of him.

Byron closed his right hand into a fist. He drew it back and threw a punch at about a quarter of his total power. He angled it so that it glanced off the side of Mills's head. It was enough to get the man's attention, plenty enough to hurt (what punch in the head didn't hurt?), but not enough to do any serious damage.

No matter how tempting it was to beat Mills to a pulp, it was not part of the plan. Quite the contrary.

Despite Mike Tyson's famous assertion that 'Everyone has a plan until they get punched in the face', Byron knew that you'd better have some kind of a strategy in place before you threw down. Your strategy might not survive initial contact but having one was better than not.

It couldn't be a quick fight. That would only further enrage Mills — if such a thing were possible: having been taken down easily at the start of the fight, he was pretty pissed.

Anger wasn't good in a fight. Anger led to bad decisions. Anger soaked up a lot of energy.

Byron raised his fist high. It alleviated the pressure on Mills. Byron waited to take the shot. The delay gave Mills enough time to throw up an open palm into Byron's face. Byron tilted his head down fractionally. It gave Mills the angle he needed to connect with the side of Byron's head.

Faking a grunt, Byron snapped his head back. He was starting to understand how professional wrestlers worked. It was a fine line between reality and fakery, with lots of room to get hurt if you got it wrong. Mills threw his other hand. It caught Byron in the side.

It gave Mills the chance to roll out from under him. Both men got slowly to their feet. They squared up, circling each other slowly. Mills was already winded, but getting out from under Byron had given him fresh confidence and a fresh burst of energy.

Byron threw a straight left that glanced past Mills's head. Mills stepped in, laying a jab hard into Byron's abdomen. He followed it up with an elbow that caught Byron's right eye. Byron took a step back. The space gave Mills the time to throw another shot. This time Byron moved out of the way.

The guards, who'd been cheering every time Mills landed a shot, lapsed back into silence. The prisoners urged Byron on, united by a common enemy.

From the frequency and depth of his breathing, Byron sensed that Mills didn't have much left in the tank. A few more exchanges and he'd be running on fumes.

Now came the part that would require some skill.

Byron stopped and put out his open palm. It was a plea for time. True to his nature, Mills took it as a signal to move in for the kill. He rushed hard at Byron, swinging a wild haymaker. Byron feinted left. He was fast enough to slip the worst of the punch, but slow enough for it still to connect. He went down onto his knees.

Mills swarmed all over him. Throwing lefts and rights at his head. There was no power behind them but they would have looked good. Mills finished with a kick to Byron's body that jarred him with pain. This time he didn't have to overplay the air rushing from his lungs.

If there was a dangerous point, this was it. A fitter man than Mills could have stomped him into unconsciousness or a coma.

Mills aimed a few more kicks that didn't carry any real power, but he was done too. He'd won. Proved his superiority. Byron lay face down in the dirt.

Byron had lost a fight he could never have won, or not in any meaningful way. Mills finally backed off, doubling over, his hands resting on his thighs, panting and wheezing. A couple of the other inmates pulled Byron back to his feet.

The shit show was over.

CHAPTER FORTY-TWO

With their cuffs and leg shackles extra-tight, Romero and Byron sat next to each other in the back of the pickup truck as it jostled its way towards the prison. Byron was bruised and sore. He had a few small cuts. He'd put good money on Mills feeling worse.

Before they had got in, Romero had thanked Byron for saving him from a beating. He hadn't phrased it exactly like that, but that was what he'd meant. Byron had shrugged it off. What else could he have done? Stand by and watch a bully like Mills beat a man old enough to be his grandfather to a bloody pulp to prove that he was in control? In a way he had done it as much for himself as for Romero and the others. He had stepped in, not to prove to himself that he had courage, but to prove his humanity. Somewhere he had always held on to the idea that he was more than a killing machine. Mills had given him the opportunity to show that he was.

Romero turned towards him. 'You are a really terrible actor. You could have beaten Mills easily.'

If anyone could have seen through Byron's performance it would have been Romero. 'I didn't think I was that bad.'

Romero smiled. 'Are you referring to your acting or your fighting ability?'

Byron didn't respond.

'I had the same plan in mind. Go easy on Mills and let him win,' Romero said, with a grin. 'Can you imagine if I'd beaten him? He'd never have lived it down.'

When Byron didn't say anything to that either, Romero added, 'I'm joking. Maybe twenty years ago I could have given him a fight.'

'I knew you were joking,' said Byron.

'It was hard to tell,' said Romero.

Byron stared straight ahead, his expression set. 'Then perhaps I'm not as bad an actor as you think,' he said to the old man.

The prisoners kept their heads down as they walked back into their respective housing units. There were more guards than usual. Where there would normally have been one in the watchtowers, there were now three, each armed. On the yard there was more of a presence too. Mills stood with a dozen other officers. For a man who'd established his position of authority, he didn't look happy.

In him now, Byron saw more red than yellow. More anger than fear. It burned at a low flame. He was still angry.

It didn't matter that the whole mess had been of Mills's making. If he had the presence of mind to grasp that, it would only make him angrier. His anger now didn't bode well. There would be payback. Byron didn't know what form it would take. Or when, for that matter, it would arrive. Or who would be on the receiving end. But it was coming. The air crackled with the promise of violence.

Byron took a metal tray and got in line. Up ahead, Red was arguing with the server. Byron didn't look down the line, but tuned in to what was being said.

'Where's the rest of it, motherfucker?' Red shouted.

'That's all there is,' said the server. 'Everyone's getting the same.'

'Bread and water?' spat Red. 'Bullshit. Where's the meat? Man's working all day, he can't do that on bread and water.'

'Move along, Rice. You're holding up the line.' A guard had strode over, thumbs hooked into his belt, more than ready to put Red in his place.

'This is a punishment, right?' said Red. 'Because of that Commie beaner and his beaner pals.'

'I said move along.'

Red moved. The next man shifted up to get his bread and water. The grumbling filtered down the line. Red walked over to eat at the whites' table. A young Hispanic inmate whom Byron hadn't seen before made the mistake of putting his tray down on the same table rather than picking another.

It was a rookie mistake. One that someone who had been in any kind of jail or prison environment before likely wouldn't have made. Red lifted his head and glowered at the Hispanic kid. 'This table's reserved.'

Whether or not the kid understood the words didn't matter. The meaning was hard to miss. He lifted his tray and moved to an empty table at the back of the mess hall.

As he took a seat across from Red, Byron was thankful that, bar some grumbling, the other inmates took the bread-and-water punishment in their stride. The best way to defuse this particular situation, Byron figured, was to let time pass. Mills would revert to his normal low-level of general annoyance. Prison food would be restored. Life would go back to being generally miserable.

Warden Castro had other ideas.

CHAPTER FORTY-THREE

In the darkness, Byron watched Red pull on his pants. He was trying to be quiet about it, which made it all the more suspicious.

Red wasn't the only prisoner in the bunkhouse getting up. A second and then a third inmate got out of bed and began to drag on their clothes. Byron recognized the other two as buddies of Red, inmates he ate with in the mess hall and hung with on the yard. They referred to themselves as 'peckers' or 'peckerwoods', which, as far as Byron had been able to tell, was some kind of lightweight white supremacist. When Red had alluded to it, Byron had wondered just how screwed the white race was if this was the best it could offer. Pretty screwed, he figured.

Byron waited until all three were dressed. They walked to the bunkhouse door and stopped. A second later, the door opened. A shaft of moonlight flashed across a guard's uniform.

Swinging his legs over the side, Byron got up. He padded across to the door on bare feet, clad only in shorts. The three were already outside. Byron stopped the door closing completely, counted to ten, pushed it slowly open, and squeezed through.

With the wall of the bunkhouse at his back, Byron watched the three inmates follow Mills to the door that led into the next bunkhouse. Mills unlocked it, and stepped back. For a moment Mills and his two buddies hesitated. Mills grabbed Red's shoulder, put his mouth to Red's ear and whispered something. Despite the moonlight and the late hour, Byron doubted it was sweet nothings.

This was the bunkhouse where Romero had been placed when he was released from solitary.

CHAPTER FORTY-FOUR

Once Red and the two other inmates were inside, Mills wandered back towards the main administration building. Byron had already noted that the lone night guard in the tower was nowhere to be seen. The cameras that would usually be trained on the bunkhouse doors were pointed elsewhere. Both these breaches of security protocol suited Byron. He quietly followed the three inmates inside the bunkhouse.

Prisoners stirred from their bunks as Red and company blundered around looking for Romero. Clearly their plan hadn't extend to such sophisticated operational details as which bunk their target occupied.

The commotion was more than sufficient to cover Byron's entry. He closed the door behind him and stood in the shadows, off to one side. Red stumbled over a pair of heavy work boots left next to someone's bunk. He lost his balance and ended up sprawling face first on top of a short Guatemalan inmate. The man shoved him off.

All around men were sitting up. Byron spotted Romero on a lower bunk in the far corner of the room. He grabbed a pillow and propped it behind his back. He looked at Red and the two white inmates with the same puzzled expression that he seemed to reserve for almost any threat that came his way. It was the look an animal behaviorist might wear while studying two gorillas fighting in a zoo. The only problem was that Romero was in the enclosure with them.

Red got to his feet. One of his buddies had spotted Romero. 'There's the old fuck!'

The three men started towards Romero. Some of the Mexican inmates traded worried looks, but they didn't move. They knew as well as anyone else in the bunkhouse that three inmates from another housing unit appearing in the middle of the night to give someone a beating didn't happen without at least some degree of co-operation from the prison guards. Someone had had to unlock the doors.

The two white inmates each grabbed one of Romero's arms and hauled him to his feet. Red pushed his face into Romero's.

What happened next, no one had seen coming. Not even Byron.

CHAPTER FORTY-FIVE

Byron had expected Romero to try to reason with Red. Perhaps to explain that they were on the same side, and that skin color was a superficial difference. What mattered more was that they were both being held unfairly, exploited to line other people's pockets, so they should be shoulder to shoulder in resisting the prison regime, not fighting each other. That was what Byron had expected Romero to say. But he didn't say anything as the red-bearded convict wound up to punch him.

That was the first surprise. No words. It was quickly followed by the second surprise. Everything about Romero's attitude and behaviour up to this point suggested that he held to broad principles of non-violent resistance. He'd struck Byron as a man who used brutality employed against him to undermine the opposition, to highlight the weakness of their position.

That didn't happen either.

Instead, Romero drew his head and upper body back six inches. Using the grip of the men holding his arms as two stanchions, he thrust his head forward, driving it with his shoulders and chest, like a soccer player attacking a ball from a corner kick to head a goal.

Romero's forehead crunched into Red's nose with surprising force. Byron heard the crack all the way across the bunkhouse.

He didn't wait for what would happen next. He broke into a run and reached Red as he drew back his fist to take another shot at Romero. He grabbed his wrist and yanked it back, snapping it. This time he screamed in pain and his body went limp. Byron let go.

The two men holding Romero released him. They hunkered down a little, making themselves smaller targets, elbows tucked in, hands bunched into fists.

It was a pitiful sight.

Maybe they'd heard how easily Mills had beaten him and figured he looked tougher than he was. Stupid, thought Byron. *Really dumb.*

He almost saw the shank a second too late. It was a long piece of metal with spikes that got shorter nearer the handle, like a Christmas tree. Like a barbed fish hook, it was designed so that the real damage would be done pulling it back out. He stepped back as it was thrust towards his left side. The sharp metal tip, honed to a fine edge, brushed against his skin, slicing it open and drawing blood.

Byron chopped out a kick to the shank wielder's leg. He followed up with an elbow that smashed into the man's face. The shank dropped to the floor. The other inmate bent down to pick it up and Byron closed in on him, put a hand behind the man's head and pulled it down, bringing his knee up into his victim's face with close to full force.

Byron spun round. Red was standing there, his hands already thrown up in surrender. 'Hey, Davis, it's me. We're cool, remember?'

They were very far from cool. Byron was all set to give Red a taste of the medicine he'd planned on dishing out to Romero. Before that could happen the bunkhouse light snapped on.

Mills and two other guards dressed in full riot gear stood just inside the doorway. 'What the hell is going on here?' Mills shouted.

A second later Byron, Romero, Red and the other two others were engulfed in a cloud of pepper spray. Byron didn't try to fight his way through it. He kicked out at the shank, sending it spinning under Romero's bunk where it couldn't do any harm. Following Mills's orders, he laced his fingers and clamped his hands behind his head. He lowered himself to his knees as the spray stung the back of his throat, and tears streamed from his eyes.

CHAPTER FORTY-SIX

The only good day was yesterday.

It was an old special-forces saying, designed to prepare operators for their work. As dictums went, it was fairly good. For once Byron hoped it might not hold true. Yesterday had started with high hopes of an escape, and ended less than twenty-four hours later in a cell for one in solitary. Romero occupied the next-door cell. The three white inmates were in the infirmary, being treated for their injuries. Sadly for them, no successful treatment had yet been developed for being dumb.

For a man who had only just been released from solitary a few days before, Romero seemed to be in remarkably good spirits. Maybe breaking Red's nose had reassured him that there was still life in the old dog yet. Byron had to hand it to the old man: as head butts went, it had been pretty damn effective. It was proof that when it came to physical violence, youth was no match for technique matched with experience.

The question now was what Mills's or the warden's response would be. Mills had sent in three inmates to teach Romero a lesson and come away with a bloody nose, both literal and metaphorical. Having an enforcer taken out by a senior citizen invited ridicule. In Byron's experience, small-time thugs like Mills hated, more than anything, being made to look foolish. Romero had made him look foolish and then some. It would not be allowed to pass without action being taken. A prison operated on the warden's authority. Take that away and you lost control fast.

Mills's response wasn't long in coming. This time, Byron couldn't do anything to stop it. All he could was sit in his cell, and listen, as a cold, dispassionate rage formed in the center of his gut.

CHAPTER FORTY-SEVEN

Given the limited scope of most inmates' interests (sport, women, and their shitty luck in life), Byron had had the good fortune to be placed in a cell next to Romero. The old man was probably the most able conversationalist among the prison population. He had a broad grasp of what was going on in the world and, perhaps more impressively, why.

Byron learned that Señor Romero had a doctorate from UNAM (the Universidad Nacional Autónoma de México), Mexico's top university. In his late twenties he had been pursuing a degree when he had become involved in a labor dispute while on a visit home. Romero had won the workers a pay rise and better conditions. That had been it. He was hooked by a job with a definite real-world outcome.

Not that Byron had ever craved a job as either a company boss or a labor organizer, but he understood the attraction of doing something that made people's lives tangibly better. Byron's government work, especially as it related to counter-insurgency, often involved setting up educational and infrastructure projects. Everyone thought it was rappelling out of a Blackhawk with a K-bar between his teeth while firing an M16 on full auto, but more often than not the real work of undermining a terrorist organization came via funding a school or arranging for fresh water to be piped to a village. So, Byron understood the appeal of working on the ground as opposed to sitting in some ivory tower telling everyone else how the world *should* work, if only they got with the program.

'You ever have regrets?' Byron had asked him, their voices echoing through the vent that fed into an air duct that ran the length of the cells on either side.

'That I didn't take the easy path?' said Romero.

'Yeah.'

'Doesn't every man wonder what their life might have been like if they had turned right instead of left? Or, in my case, left instead of right,' Romero said.

Romero had a bone-dry sense of humor that made Byron smile. For someone who must have carried his fair share of ideological baggage, he still appeared to have an appreciation of the absurdity of life, and of his own absurdities.

'I guess they do,' said Byron. 'Not sure that's the same as having a regret, though.'

'Neatly sidestepped, Mr Davis,' said Romero. 'If there were a prize for never giving a straight answer you would be some kind of Olympic champion. It may not be too late for a career in politics.'

Byron laughed. 'Think I'll pass.'

Lunch arrived a few minutes later. To Byron's surprise it was better than what was dished out in the mess hall. The bread was fresh. The stew contained what appeared to be chunks of real meat. The fruit, an apple *and* an orange, was free of mould. It was only when he heard the prisoner delivering it whisper to Romero in Spanish, asking how he was and whether he needed anything, that Byron realized this might be the special 'Romero' tray.

He took his time eating. Having food that was actually edible rather than something to be choked down made a pleasant change. It wasn't Michelin-star quality, but after what he'd been eating since his arrest it tasted pretty damn good. Or should that have been simply 'it tasted'?

He finished eating, fed his tray back through the slot, and lay down on the concrete slab topped with a sliver of mattress that passed for a bed in the SHU. That was the other upside of solitary. Any time was nap time. No slaving away in the scorching sun. Privacy. No having to listen to dozens of other men snore or fart or talk in their sleep.

Peace.

It didn't last.

It never did.

This time, Byron was awake when they came for Romero. Three sets of boots marching slowly down the corridor outside. Three guards, faces obscured by bandanas underneath their riot helmets so that all that showed was their eyes. Business eyes. Pupils pinprick small. The dead-soul gaze of men on a mission.

CHAPTER FORTY-EIGHT

Ten minutes later Romero, an oxygen mask placed over his face, was wheeled out of the cell on a gurney. At least, thought Byron, they hadn't just left him to bleed out. It was a small mercy but a mercy none the less. Even Mills, or maybe the warden, had a limit. Or perhaps they knew that there was a world of difference between beating the shit out of someone and killing him.

A hushed reverence seemed to descend upon the SHU as the gurney passed. Eyes peered through tray slots. No one shouted. The whole atmosphere had changed. It was as if a terrible storm had passed and all that was left was the debris.

Byron had no way of knowing if Romero would make it or not. It had been a sustained beating. The old man was not in the best of health, despite evidence to the contrary in how he had handled Red. Even if he survived and made at least a partial recovery, his health would be damaged, if not physically then psychologically.

A beating like that would alter a man like Romero, someone who believed in the fundamental decency of people. A hardened con could take a beating and not think much of it. Their cynicism and the division of the world into predator and prey provided them with psychological armor. Not so with a regular person. Unwarranted brutality affected them in a different way.

Byron lay back on his bunk. When dinner came, he ate reluctantly. Even though the food was still better than it had been in the mess hall, it didn't taste as good as lunch had. His appetite wasn't there. He made himself eat it because he would need the calories.

What had happened to Romero had been a wake-up call he shouldn't really have needed. There was no doing the decent thing in a place like this. No greater good. The only responsibility Byron had was to himself. Whatever chance arose to get out, he had better take it. If he got a chance to even things up with Mills in the process then all well and good. But he wasn't going to allow Romero's welfare or anyone else's to keep him here a second longer than was absolutely necessary.

After Romero had been taken away the inmates had quietened. Even the one or two Byron assumed were housed there because they had psychological problems, and usually kept up a fairly constant litany of screams and obscenities, fell silent.

The night was the same. The atmosphere was subdued. It was as if there had been a collective recognition that you couldn't beat the system so why bother trying?

The next morning that had changed.

CHAPTER FORTY-NINE

At first Byron assumed the whispered conversations between cells heralded news that Romero had died. He braced himself. A man twenty years younger than Romero might not have survived such a physical ordeal. That was why Byron had always questioned the use of physical violence to bring someone into line. Even if the force was measured there was no way of knowing whether some underlying condition would lead to the person's death. An undetected heart murmur, a skull that was thin where it should have been thick, a sudden fall back onto the edge of a sidewalk. The human body was resilient but could prove vulnerable when least expected. You just never knew.

Once the blood had been hosed from the floor, Romero's vacant cell had been occupied by another inmate. Byron hadn't spoken to him, even when the man had tried to introduce himself through the vent as Dallas, a drifter, originally from Seattle. He had been picked up on some bullshit vagrancy charge by some asshole cop. From the way he talked Byron got the impression that this wasn't Dallas's first rodeo. For once it sounded like Kelsen County had leveled a vagrancy charge against someone who was actually a vagrant.

Now Dallas was back at the vent. 'You hear what happened this morning?'

Here it comes, thought Byron. Nothing traveled faster than bad news. Especially in a place like this. He was sitting on the floor, his head back against the wall. He closed his eyes. 'No,' he said.

'They called a strike.'

His eyes opened. 'What d'you mean?'

'This morning. After breakfast. The cons wouldn't

move. Wouldn't get in the trucks. They say they're on
strike,' said Dallas, unable to keep the excitement out of
his voice. 'Guards went crazy. Threatened 'em with all
kinds of shit. Didn't make no difference, though. I mean,
what they gonna do? Throw everyone into solitary? Don't
have the cells.'

'Everyone's on strike? All the prisoners?'

Byron didn't see the white inmates going along with a
strike that had been called by a man that at least of some
of them referred to as a 'Commie beaner'.

'All of 'em. When the beaners wouldn't go out on
work duty, no one else would either.'

It wasn't exactly a show of solidarity across the racial
divide but the end result was the same. Byron smiled.
Romero. Even from a hospital bed he could still piss Mills
and Castro. It didn't even matter whether Romero had
called it or not. In some ways it was better that the leader
of at least a section of the inmates was out of commission.
What else could they do to him that they hadn't already
tried?

'You hear anything about Romero?' Byron asked
Dallas.

'Nope,' said Dallas.

That was good. If Romero had died it would have
gone on the bush telegraph faster than news of a strike.
Now, given what had already happened that morning,
Byron guessed that the prison authorities were praying that
Romero kept breathing. Prison strikes, if they weren't
resolved or met with reprisals, were usually a precursor to
something else. Often a riot.

Dallas took the opening of a dialogue between them
as the green light to start telling Byron his life story.
Although Byron didn't respond, or offer any
encouragement, he kept going. He rolled from birth to his
present predicament with barely a pause for breath. A
daddy he never knew, a mom whose taste in men never

got any better, no matter how many she tried to settle down with. It came off like a bad country song. There was even a dog somewhere in there. Byron let the words wash over him as he thought about the levels of rage that would be washing over Warden Castro now.

Whether Romero had called for the inmates to strike or whether it had been a spontaneous reaction to him being attacked in his cell didn't really matter. If Mills hadn't beaten Romero, the inmates would have been at work this morning.

Word was also filtering through that the women prisoners were staying in their units and refusing to work. While much of the men's labor struck Byron as 'busy work', the women assembled electronic goods for sale. Over the last few years a new wave of factories had sprung up in Mexico, driven by high shipping costs between Asia and the US, but why pay even a few pesos when you could have the work done for free, using essentially the same workforce you would have used anyway?

As business models went, free labor was hard to beat. And if anyone from outside questioned what was being done, there was an easy get-out. These people were criminals. After all, they were in prison, weren't they? Work was a tried and tested way of rehabilitating criminals.

But if the prisoners wouldn't work? If they refused? Factories had fixed costs. They had components coming in at one end, being assembled and shipping out again at the other. Even a day's lost production would cause major problems and questions would be asked.

Shit rolled downhill. The warden would be getting pressure. In turn he'd be asking questions of Mills. Like whose idea it had been to get into a completely unnecessary dick-measuring contest with an old man. Never mind allowing it to escalate to a point at which all of the prisoners had stopped working.

There was also the issue of money. Cops and judges didn't behave in the way they did in Kelsen County without there being something in it for them. With everyone in it, and no one prepared to pay any attention to Thea Martinez, the lone objector, it was low risk. But a risk existed. If the Feds decided to take an interest in the lack of due process, and breaches of civil and Constitutional rights on an industrial scale, a lot of people would have a lot of explaining to do. So, the money offset the risk. When it dried up, it was a shitty deal all round.

The warden's next move would be crucial. He couldn't afford to get it wrong. It occurred to Byron that what had started as yet another setback to any chance of escape might just be an opportunity in disguise.

CHAPTER FIFTY

'I'd like to speak with the warden.'

The guard smirked at Byron through the slot in the cell door. 'In case you hadn't heard, he's kind of busy right now.'

'That's okay. Just tell him I can get everyone back to work.'

Back to work. The three magic words. Better than *Open Sesame*, or *Alakazam*, or clicking a pair of red shoes together three times and wishing you were back in Kansas.

CHAPTER FIFTY-ONE

Lauren Stanley had hoped to be the first person to arrive at the meeting. She wanted to secure a seat near the top of the table, next to the deputy director, who usually chaired the meetings, but Nick Frinz from the State Department had beaten her to it. A Yale and Harvard graduate, Frinz had scaled the heights as quickly as she had.

'Hey, how's it going?' Frinz asked her cheerfully, as she sat down across from him.

'Good.'

Lauren liked to keep chit-chat to a minimum. That went double for Frinz, who was apt to turn the most harmless remark to his advantage.

'How goes the search for Tibor?' Frinz asked, all smiles.

'It goes.'

'You know they're thinking of dropping him down the list?' said Frinz.

She did. It was why she had made sure to get here early to grab the prime seat that Frinz was currently occupying. Resources were scarce, and Tibor was no longer seen as high priority. That happened if someone went long enough without causing the government any further trouble. Like an elephant, they never forgot, but they always had bigger fish to fry.

Tibor dropping down the list would be bad news for Lauren's career. No doubt that was why Frinz was grinning at her, like an idiot. To him, it was a game. Nothing more and nothing less. 'Yes, I'd heard,' said Lauren, matching Frinz's smile with one of her own. 'I don't think it's going to happen, though.'

'How come?'

Frinz seemed temporarily thrown by her good-humored reaction to his needling.

'Just a hunch,' said Lauren, tapping the edge of

the file that lay on the table in front of her.

Inside was a picture of Tibor. It had been taken at a rest stop ten miles east of a town in south-east Texas called Kelsen. Two sightings in the same state, taken less than a week apart. It was m

ore than enough to keep the search live.

CHAPTER FIFTY-TWO

The warden's office door was firmly shut. Byron could hear at least three men, including Warden Castro, inside. For once, the warden wasn't doing most of the talking.

The two other men's voices rose and fell. One was louder, and more vociferous, than the other. Byron didn't have to be able to hear what was being said to get the gist.

The door opened. Byron put his head down and studied the floor as the two men emerged. Both were white, in their late fifties, with the middle-age spread that suggested too much good living. He studied them from the corner of his eye as they sauntered out. One was Sheriff Martin. Byron didn't know who the other was.

Martin was dressed in civilian clothes: grey slacks, a lemon yellow polo shirt and black loafers. It was only seeing him up close that Byron realized the election posters he'd seen on the way into town must have been Photoshopped. If anything, Sheriff Martin was less becoming in real life. If beauty was only skin deep, in his case ugly went right to the bone.

The other man was wearing a navy suit with a white shirt and red tie. His shoes were expensive Italian leather, polished to a high gleam, and he was sporting a Rolex watch. The way Martin fell in behind him as he strode out towards the visitors' parking lot at the front, Byron could see that the second man was the boss. And the boss didn't look pleased.

Byron waited. No doubt Warden Castro was assessing the damage to his ass, the man who'd just left having chewed it out.

'Davis!' Warden Castro called from the office.

Byron got up and walked inside. Castro was behind his desk, trying to look like a man in control of his domain and doing a poor job of it. He had bags under his eyes, and the air smelt vaguely of rye whiskey and vomit.

Castro rose from behind his desk and jabbed a chubby index finger at Byron. 'I hold you partly responsible for this, Davis.'

'And which part would that be?' Byron said. 'Making inmates work in an unsafe environment? Beating the living shit out of an old man?'

Castro's voice rose. He probably felt pretty good for being able to shout at Byron when he'd just been shouted at. *Shit rolls downhill. And keeps on rolling.* Byron guessed he was nearer the bottom of the hill than Castro.

'You came here to bitch at me and you can head right on back to the SHU. I asked you to deal with Romero. That didn't mean becoming his best buddy and going native on me.'

Native? thought Byron. *Really?* 'That's precisely why I'm the person who can talk to him and get him to tell the others to go back to work.'

Castro blinked across the desk at him.

'That's what you want, right?' said Byron.

'You think he'll listen to you?' Castro sounded tentative. The idea of solving a dispute though dialogue and negotiation was certainly not the go-to solution for a man like him.

Byron guessed that was what happened when you were used to getting what you wanted, when you wanted it, without being challenged. Over time it made for a narrow view of how the world operated. It was fine while it worked, but when the world stopped doing what you wanted it to do, what then?

'I think he might,' said Byron.

Castro was still chewing the idea over. But at least he'd taken the bait.

Byron took a breath. 'You'll have to offer him something in return for calling off the strike.'

That seemed to go down less well. 'I ain't offering him or those other animals jack shit. You hear me?' he spat across the desk.

Byron could see where Mills had got the idea that everything involving the prisoners was some kind of dick-measuring contest. It was clearly the management ethos. Byron understood that, in a prison, boundaries were important. So was control. But it had to be tempered at times. All stick and no carrot was a recipe for trouble. Most dictators found that out eventually. Too late. But they found out.

There was no point in arguing with Castro. Byron decided to circle back and come at it from a different angle. 'This strike is a problem for you?' he asked, feigning innocence.

'Damn straight. We have people waiting on the stuff from the assembly plant, components stacking up. The whole chain's already jammed,' said Castro.

'How many days before it gets really serious?' Byron asked.

Castro seemed to study him. Who the hell was this guy? That was what he appeared to be thinking. 'It's already serious.'

Byron hadn't expected a straight answer. For all Castro knew, Byron was there to gather what intelligence he could to feed back to the prisoners who'd organized the strike. After all, hadn't Byron taken the beating that Mills had intended for Romero? That alone was a huge question mark over whose side Byron was on.

'Okay,' Byron said, deciding to rephrase the question in a way that would draw Castro's ire but that he would understand. 'How long before they're looking for a new warden to come in and sort it out? That's usually how these things go. Get a fresh face in to make the offer that you could have put out there right at the beginning.'

'I'm not going anywhere, Davis. You can go back

and tell your Commie pals that.'

'They're not my pals, Warden,' said Byron. 'I came here to see if I could help get this resolved because I want a favor in return.'

Castro might not get reason and logic and negotiation. But naked self-interest? Byron was confident the man would be able to grasp it.

'What's the favor?' he asked Byron.

'I get the strike called off and you let me walk out that front gate as a free man.'

The warden's reaction wasn't the one he'd been anticipating. Rather than curse or tell him to forget it, Castro threw back his head and laughed. He laughed so hard he started to cough. He pounded the desk with his fist. When he caught his breath again, he said, 'Oh, Davis, you're a comedian. You tell 'em to call off the strike and I let you stroll out of here?'

'That's the deal. If you want to end this and get everyone back to work. That is what you want, right?'

'I think this conversation is over,' said the warden.

'Okay, but you know they have you over a barrel here? Most strikes are broken because the employer has deeper pockets than the workers. But you don't pay these people, so that isn't going to work. You could stop feeding them, I guess, but you need them able to work, and starving people have low productivity. Plus they may just call your bluff and run with a hunger strike if you do that. The way I see it, you have the problem and they have the time.'

CHAPTER FIFTY-THREE

The atmosphere bordered on festive. Prisoners lolled on their bunks, played cards, read and talked. In one corner the prison equivalent of a book club seemed to be discussing the rise of female erotica. More specifically, the wildly popular sub-genre, whose plots tended to revolve around misunderstood billionaires with strange sexual predilections and naive young women who blushed a lot.

'See, I always knew that shit worked with bitches,' one inmate was saying.

'Only if you got the cash,' retorted another.

'No. The money is the icing. Dominance is the cake. Men got to be men. That's what bitches dig,' said the first inmate.

Byron left them to debate the finer points of gender equality and power as it related to human sexuality. He walked over to his bunk, lay down and surveyed the scene.

His first impression had been correct. The usual sullen, tense atmosphere had gone. Even Red and his buddies seemed to have caught the good mood. There must have been something about sticking it to Mills and Castro that overrode any bad feeling between the different racial groups. Even if the whites had only joined the strike because they didn't want to work while the others stayed in the bunkhouse playing poker, their decision had created a bond. Battle lines had been drawn. Prisoners versus guards.

Right now the prisoners had the upper hand.

Things wouldn't stay like this indefinitely, though. Whoever controlled Castro needed the factory open and work being done. They would make sure that happened. One way or another. No one smart enough to engineer a set-up like this was going to stand idly by and watch it collapse.

Something would change. The only questions that

remained now were what, and when.

The party atmosphere carried on through lunch. In the mess hall, Byron even noticed a couple of white inmates sharing a table with Mexicans. Almost as surprisingly, even the guards appeared happier. Mills was nowhere to be seen, but the guards supervising the meal seemed relieved to be inside the relative cool of the mess hall rather than out in the dusty Texas sun.

Mills's absence suggested that perhaps the warden was trying to take down the tension a notch. Or at least not make things worse. Byron hoped it stayed that way. The last thing the present situation needed was Mills on the rampage.

After lunch the prisoners filtered out into the yard. They were greeted by a cloudless blue sky. Someone produced a soccer ball and an impromptu pickup game began. Byron stood in a corner and watched. For big, muscular men who did manual labor all day, some of the prisoners were skilled players.

The game was raucous but good-natured. Prisoners waiting to come into it warmed up on the sidelines. Someone would get tired and another would take their place, jogging onto the 'pitch' like it was the Bernabeau in Barcelona or some other famous stadium. For a while it was hard to remember that they were all inside a prison – or, as Byron had come to think of it, a semi-legal forced-labor camp.

The game rolled on. The score ran into double figures for both sides. Players switched in and out. The guards watched, arms folded across their chests. One of the watchtower guards leaned over the edge, following the action below.

After an hour, the heat became too much, even for the hardiest of the players. A break was called. A few minutes later the guards shepherded the prisoners back into the bunkhouses. They went without complaint.

Some of the soccer players hit the showers. Others lay down for a nap. Cards groups and conversationalists reconvened.

Byron lay down on his bunk, and closed his eyes. He didn't fall asleep, but he let his mind rest, tuning out the noise around him until it was a dull thrum.

Half an hour later he heard the first voice being raised. It registered but he tuned it out. Then the tenor of many voices began to change. Their owners spoke more softly. There was a sharper rise and fall in volume.

Byron opened his eyes. He turned onto his side and scanned the room. In one corner half a dozen Mexican inmates were deep in conversation punctuated by lots of finger jabbing.

Sliding off his bunk, Byron stood up. 'What's going on?' he asked Red, who was leafing through a girly magazine that had been passed around so much it was a wonder that any of the pages opened.

Red's eyes ferreted around the room. 'Shit's gonna kick off.'

As answers went, it was hardly informative. Byron had already worked out that some of the prisoners were animated. 'Because?' he said to Red, struggling to keep the sarcasm out of his voice. Not that Red would register it.

'Romero's dead,' said Red.

CHAPTER FIFTY-FOUR

From the way Red gave Byron the news, it was as if Red and his buddies hadn't been ready to do precisely what the guards had done to Romero. His mind had already excised the fact that not much more than twenty-four hours ago he had been on the guards' side of the present conflict. Not only did he sound upset at the news of Romero's death, he was outraged.

'Fuck these punk-ass guards,' said Red, a fleck of saliva spraying from his mouth. 'Take away those billy clubs and that pepper spray and they ain't shit.'

'Do we know for sure that Romero's dead?'

That question was met with less certainty. 'Well, no one's seen the body or anything, but Hector over there,' Red said, thumbing towards a group of Mexican inmates in the corner, 'his wife works in the prison hospital and she heard the guards talking, so, yeah.'

'So she didn't see him either?' said Byron.

'Well, no, but she was a nurse back home and stuff so …'

Byron walked past Red towards the bunkhouse door. He pushed through it into the yard. It was late afternoon. The searing heat had died down a little.

By the time he hit the gate he could feel eyes on him, both from the prisoners behind and the guards in the watchtower. One of the younger guards stood by the gate. He hitched his thumbs into his belt as Byron approached. 'What you want, Davis?'

'Is Romero dead?' Byron asked him. There was no point in beating about the bush. Either he was or he wasn't.

'Where'd you hear that?' the guard said, with a smirk that could either have been confirmation or amused denial.

'Doesn't matter. Is he or isn't he? If he is, you boys

better make sure you have your body armor on because there'll be trouble. If he isn't then someone needs to tell the men back there,' Byron said, nodding back towards the bunkhouse. 'Even the peckerwoods are spoiling for a fight.'

The guard snickered, and Byron had to admit that the peckerwoods were unlikely to strike fear into the heart of any authoritarian institution, like a prison.

'Look, Davis, if we had to run round stomping on every bullshit rumor that these idiots start, nothing would get done,' said the guard.

'Well, this is one that's worth putting to bed,' said Byron. 'You might want to let the warden know.'

The guard spat a gob of chewing tobacco onto the ground. 'Wait here.'

He walked towards the administration block. He took his time about it. The heat may have slowed him down, but Byron guessed it was another petty show of power.

Byron waited for ten minutes in the direct sunlight and searing heat next to the gate. Finally, the guard sauntered back. He took out a key and unlocked the gate. 'Warden wants me to take you to the hospital wing.'

Romero looked at Byron as he pulled up a seat next to the old man's bed. His face was swollen and bruised and his arm was in a cast. He was hooked up to a heart monitor and an IV. He didn't look great, but he wasn't dead either.

'You're my first visitor,' Romero said, his voice a gravelly croak.

'Sorry, I didn't have time to get you anything,' said Byron. 'The gift store was closed.'

Romero managed a smile. Byron was relieved to see that the twinkle was still in his eyes. It was more important than the physical injuries. Those would heal. But if the beating had somehow splintered Romero's spirit, or reduced his humanity, he would have been more concerned. The gleam in the old man's eyes told him that whatever Mills and his thugs had set out to achieve they had failed.

'I heard you were dead,' Byron told him.

'I'm sorry to disappoint you.'

Byron smiled. 'How you feeling?'

'Well,' said Romero, 'when you get to my age you pretty much wake up feeling bad and it doesn't get much better. This is worse than that. Which proves that anything is possible. Even feeling worse.'

'Something for me to look forward to, I guess,' said Byron.

'So who was saying I was dead? Castro?'

Byron shook his head. 'Mainline gossip. Everyone's gotten worked up about it. You hear they're on strike?'

The gleam grew brighter. 'I'd heard something. It's good to know that, even at my age, I can still cause trouble.'

'You sure did that. Castro's having kittens. You know the women are on strike too?'

Romero gave a little nod. His chin settled on his chest. He was getting tired.

'So maybe now you've proved your point it'd be a good time to call it off,' said Byron.

Romero's head snapped up. 'Castro sent you to ask me this?'

'Not directly,' said Byron. 'It was originally my idea to come talk to you.'

'And why do you care so much? You have shares in the Kelsen County Corporation you haven't told me about?' Romero asked.

'They're incorporated?'

Romero smiled. 'Via a series of companies in the Cayman Islands. You think I'm just an old rabble-rouser?'

'Your word, not mine.'

'I did my homework before I came here,' said Romero. 'But in answer to your question, I can't call off the strike. And even if I could, why would I? We're hurting them in the only part of them that is sensitive to pain. Their pocket.'

Byron wasn't so sure. 'You think they'll just suck that up? Stand by while they watch their profits go down the drain?'

Romero's head sank down into the pillows. 'No, I don't.'

'So what's the point of doing this?' Byron asked.

'What's the point of doing anything?' Romero said, his question seemingly directed at the ceiling. 'What do you think the world be like if everyone had always accepted their lot in life? If no one had ever stood up for themselves when faced with injustice?'

Byron moved his chair a little closer. He was aware that the guard who'd escorted him there was waiting in the corridor to take him back. 'I'd agree with you. I just think that, in this case, you can't win. Worse, I'm worried about what they'll do if this thing rolls on. Say they leave the men alone and target the women's prison. Try to force them back to work. What then?'

Romero rolled his head so that he was looking straight at Byron. 'If you think that women are easier to push around than men, perhaps you understand less about how this world of ours works than I thought you did.'

'I don't want to see anyone get hurt. That's all.'

'If I didn't know better I'd say that sounded like a threat,' said Romero.

'Hey, I'm the one who took an ass-kicking on your behalf and stopped another. You forgotten that already?'

'You're quite right. That wasn't fair of me.'

The green line on Romero's heart monitor was peaking

higher and more frequently. Byron didn't want to wear him out. He'd come to say what he had to say. He wasn't going to get anywhere. At least, not right now.

Byron pushed back his chair. He reached out and touched the back of Romero's hand. 'Just get better, okay?'

'A few more days and they say I can get out of here,' said Romero. 'Maybe then I'll talk to the warden. Present our demands. When I know that I have his attention.'

Byron said goodbye. There were some people whose attention he'd rather not have. Castro was one of them.

CHAPTER FIFTY-FIVE

The prisoners were already gathered, awaiting Byron's return, when he walked back into the bunkhouse. There was a crackle of tension in the air. Byron was familiar with it. It was the human equivalent of the tight, clammy air in the hours before a thunderstorm.

'Romero's fine,' Byron told them. 'I just saw him. He has a broken arm and a lot of bruises but he's alive. In fact, he's been told he may be able to get out in a few more days.'

That was not what the assembled prisoners had expected to hear. More than that, he suspected it was not what they had hoped to hear. Not that they wished Romero dead. They didn't. But they might have been looking forward to the righteous anger that could be unleashed upon the news of his death.

The inevitable challenge came a few seconds after Byron finished speaking.

'Why should we believe you?' a heavily inked Mexican prisoner asked Byron.

Byron wasn't about to play that game. He hadn't wanted to intervene on Romero's behalf. It had cost him his chance to escape. He didn't want to help Castro either. He flat-out didn't want to be on anyone's side in all of this. Yet he found himself being constantly asked to pick either one or the other. It was beyond old by now.

'You don't,' he said. 'Believe me or don't believe me. I couldn't give a fuck. But Romero's fine. He told me he may be out in a few days and then he plans on sitting down with the warden and working out some kind of compromise.' He threw up his hands. 'That's all I got.'

Word came back a few hours later, from another source in the prison hospital, an orderly who took food over there, that Romero was indeed alive. Those who had doubted Byron went back to their card games.

The mood was more somber than before. Now they were dug in. The novelty of thumbing their nose at the warden and guards had begun lose its sheen. A good number of the prisoners had been hyped up by the rumor of Romero's death. It would have lit the touch-paper of a riot. Now it was back to the dull mundanity of trying to hurt the warden and Mills by doing precisely nothing.

The prisoners had dinner. They had an hour on the yard. Then they went back to the bunkhouse. A few hours later it was lights out.

The morning would bring more of the same. More nothing.

CHAPTER FIFTY-SIX

It was just after lunchtime on the fourth day of the strike when a guard appeared at the gate leading Romero into the yard. His arm was still in a plaster cast, and he was walking with the help of a stick, but he was walking. Or, rather, hobbling.

Byron could tell from the drawn look on the old man's face that he should still have been in hospital. He wasn't fit enough to be discharged. But he wasn't about to lie in bed a day longer than he needed to. Not when the action, or what passed for action, was out here.

The guard let him pass through the gate and beat a fast retreat. Mexican prisoners swarmed around the old man, clapping him on the shoulder and trying to shake his hand. No doubt about it, he was the conquering hero. Byron pushed through the melee. 'Okay, give him some space,' he said, falling into impromptu bodyguard mode, pushing a few over-eager supporters out of the way.

'Didn't I tell you I would be out in a few days, Davis?' Romero said.

'Your idea or the warden's?' Byron asked, squaring his shoulders against the press of bodies.

'It was mutual. I don't like hospital beds and he wants to sit down so that this matter can be settled.'

'Is that so?' said Byron.

Romero struggled to keep his balance as a hand reached through the wall of bodies for his. He stopped, hooked his walking stick over his wrist and shook it. Byron tried to keep him moving to get him inside the bunkhouse where he could sit down for a few minutes. He wasn't a fan of crowds like this. He wouldn't have put it past the warden to pay off an inmate to finish the job that Mills had started. A crowded prison yard was an ideal location for an assassination attempt.

A few more steps and Romero took Byron's arm for support. 'Let's go talk to the warden. You can come with me.'

'You don't want to rest up first?' Byron said.

'What do you think I've been doing? No, the quicker I can speak with Castro, the quicker this can be settled,' Romero told him.

'Why do you need me with you?' said Byron. Once again he was being pulled inexorably into a situation that he wanted no part of.

'I don't need you there. But it would be good if you were.'

The crowd was still pressing around them. If Romero didn't want to go back to the bunkhouse then the warden's office was as good an alternative as any. At least it had chairs.

Byron helped Romero turn back towards the gate. The crowd pivoted with them. Slowly they made their way back. The guard eyed them as they reached the fence.

'I would like to speak with Warden Castro,' said Romero.

The guard rolled his eyes but opened the gate. A cheer went up from the crowd of prisoners. As Byron began to escort Romero through, the guard's arm fell across his chest. 'Where do you think you're going, Davis?'

'I'm helping him.'

The guard stepped back. 'Jesus, it's like you people are running this place, these days,' he said, through teeth so gritted that Byron could almost hear the enamel chipping off them.

This time there was no wait to see Castro. Romero and Byron were shown straight in. They took a seat as the warden made a show of finishing up some paperwork. He signed his name, put the papers in a folder and closed it.

'How are you feeling, Señor Romero?' he asked.

'All things considered, I feel good, Warden Castro,' said Romero. 'Thank you for asking.'

The forced politeness between the two men was entertaining to watch. Both would have happily seen the other dead. Yet they moved through the dance that was expected of them, as if they were old friends sharing late-night brandy and cigars.

'Okay, shall we get this done?' said Castro.

The bluntness drew a grin from Romero. 'Texan charm. And I always thought it was a myth.'

Castro glared at him. There were few things that Texans disliked more than someone who wasn't Texan criticizing their beloved Lone Star State. They might bitch about it, but that was different.

'Our demands are very simple, Warden,' Romero began. 'Nothing that will trouble you too much. Or cost you too much money. At least, not as much as a prison strike.'

Castro was still glaring at Romero. There was something else that Byron detected. A smugness that suggested Castro was already at least three moves ahead. That he'd been planning for this discussion, that he had Romero all figured out and knew just how to deal with his demands.

'I'm relieved to hear that,' said Castro. 'Please, do continue, Señor Romero. Though I should counsel you that I had a very similar discussion not too long ago with a young man from your side of the border. I believe he was your nephew.'

If the jibe was intended to provoke a reaction from Romero, it failed. He smiled politely, though Byron saw, below the desk, his hand tighten around the top of the walking stick so hard that his knuckles went white.

'Shall I tell you what we require?' Romero asked.

'Please do.'

Castro picked up the folder he'd just put down and opened it. He studied the piece of paper on top. His finger ran across it, tracing the text.

Romero began, 'First, we ask that efforts are made to ensure safe working conditions for the inmates. We believe that the same standards should apply inside this institution as outside.'

'That seems very fair, Señor Romero. Certainly something we can look into. The accident that happened was very regrettable. Not something I'd want to happen in any prison that I run.'

Romero looked surprised at this response. It was not what Byron had expected either. Not by a long way. Castro had never struck him as the apologetic kind.

'I appreciate that. Thank you,' said Romero. 'Second, we would like to see . . .'

'If I could stop you there,' Castro said, holding up his hand. 'Perhaps if you could write all these demands down for me before you leave.'

'Leave?'

Romero looked as if the floor had disappeared from under him. Byron guessed that was the reaction Castro had intended. Let Romero come in, be polite and agreeable, then tell him they were releasing him.

'Yes,' said Castro. 'Judge Kelsen has granted you an immediate release. Medical grounds. We're concerned about the state of your health.'

The bitter irony of Castro's concern for the man's health wasn't lost on either Byron or Romero. Romero gave a nervous laugh, as if he knew he'd been outmaneuvered but still couldn't quite believe it.

As switches went, its beauty lay in its simplicity. Byron was just surprised that Castro, or whoever had come up with it, hadn't thought of it sooner. This wasn't like releasing some political dissident back into the general population, returning them to their supporters, where they could foster further trouble. Quite the opposite. Romero's cause was contained within the footprint of the Kelsen County Jail. Place him outside and that was that. Romero was being released into obscurity. Or, potentially, something much worse.

'Sorry, Davis,' Castro said, as he slid the piece of paper across the desk towards Romero. 'You'll have to wait. No extenuating circumstances.' He turned his attention back to Romero. 'Actually, Davis here gave me the idea. Kind of kills two birds with one stone. Everyone's happy. Ain't that right, Davis?'

Romero glared at Byron. 'This was your idea.'

'Indirectly, I guess,' said Byron, as, in turn, he stared at Castro.

'You just need to sign here and here,' Castro said, tapping two dotted lines on the release form.

'Can I at least read what I'm signing first?' Romero asked.

'Never known a man who wanted to read the fine print when he's being offered his freedom,' said Castro. He seemed more delighted with himself with every passing minute.

'That's strange,' said Romero. 'I've known a few.'

The comment flew straight over Castro's head. Byron, too, knew of many dissidents or leaders who had refused their freedom because their release came with conditions they found unacceptable. Somehow, though, he doubted that Romero would be offered a choice in the matter. They wanted Romero out and that was what would happen. If they had to, they would pick him up and carry him out of the gate.

'I'll have to arrange transport home,' said Romero.

'Oh, don't you worry about that, Señor Romero,' Castro said. 'Sheriff Martin has it all worked out. Concierge-level service, if you will. A Kelsen County deputy is going to drive you right to the border crossing.' Castro's eyes narrowed. 'As you entered illegally we want to be sure that the Department of Homeland Security has your name on file so you don't come back. Not that we haven't enjoyed having you as a guest, you understand.'

Byron watched as Romero, very reluctantly, took the pen that was handed to him and signed his name twice. Castro put out his hand to take the form but Romero began to write something under each of his signatures in block capitals.

He finished and handed the paper back across the warden's desk. Byron caught a glimpse. Under both signatures Romero had written: 'I SIGN THIS UNDER DURESS.'

Castro didn't miss a beat. He took the paper and placed it back in the manila folder. 'Thank you, Señor Romero. Your transport is waiting outside. Davis, you may return to your cell. If you like, you can share the good news of Señor Romero's release on compassionate grounds with your fellow convicts.'

CHAPTER FIFTY-SEVEN

There was added poignancy to Byron and Romero's goodbye because both men knew what had happened to Romero's nephew when he was released. Byron's mind was racing as he tried frantically to think of some way around it. He had nothing. If he hadn't been able to extricate himself safely from this situation, how could he possibly help Romero?

Of course they might just be getting ready to drive Romero to the border crossing in Laredo and hand him over to the INS for deportation, but Byron doubted it. Castro wanted to make an example of him, just as they'd done with the nephew. Come across the border to create trouble and you'll be sent back home in a box. It was justice, with a Texas twist.

If anyone asked the county sheriff's escort what had happened, all he would need to say was that Romero had escaped the patrol car. It would be the word of a deputy against that of Romero. And Romero wouldn't be alive to give his account of what had gone down.

Byron's best guess was that Romero would be found somewhere in the desert with a gunshot wound to the back of the head. Assuming he was found at all and the coyotes hadn't eaten him. As soon as he climbed into the back of the Crown Vic that was waiting for him outside, engine idling, his fate would be sealed. Strangely Romero seemed resigned to his fate. He had registered his final protest in ink. It struck Byron as a lame way to go for a man who must have fought so hard through his life. Maybe he was just done. Byron had experienced moments like that. He'd had times when he'd contemplated giving up and surrendering to his fate. Losing his wife had brought him to that point.

What must it have been like for Romero, who had

fought so hard for what he believed in, and for longer? Perhaps the beating, or the humiliation of it and what it demonstrated about human nature, had taken the fight from him.

'This wasn't my idea,' Byron said to Romero.

'I know that, Davis, not that it matters.'

'It matters to me.'

Romero nodded. 'I understand. So this is goodbye?'

He put his working hand out. Byron shook it. He was still trying to think of some way out for Romero. 'When you were arrested, what did you have with you?' he asked. Any personal property he'd had that had been confiscated should be returned to him upon release.

The question seemed to puzzle Romero. 'My wallet, bank cards, some cash, family pictures. My clothes. My phone. I switched that off when I gave it to them so the battery wouldn't run down. Nothing, really. I was traveling light.'

'Make sure you get it all back before you go. Especially the phone. Don't leave without it,' said Byron. He looked around to make sure they weren't being watched, plucked a pen from a nearby desk, grabbed Romero's good hand, and scribbled a number on it. 'Her name is Thea Martinez. She's an attorney here. Tell the deputy you need to take a leak. Insist on using a gas station so you have some privacy. When you're alone call her. Explain who you are and what your situation is. Tell her your life is in danger and ask her to come meet you. Once you've done that, sit tight. If the deputy tells you to move, you tell him about the call you just made. Tell him that she's contacted the US Justice Department and the FBI field office in San Antonio.'

'You really think that will stop them killing me or dropping me out in the desert with no water and a broken arm?' Romero asked.

'I don't know. But it'll give them something to think

about. A man going missing is one thing. A man who goes missing after he tells an attorney that he's about to be snuffed by the county sheriff is something else.'

Romero glanced down at Thea's number on the palm of his hand. 'I can trust her?'

'More than you can trust anyone else around here,' said Byron. 'All I know is that the judge, the sheriff and the warden all seem to hate her.'

'An excellent set of recommendations.'

One of the guards walked into the outer office where they were standing. 'Hey, Davis, you ain't going anywhere. I want you back on the mainline. We have to finish processing Romero.'

'Good luck,' Byron said.

'The same to you,' said Romero.

CHAPTER FIFTY-EIGHT

He didn't know how it had happened, but by the time Byron walked back into the bunkhouse, word had already got round that Romero was gone. From the fallen faces and stooped shoulders, it looked like his release was already having the desired effect. They were only a few days into the strike, but removing Romero, so soon after his triumphant return, had sent morale plummeting.

No matter the righteousness of the cause, Byron had no plans to rally the troops. The sooner they were back to work and out on those trucks, the sooner he could get out of there.

A couple of the Mexican prisoners walked over to him. They wanted to know if he'd seen Romero. He told them some of what he knew. There was no point in mentioning the ride they had planned for Romero to the border. It would only make an already tense situation even worse. If they killed Romero the inmates would hear about it eventually and the whole place would go up. Byron didn't plan on being there when that happened.

As he reached his bunk, Red sidled up to him. 'We need to talk.'

Byron doubted they did, but he humored Red and walked with him to a quiet corner of the bunkhouse. 'What's up?' he asked.

'Me and some of the other guys are going back to work tomorrow,' said Red.

Byron shrugged. 'Okay.'

'If you're smart you'll do the same.'

'I'll be happy to,' Byron told him. 'What's with the change of heart?'

Red shot Byron a smile that suggested he was holding on to some special secret. It was the kind of look that made Byron want to punch him in the face. 'Mills is telling us that those who go back tomorrow are going to get some goodies.'

'Goodies?' Byron asked.

'Whores. Hookers. Women,' said Red.

'And where are these women going to come from? I sure as hell didn't see anything that even looked like it might be a bordello in town.'

Red's smirk grew broader. 'The women's prison.'

Byron folded his arms across his chest. 'What the hell are you talking about? Those women aren't hookers.'

'Sure they are,' said Red.

Byron reached out and clapped a huge hand on Red's shoulder. 'You or your peckerwoods lay a finger on any of those women, regardless of whether you think they're hookers or not, and I'll kill you. Do you understand me?'

Red tried to push Byron away. 'What's it to you?'

Byron squeezed a little harder. Red winced. 'You heard me. Touch any of them and you're a dead man.'

The first punch was thrown in the mess hall. Red and a couple of his white peckerwood buddies had made a passing comment to a table of Mexicans. Byron didn't catch what was said, but he didn't have to. He could make an educated guess about its nature from the reaction it garnered.

A Mexican prisoner with full sleeves and a chest like the front of a Mac truck stood up and popped Red in the face with a looping right hand that seemed to start in the next county.

Red fell back, blood gushing from a broken nose. His two buddies double-teamed the Mexican, tackling him to the floor and laying in with a flurry of kicks and punches. The inmate's buddies got to their feet, metal trays flying, and waded in.

It was one of those fights in which someone could

have been badly hurt, if the participants had been focused on inflicting damage rather than flailing wildly at whoever was within their immediate reach. If it had been set to music, the score from an old Buster Keaton movie would have been the most appropriate accompaniment.

The three guards on mess-hall duty stood back and watched. When the dozen or so participants had tired themselves out, they stepped in. They pulled Red and his buddies clear, saving their batons for the Mexicans who'd been involved, and a few who hadn't.

What little solidarity that had existed was well and truly ruptured. It seemed like the promise of a woman was a pretty good motivator for men like Red, who didn't care whether the person they wished to have sex with was willing or not.

If this fight was the product of an incendiary comment, Byron could only imagine the shit show that would go down if Red and his pals were let loose inside the prison's sister facility. The women they were talking about were mostly the wives and girlfriends of the men in here. More likely it was a power play by those in charge. If you don't get back to work then we won't punish you: instead we'll punish your loved ones. In the worst way imaginable. The threat of such a thing was usually enough to get someone to buckle under. It was so horrific that very few men would risk such a thing happening, even if the chance was remote. Usually threats had to be credible. If a man told you he was going to stomp you into dust, he'd better look like he was capable of doing so.

Byron's first thought was that the idea had been floated to get some leverage over the striking Mexicans. Then he had started to think about it a little more deeply. Rape as punishment, or the threat of it, had gained traction in places like sub-Saharan Africa and the Middle East. Before that it had been deployed in places like Bosnia. But in America? No way. Another force was at work here. A much darker one. And he had a fairly good idea what, or who, it might be.

CHAPTER FIFTY-NINE

The prisoners from Byron's bunkhouse filed into the mess hall for breakfast. Mills and about four other guards were waiting for them. They stood in front of the serving area where the inmates usually picked up their trays. Byron was about ten back in the line.

'Okay. You men who are working today, pick up your tray and go ahead. The food's so good that even I ate it this morning. There's plenty of it too.'

Mills looked at the inmates who were shuffling towards the back of the line: the men who planned on continuing with the strike. He tilted his head back theatrically and sniffed the air. 'Mm, damn, that smells good. Might have some more.'

The prisoners exchanged looks as Red and his buddies pushed through to the front of the line. 'Make way for the workers,' said Red, as subtle as a house brick. He grabbed a tray and started to move down the line. Byron had to admit the food did look good. Real eggs. Crispy bacon cooked to the sizzle. Biscuits. Gravy. Hot coffee that might have seen a coffee bean somewhere along the line.

'Slap that shit on,' said Red to the server. 'I got a long day ahead of me and an even longer night.' He nudged the man next to him. 'Know what I'm saying? A man needs his protein if he's going to be doing a lot of fucking.'

For a second Byron thought the scrap might kick off again. A couple of the Mexicans were glaring at Red and his buddies. It took Mills drawing his baton and slapping it into his open palm to settle them down.

'Going to get me some sweet brown sugar,' Red continued on.

Mills had heard enough. 'Shut your pie hole,' he bellowed at Red. 'Keep moving along the line. Workers only.'

Byron found himself hesitating. He was going to join the work detail. His freedom required it. But this display turned his stomach.

One of the Mexicans pushed past the others in line and picked up a tray. Others muttered at him. Mills lowered his baton across the man's chest. 'You eat, you work. You take this food and don't work, it's all kinds of bad news for you.'

The man lowered his head and gave a little nod that he understood. Behind him the muttering grew louder and moved down an octave. The Mexicans were growling. The man took his tray and moved on. He kept his gaze focused on the food and took a table across from Red and the others.

Byron could feel eyes on him as he moved back towards the stack of trays. A couple of inmates' shoulders checked him as he made the short journey but he shrugged them off. He had gone above and beyond what he'd ever intended. He had his own war to wage, and he couldn't fight it while he was here, never mind if he was caught by his pursuers.

The server looked up at him. 'What you want?'

'Everything,' said Byron.

His plate heaped with food, Byron took an empty table. It was better that he ate alone. He didn't want to talk. He wanted to eat his breakfast and get out on the truck, pick his moment and not look back.

Not look back?

He wasn't sure that would hold true. He was already worried about Romero. Had he managed to contact Thea? Or was he lying dead somewhere? Had the warden actually returned him to the border? Maybe he would find out what had happened to him once he was out of there.

He ate slowly and methodically. The lone Mexican breaking the strike was joined by a couple of others. They sat together, and ate, not looking at each other, not speaking.

The food was good. Mills hadn't exaggerated. It was the best meal Byron had eaten since he'd been arrested. He always enjoyed breakfast, not that he had had time to eat it on the road.

At the serving hatch, the metal containers filled with eggs, bacon and biscuits were being removed. They were replaced with others. Mills waved the striking men forward with a grin. 'Chow time, *muchachos.*'

The men took their trays and filed along. They looked with disgust at the watery porridge, but didn't complain.

Mills was enjoying every second of this. 'Hey, don't bitch at me. You had a choice. Work and a good meal, or lay on your ass and eat this shit. I wasn't twisting anyone's arm. Oh, and sit on the other side. Don't want you disturbing men who want to earn their keep.'

Mills was as dumb as Byron had figured. The more he tried to humiliate the men who were striking, the harder their resolve. If he'd simply laid out the options, Byron was fairly sure that more would have come over to the work detail. It would have suited Byron too. The more men to supervise, the busier the guards would be, and the easier for him to make his move.

Apart from Red, the men sitting near Byron ate in silence. The other, larger, group spooned their porridge and stared over, eyes filled with hatred. The oldest trick in the book: divide and rule.

Breakfast finished, the first group filed over to deposit their trays. Mills was waiting for them. 'This way, gents. Don't worry, we don't have anything too strenuous for you today seeing as you're on your own. No ladders.'

Men from the other units joined them at the trucks. They

were mostly white, but with a few of the Mexican and Hispanic inmates. Byron was on the truck before he noticed that, while they were all handcuffed, the guards had dispensed with leg shackles. The only explanation was that Mills or whoever made the call didn't figure strike-breakers as flight risks. Byron smiled to himself as he climbed onto the back of the truck.

The guards were also light in number. Two guards per truck with no advance or rearguard security. Mills was riding in the cab of Byron's truck.

CHAPTER SIXTY

They drove into town, along the trash-free sidewalks, past the McMansions, the upscale shopping mall and new office buildings. They turned, finally, through a rear access gate of Kelsen Country Club. A sign informed them that it had been established in the late nineties. Byron wondered if that was around the time the prison had opened and business started to boom.

The trucks pulled up to next to a long, low building filled with green and white canopied electric golf buggies. Through some trees Byron could see a fairway and four middle-aged white men in slacks and polo shirts hacking their way towards a perfectly manicured green. His fellow inmates had the look of men who might have landed on Mars. Byron doubted any of them had ever been so close to a place like this.

Mills seemed fairly uptight. Byron wondered if maybe he was up for membership and wanted to impress the committee. He thought about asking him, but decided against it. Better to let the man think he'd fallen into line and was playing along.

The inmates were divided into three work parties of eight men each. Byron was paired with one of Red's toothless buddies and six Mexicans. They followed Mills and another guard over to a practice area where the members could hit some balls or refine their swing, in relative privacy, before going out to play.

Byron watched Mills and the other guard, the truck's driver, carefully. He had seen Mills tuck the keys into the front pocket of his pants.

Each prisoner was set to work raking leaves. Byron made sure he was standing next to the other white inmate when the rakes were handed out. 'Going to be pretty tough to work with our hands cuffed,' he said to him.

It took the man all of five seconds to pass the complaint on up the chain. 'Hey, guard, how we expected to rake this shit with cuffs?'

The guard looked to Mills for a ruling. Mills raised his mirrored sunglasses and looked at the eight prisoners. 'Sure. Take their cuffs off.'

The inmates held out their hands and the guard moved along the line using his key to unlock them. They were ordered to place the cuffs in a neat pile and step away. They did so, rubbing their wrists and smiling. A day raking leaves on a golf course? Easy work, with trees for shade. It didn't get much better.

Byron picked up his rake and went to his spot underneath a large beech tree. He set to work, paying no attention to either the other prisoners or, more crucially, the guards. The compliance of the work details must have softened the brains of Mills and the other guards in one other way. It was often harder to note something that wasn't there as opposed to something that was, and it was only when he glanced up at Mills after a half-hour of raking that he realized Mills and the guard with him had no shotguns, only their sidearm. The shotguns must have been in the truck.

Not that this helped Byron. As long as you got in close, it was usually safer to take a shotgun or rifle from someone than a handgun.

Mills lay in the shade, his back to an oak tree, and watched the workers. He had pulled a pack of cigarettes from his shirt pocket and lit one. He'd wait twenty minutes, then light another. He didn't move.

Byron could simply have slipped out of sight and started to run, but that seemed like a great strategy for being caught quickly. The two most important elements of a successful escape and evasion were time and distance. Running from a standing start offered neither of those advantages.

The morning wore on. Byron kept watching Mills and the other guard, but they stayed where they were. If an opportunity wasn't going to present itself, there was only one thing for it.

'Officer Mills,' Byron called.

Mills turned to him, clearly irritated that his smoking and lazing about had been interrupted. 'I swear, Davis, you're worse than my ex-wife,' Mills growled.

Byron bit back the wisecrack that was on the tip of his tongue. 'I think my rake's busted. Do we have any more in the truck?'

Mills scowled, slowly getting to his feet. 'How the hell do you break a rake? All I asked you to do was rake leaves.'

Byron wasn't going to share his method, but he knew exactly how he'd done it. A minute before, he he'd propped the rake against a tree at a forty-five-degree angle and stood on it, snapping it clean in half. 'Guess I don't know my own strength.'

'You ain't that strong, Davis. I kicked your ass, remember?' said Mills, strolling over to inspect the damage.

The male ego was a wonderful thing, thought Byron. The possibility that he'd been allowed to win hadn't occurred to Mills. That was just how Byron wanted it. 'Must have been cracked already then,' he said.

'Bullshit,' said Mills. 'You must have done something dumb.' He shook his head in disbelief, but he was buying it. Mills got closer. 'We don't have any spares. You're just going to have to use what you got.'

Byron bent down and picked up both pieces. He held the top of the wooden shaft in his right hand. It was about eighteen inches long and splintered where it had been broken. 'I can't work with this,' he protested.

'Then you should have been more careful, Davis.'

Mills was within a few feet now. He was so busy lording it over Byron that his cigarette was still dangling from his right hand.

Byron gave an apologetic shrug. 'Do we have any tape? Maybe I could tape it back together or something.'

Mills laughed at the absurdity of the suggestion. He raised his cigarette to his lips, and began to take a long drag.

Byron pushed off with his left foot, shifting his weight forward, pivoting with his hips and plunging the jagged edge of the wooden shaft towards Mills's neck.

Mills tried to sidestep it but it tore into the side of his neck, leaving a long gash.

Byron followed up with a left elbow strike to the man's face, and a knee to his groin. Air rushed from Mills's lungs in a single burst. He started to fall. Byron grabbed his shirt with his left hand, keeping Mills on his feet long enough to unclip his belt and holster. He threw them behind him, with Mills's sidearm, then sent Mills reeling back with another fierce left elbow, this one catching him in the side of the head.

Byron bent down and picked up the belt and holster. He drew the pistol, a Glock 21 Gen 4. He snapped the belt, with Mills's pepper spray and baton, around his waist and made sure there was a .45 round in the chamber of the Glock, ready to go if he needed it.

He needed it sooner than he'd thought. Looking up he saw the other guard, a skinny white dude, booking it towards them, his firearm drawn but low by his side. Byron raised the Glock and aimed it. 'Drop your weapon,' he shouted at the guard, who had closed within twenty feet.

Stupidly the man didn't. Instead, he stopped and began to bring his pistol up. Byron sighted his chest and fired a single shot. The guard went down, thrown back hard by the impact of the Glock's .45-caliber round, and landed on his side.

Byron jogged over to him. He picked up his gun, and bent down to take a look at the damage. The round had smacked into his body armor, splitting it open and passing through into his left side just below his ribcage. He was screaming and crying with pain. Byron didn't blame him.

Chances were, with medical treatment, he would live. The body armor had absorbed some of the impact, and taken the sting out of the shot. It had missed his heart and lungs. Byron reached down to the guard's neck and found a pulse that was regular and strong.

Red and the other prisoners were gathered around, rakes still in hand, staring, open-mouthed, at Byron and the chaos that had erupted from nowhere.

'Red,' Byron said, waving him over.

Cautiously, Red began walking towards him. 'We're good, ain't we?' Red said. 'I mean that shit I was saying about those women. That was a joke. I wouldn't have—'

'Shut up,' Byron said.

The other white inmates had taken to their heels, running into the trees. Red glanced back to them, wondering if he'd made a bad call.

'We're fine,' Byron said. 'Stay with this guard. Make sure he doesn't close his eyes. Try to get some pressure on the wound, if you can. That should slow the bleeding. When the other guards get here, tell them they need to get him to the emergency room as soon as possible.'

Red knelt down by the guard. 'You'd better get out of here,' he said to Byron.

'No shit.'

Byron jogged back to Mills, who was crawling on his elbows and knees towards a stand of pine trees. When he heard Byron coming back, he picked up the pace as best he could. Byron reached him in six strides, grabbed the back of his shirt and hauled him up. 'You're coming with me,' he told him, pushing him forward through the trees and back towards the parking lot where they had left the pickup.

Behind him, Byron heard a radio crackle. He looked back to see the injured guard with his thumb on the call button of his radio. 'This is Officer—'

Red grabbed the radio before he could finish his transmission. He glanced at Byron and threw it away.

Byron half pushed and half carried Mills forward. Behind them, he could hear panicked shouts from the other guards as they tried to get a handle on why they'd just heard a gunshot and screams and why an officer had begun a panicked message that had been abruptly cut off.

When they reached the pickup, Byron scoped out the one they'd arrived in. 'Keys,' he said to Mills.

Mills laughed. 'Asshole. They're with the other guard.'

Byron shoved a hand into Mills's pants pocket and came up with the keys. 'Nice try.'

He clicked the button to unlock the doors, then opened the cab's passenger door and shoved Mills inside. He walked round the front, the keys in his hand, and got into the driver's side. He started the engine, put the truck into drive and hit the gas. He steered with one hand, using the other to cover Mills with the Glock.

In the side mirror as they powered down the track towards the rear entrance to the Country Club, Byron could see a couple of guards racing into the parking lot they'd just left. Mills's head was resting against the window. His shirt was soaked in blood but the bleeding from his neck had slowed.

'You're crazy, Davis. You know that? Who the hell pulls something like this to get out of the county jail?' said Mills.

Byron ignored him, focusing on the road ahead as they pulled out of the back of the country club and onto a street.

'You know Texas has the death penalty. Trying to kill

two prison guards, they'll fry your ass for this,' said Mills.

Big deal, thought Byron, spinning the wheel hard to avoid rear-ending a soccer mom, who had slammed on the brakes of her Porsche Cayenne as soon as she caught sight of the pickup truck with the blood-soaked prison guard in her mirror.

'Believe me,' Byron told Mills, 'if I wanted to kill you, you wouldn't be here right now.'

CHAPTER SIXTY-ONE

As Byron passed the Porsche he glimpsed the blonde driver on her cell phone. No prizes for guessing who she was talking to. He flashed back on the Sheriff's Department motor pool, which held enough vehicles for a town ten times the size of Kelsen. All brand-new vehicles, all well maintained, all of them fast enough not to be outrun by the truck he was driving.

The man nursing his wounds in the passenger seat had obviously just had the same thought. 'You're screwed, Davis. There's no way you're getting out of here alive,' he said. 'This town might look nice, but it's a goddamn fortress. And outside, what you got? A whole bunch of nothing, and nowhere to hide.'

Mills kept ranting. Byron tuned him out as the soccer mom took evasive measures, rounding the next corner so that she almost flipped her SUV over in her eagerness to get away from the pickup. If Mills wasn't venting, if he actually intended to throw Byron off course, it wasn't working. If you were a dead man walking for long enough, you tended not to worry too much about threats. And there was something Mills didn't understand. Fear was an idea to Byron, not an emotion.

The parking entrance to the town's main shopping mall, Kelsen Fashion Square, was up ahead. Byron turned into it, driving down the entrance ramp, plucking a ticket from the machine, and waiting for the barrier to rise.

The pickup nudged past the barrier and into the gloom of the underground parking garage. Mills started to tell Byron just what a dumb move this was, and Byron's finger fell from the side of the trigger guard to the trigger. 'Be quiet,' he told Mills.

Mills fell silent. The calming power of a loaded gun

pointed at you was never to be underestimated. It tended to focus the mind in a way that few other objects did.

Byron drove down two levels to the lowest level. It was where he guessed there would be most empty spaces (the sign outside had informed visitors that there were three hundred vacant spots). Consumers who arrived at a mall in their car tended to minimize the distance between where they parked and where they were heading. God forbid that someone had to walk an extra twenty yards when they could wait five minutes for someone to exit some prime real estate next to the elevators.

Byron pulled into a spot next to another pickup. Mills shot him a 'Now what?' look. The bleeding from his neck had all but stopped.

'Take off your clothes,' Byron told him.

The instruction was enough to override Mills's fear of being shot in the gut. For Mills, a man whom Byron had seen humiliating others, the prospect of his own humiliation was clearly a matter of some sensitivity.

'Now hang on a goddamn minute,' Mills protested. 'I know some guys turn faggot in the pen, but I ain't no homo.'

'Relax,' said Byron. 'If I were gay, I'd have better taste.'

From Mills's reaction, Byron wasn't sure if the guard was relieved or his ego bruised. He didn't have time to seek clarification. He jabbed the Glock into Mills's face. 'Do it.'

Mills shuffled along the seat a little and began taking off his clothes. He stopped when he got down to his jockey shorts. Byron couldn't help but notice the piss stain that had blossomed through the front of the white fabric. It was no great disgrace, but Mills flushed. From the yellow hue, he needed to drink more water.

'Everything off,' said Byron.

'Fuck you, faggot,' Mills said, his voice high and

hoarse.

'I think we've already established that the sweet act of love is off the table,' said Byron.

Mills slipped off his shorts and threw them into the foot well.

Byron grabbed the door handle. 'Don't move. I'll be right back.'

He got out of the cab, and walked to the back of the truck. He climbed up onto the flat-bed and rummaged through the detritus of work gear that had been left behind. He found what he needed, picked it up and jumped back down.

He went to the driver's door, opened it, got in, and tossed what he had collected down onto the seat next to Mills. Mills's eyes grew as wide as saucers.

'There's good news and bad news,' he said to Mills. 'What do you want first?'

Mills was on the edge of screaming. If it hadn't been for the gun, Byron was fairly sure he would have started by now.

'The bad,' said Mills.

'The next few hours are going to be very unpleasant for you.'

'And the good?'

'Unless your colleagues in the Sheriff's Department get overexcited, you're going to live.'

Looking down at the gasoline can, duct tape and box cutters sitting next to him, Mills didn't look too convinced. Byron didn't blame him. Faced with the same set of objects, there was every chance he would have asked for the bullet, and hoped for a clean headshot.

CHAPTER SIXTY-TWO

'You have got to be shitting me!'

Legs planted wide, Sheriff John Martin stood on the third level of the now evacuated Kelsen Fashion Square mall, and stared at the pickup truck sitting, engine idling, with a naked correctional officer cuffed and duct-taped to the steering-wheel. Sheriff Martin couldn't help what happened next. He'd never be able to explain it. Later, he would try to, without ever getting close to the truth.

He looked at the truck and Mills inside and burst out laughing. The looks he drew only made him laugh all the harder.

'Oh, my Lord,' he said, when he had regained enough breath to speak. 'Some dipshit drifter did this? Man, that is too much. Guess we finally caught ourselves a real criminal and never even knew it.'

Two years ago Bobby Slaw, a former Marine, had persuaded the department to allow him to establish a bomb squad. Now he stood behind the sheriff. All those days of training in the yard, the rest of the officers sniggering at him from behind reflective glass, and now he was going to have his moment in the sun. He'd be able to justify all the cash they'd thrown at that garbage can on wheels he'd insisted the department purchase to 'facilitate remote control explosions'.

That poor bastard Mills, thought Sheriff Martin. The guy was a grade-A asshole, and not the brightest, which was saying something: the correctional officers were guys who couldn't pass a Sheriff's Department entry exam that consisted primarily of being able to hit the door. But Mills didn't deserve this. If Slaw's assessment was correct, Mills would go up like a Roman candle if they put a foot wrong.

CHAPTER SIXTY-THREE

Byron waited in an abandoned lot across the street from a gas station in the south-east corner of Kelsen. It had a sign promising future development by the Kelsen County Corporation. It was secured by chain-link fence, but someone had already cut a hole in it on one side. Not that there was much of anything to secure.

Behind a large dumpster near the back of the lot he'd spotted a couple of well-fed rats and some discarded hypodermic needles. Like any town, if you scratched under the surface of Kelsen you could find a place that was way less Stepford than a visitor might have assumed. He had spent months traveling the country so the needles hadn't surprised him. Like all things eighties, heroin was making a comeback, fueled by the country's recent flirtation with prescription opiates, like OxyContin.

Byron had been in the lot for twenty minutes and the wait was already making him nervous. He was starting to wonder if the person he was expecting would show. He planned on giving it another ten minutes before leaving. It seemed like every few minutes a Sheriff's Department vehicle rolled past. They seemed to be heading in either direction, criss-crossing the avenues, two or three cars passing five minutes apart. It was evidence that they didn't yet have a solid lead.

The time to worry would be if and when it went quiet. When cops had solid intel of a suspect's location they tended to withdraw from the immediate area and establish a perimeter. Only when that was done would they appear, and even then, if they did it right, it would be sudden and with overwhelming force. So, for now, a few patrol cars with spotlights didn't concern him. Waiting on someone he didn't truly know, and certainly didn't know if he could trust, was another matter entirely.

Another patrol slid by. It stopped, put on its turn signal, and drew into the gas station. Not good. Not good at all. That was Byron's meeting point. He watched as the two sheriff's deputies got out and walked inside. For a second he thought about the possibility of jacking the patrol car but swiftly dismissed the idea. Too risky. It was parked within sight of the front of the gas station.

He watched the two deputies head for the coffee stand. They each poured themselves a cup, topped up with cream and sugar. Byron didn't blame them. He could have used some caffeine himself right now.

The deputies crossed to the cashier. He didn't appear to ring up the sale. That was standard protocol. Gas stations got robbed. Gas stations popular with cops, not so much. Free coffee provided an excellent return on investment if you were a gas-station owner trying to keep your insurance premium down.

A dark sedan rolled down the street. Tinted windows made it hard to see the driver. The vehicle slowed near the gas station, looking like it might turn in, then kept going, maybe spooked by the cops but it was impossible to know.

The cops idled at the counter, shooting the breeze with the elderly lady behind the cash register. For a second Byron flashed onto another gas station. Another woman who'd just been doing her job when their paths had crossed. He pushed out of his mind the memory of what had happened, of the terrible thing he'd done. It wasn't as if he could change the past. If he could, he would. All he could do was try to ensure that he didn't repeat it.

In some ways, Mills had been a start. Byron could have killed him. Not only did he have opportunity, he had motive. It would have made escape easier. Rigging the truck, or rather faking the rigging, had taken time. It had exposed him to capture far more than just dropping a round into the back of Mills's head. If a patrol car had cruised through the mall parking lot while he was in the middle of it, things would have been bad.

As personal improvement went, claiming to have terrified someone he could have murdered in cold blood wouldn't earn Byron any points. But knowing what he did about his capacity for violence, it felt like a start.

Still, he could feel the rage within him, which worried him. Not only because he might hurt another innocent person, but also because he feared that once the genie was out of the bottle, he might not be able to push it back in. That was what he feared more than anything. Certainly more than capture. More even than death, though the will to live had proven far more potent than he could have imagined.

The cops picked up their coffee and moved back towards the door. The same dark sedan turned onto the street again, on its second go round.

The cops climbed slowly into their patrol car. The sedan slowed near the gas station. The cops were taking their time leaving.

The sedan's brake lights flared red. The cops looked at it. The driver seemed to hesitate for a moment. Finally, the car pulled into the gas station. The cops were still watching it.

The sedan pulled up next to a gas pump. Its lights died along with the engine. The cops seemed unsure as to whether they were leaving or not.

The driver's door of the sedan opened. Byron couldn't see the driver, his view blocked by the street-side gas pumps. He narrowed his eyes, trying to focus through the gloom. To see if it was who he thought it was.

The cops were equally curious. Curious enough to kill their engine and get back out. They walked the short distance to the sedan.

Byron studied their body language for clues. Everything about their manner suggested they recognized the person. Their hands stayed by their sides rather than falling to their service weapons. They appeared to be smiling.

'Come on. Come on. Let me see you,' Byron whispered, in the darkness.

Was it another cop? Someone in plain clothes? It would have made sense to have law enforcement out in civilian clothes and vehicles to aid the search. A fugitive would hide at the first sight of a black-and-white. Much less so with a regular car. They might still hide, but a second or so later than if someone in uniform had been cruising past, and a second would be all a vigilant cop would need to see them.

The cops were standing next to the sedan now, smiling while they talked to the driver, completely relaxed. The driver was moving to the rear of the car, ready to start pumping gas.

The cops said their goodbyes and started back to their patrol car. Thea Martinez stepped away from the sedan and looked around, searching the shadows.

CHAPTER SIXTY-FOUR

Thea's car sat parked in the side street next to the gas station. Byron watched it for a long moment. Her friendly chat with the cops had thrown him off. It wasn't that she'd run into them. With all the cops out on the road, it was likely that she would. No, it was their manner. Thea had painted herself as Enemy Number One of the Kelsen County establishment, yet they'd all but given her a hug.

He pulled up the chain-link fencing where it had been cut away, and squeezed through the gap. He had picked up some clothes from a charity deposit point, but even without prison blues, he still looked every inch the fugitive from justice. Hell, even in a Hugo Boss suit and wingtips he carried that air. That was part of why he'd made such an effective overseas operator, especially in high-risk areas.

He skirted the edge of the lot, staying where there was least light, then walked down the sidewalk and crossed the street a half-block past the gas station. He doubled back and turned down the street where Thea's sedan was parked.

Looking for signs of a surveillance operation he came up blank. Not that he would know. At least, not if it was being conducted properly. He reached the car and opened the rear passenger door.

Thea started as he settled onto the back seat. He still had Mills's Glock but he kept it out of view. 'Thank you,' he said.

'You're welcome.'

It was a strangely formal exchange for such an out-of-the-ordinary situation.

She half turned to look at him. He didn't need his psycho-neurological synesthetic powers to see that she was scared. Her widened pupils and shaking hands, clamped to the wheel to minimize the obvious tremor, told him that much. 'What should I do now?' she said. 'I don't think it's the best idea to stay parked up here. Martin's got every single deputy he has out looking for you.'

'You're right. You should drive.'

'Where? There are roadblocks on every road out of town.'

'Your office?' Byron offered.

'My office is in the basement of my home.'

She must have registered something in Byron's expression because she quickly added, 'I'm trying to keep the overheads low. Being St Thea Martinez of Kelsen County, pro bono work a specialty, doesn't exactly leave me rolling in dough at the end of the month.'

'Wherever you feel comfortable. My continued liberty isn't your responsibility.'

'No kidding,' Thea shot back. 'And to think you wouldn't let me try to get you off. I'm still trying to work that one out.'

Byron looked through the rear window as headlights flashed past on the road behind them. Thea took the hint. She started the engine, put the car into drive and pulled away from the curb, heading down the side street and taking a right down a narrow alleyway. Driving seemed to relax her a notch or two. It did the same for Byron. He had spent most of the afternoon and early evening in perpetual motion.

Thea glanced at him in the rearview. 'An advantage of staying in the same one-horse town all your life, apart from college and law school – you get to know all the back alleys.'

Byron remained silent.

She took a deep breath and blew a stray strand of hair out of her eye. When it fell back, she pushed it away with her fingers. 'I can't believe I'm actually doing this,' she said, more to herself than Byron.

'Why not? You strike me as someone who's fairly accepting of risk.'

'There's risk and then there's risk. Know what I mean?'

'Not really,' said Byron.

She slowed the car, took another turn, straightened back up and gave him a long rearview glance. 'I saw what you did to Mills.'

For a second Byron was panicked. What did she mean, she'd seen what he'd done? 'He's fine, right?'

'Physically, yes. Mentally, I wouldn't be so sure.'

For a second Byron had worried that Martin and his merry men had blundered in rather than following standard protocol when dealing with a suspected explosive device. Byron had constructed the scene to look like an honest-to-goodness IED but, apart from the can of gas, there had been nothing to cause any harm. Unless, of course, someone lit a match or started firing, which he hadn't entirely ruled out. 'I don't think Mills was ever fine mentally,' he said drily.

Thea didn't laugh. 'He's a bully. But he's still a human being.'

Safe in the gloom of the back seat, Byron rolled his eyes. If there was one thing that worried him more than a reactionary with totalitarian tendencies, like Mills, it was a bleeding heart. At least with someone like Mills you knew what you were getting. With someone like Thea, the consequences of their actions were often unintended and consequently much harder to predict.

'I had to buy myself some time. Keep Martin and his posse occupied for a while.'

This time it was Thea's turn to roll her eyes. 'And you didn't enjoy teaching Mills a lesson?'

'Do I have to answer that question, counsellor?'

'You already did.'

'Did you get a call from Romero? When they released

him I gave him your number.'

She fell silent at the mention of the name. Her eyes flicked back to the road. 'We can talk about that later.'

They had reached a quiet residential neighborhood of older, smaller wooden houses. They looked neatly kept with fresh paint and mown lawns. McMansions they were not.

They turned into a driveway. Thea reached up to the sun visor and hit a clicker. A garage door opened. She drove inside, and hit the clicker again, closing the door behind them. She got out, looking back at Byron. 'If I'm going to be murdered by a homicidal psychopath then I may as well have it happen in the comfort of my own home.'

CHAPTER SIXTY-FIVE

Thea slid a key into a rickety back door and pushed it open. Byron followed her inside. A short hallway led into a kitchen. A cat yowled from the far doorway and padded across to Thea, rubbing itself against her legs.

"I know, cliché, right?" Thea said.

'What is?'

'Single cat lady. I'm working my way up to a full dozen.'

'How many do you have so far?'

'Three,' she said. 'And maybe a couple of neighborhood strays, but I'm not sure whether they count.'

Byron wasn't sure how to respond so he didn't say anything.

'You have any pets?'

Before he could answer that one, Thea laughed. 'Who am I asking?'

'What does that mean?'

'Well, for a start, you don't actually exist, do you? Not on any official database. Not with the name and details you gave when you were arrested.'

She crossed to the sink, reached down and picked up a water bowl, filled it from the tap and put it down on the floor. By the time she straightened up, Byron was standing directly behind her. He reached over and grabbed her wrist. 'You ran my fingerprints?'

She spun round, breaking his grip on her wrist. Her hand raised and shoved him hard in the chest. He stepped back.

'I'm sorry,' he said. 'I shouldn't have touched you.'

Her left hand was feeling in the sink behind her for a knife that Byron could see lying in a pool of soapy water. 'Don't do that,' he said. 'Please. I promise I won't touch you again.'

She stopped feeling for the knife but kept her hand where it was.

'Please,' he said again. 'This isn't ... I'm not who you might think.'

'So who are you?'

'You want my name, or do you want to know who I am?' he asked. A better question might have been, did she want to know what he was? The only problem with that was that he wasn't entirely sure of the answer. Objectively he guessed he was . . . what? Part man, part machine? A cyborg? But that word conjured a creature, at least in his own mind, that was far more machine than he felt.

'Is there a difference?' Thea said.

If someone had run his prints, it didn't really matter now whether he lied or told the truth. If his prints were run on any system that connected in any way to any national or international database, it would set alarm bells ringing. Alarm bells that would ripple outwards until they hit someone in the State Department, the CIA or the Pentagon, and likely all three. The Kelsen County sheriff would be the least of his worries.

'My name is Byron Tibor.'

She studied him. Her hand moved out of the sink. 'Sorry, is that supposed to mean something?'

Byron rubbed at his face. 'Tell you what, you tell me about Romero and I'll answer whatever questions you have as truthfully as I can.'

'As truthfully as you can?' Thea said. 'Thought I was supposed to be the attorney.'

'I don't have all the answers. Nor do I understand everything that's happened to me. That's what I was trying to get at when I said that.'

'Now you have me interested.'

She walked past him to a refrigerator. 'Does Byron Tibor drink wine?' She pulled it open, took out a bottle, crossed to a cupboard for two long-stemmed glasses and put it all on the small table in the middle of the room.

'Would you mind if I took a few minutes to get cleaned up first?' he asked her.

'Sure. The bathroom's at the end of the hall.' She nodded towards the door leading out of the kitchen. 'Don't take too long. I really want a glass of wine and I don't like drinking on my own.'

Byron walked past her to the door. He could smell her perfume. He couldn't imagine a woman like her having to drink alone, except by her own choice.

Closing the bathroom door behind him, Byron laid the Glock on a shelf over the sink and within easy reach of the shower. He took off his clothes, turned the shower on hot, and got in. He scrubbed himself clean and got out. It was only then he realized that he couldn't see any towels. There was only a wash cloth, but that wasn't about to do the job.

He padded to the door, opened it and called down the hallway, 'Hey, do you have a towel I could use?'

There was a moment's silence.

'Oh, shit. Sorry. I just did laundry and haven't put any towels back in there. Hang on.'

He closed the door again and waited. There was a tap at the door. He opened it a crack. Thea handed a towel through the gap. 'Thank you,' he said. He caught her eyes lingering on what was visible of his broad shoulders, wide chest and muscular arms.

She saw that he'd caught her checking him out and got flustered. 'You're welcome. I'm just opening the wine.'

He closed the door, dried off, finger-combed his hair, and got dressed.

Thea held out a glass of white wine as he walked back into the kitchen. 'Thanks,' he said, taking the glass and sitting down at the kitchen table.

He took a sip. It wasn't bad.

She watched him over the rim of hers as she drank. 'So,' said Thea. 'I have bad news about your friend Romero.'

Byron wondered if that was why she had needed the wine. To fortify herself to break bad news.

'It's partly what happened with him that made me decide to come and meet you,' Thea added. 'I'm not sure if that'll be any consolation or not.'

Byron wanted to ask her what that meant. Had she ignored Romero's plea for help? Byron didn't want to believe that, but maybe she hadn't wanted to get mixed up in it. Or hadn't realized what was at stake. He guessed that she would tell him in good time, and even then it would be in her words with no way for Byron to know if what she said was true or not.

'He's dead?'

Thea took another mouthful of wine. 'Yes. His body was found this morning. Out in the desert. I've asked for an autopsy by someone outside the county, but I don't hold out much hope.'

'You don't trust the county coroner?' Byron asked.

She laughed. 'For one, he's not exactly a coroner, more a family doctor who was given a pathology lab and some scalpels. And, like most everybody else around here, he's not about to rock the boat.'

'Everyone apart from you, you mean?'

'For all the good it's done me.'

'So why do you feel guilty about what happened with Romero?'

'Who said I felt guilty?' Thea said.

'You said that you only helped me because . . .'

Thea waved her hand as she took yet another sip of wine. Her glass was already a third gone. 'I hesitated when I got his message. Made some phone calls instead of getting in my car. By the time I went to try and catch up with the deputy who had him, he was gone. My calling them had only sealed the deal. I think so anyway. I was hoping that if they knew I was aware they had him, they might have second thoughts about hurting him. More fool me, right?'

Byron was relieved. She hadn't ignored Romero. She just hadn't been decisive enough. 'A man tells you he's going to be killed and then he turns up dead? Isn't that going to pull in someone from outside?' he asked.

Thea topped up her glass. 'It didn't last time. Or the time before that. Or with the one before that. Why would this be any different?'

Byron took her point. Somewhere like Kelsen, where everyone who mattered was in on whatever was going down or at least was enjoying the benefits, it was hard to break the cycle. 'So how did they do it?' he asked.

'Drove him out to the desert and left him without water. Probably beat him up before they left. No water and this heat for an elderly man who was injured? It wouldn't have taken long.'

Byron raised his glass in a silent toast to Romero. What a chickenshit way to kill such a brave man. They hadn't even had the balls to end his suffering and put a bullet in him. That would have been difficult to explain away, even for them.

'He was a good man,' said Byron, the wine tasting bitter at the back of his throat.

'A lot of good men have died here. And women for that matter. That factory is a death trap,' said Thea. 'At least a dozen women have been either killed or seriously injured working there. When it happens they just ship them back over the border, either in a wooden box or a wheelchair, and carry on like it was nothing.'

They took a moment to contemplate those who had passed. Byron was sure of one thing. If the warden or the sheriff wanted to take him down, he was taking them with him.

'So,' said Thea. 'Now you know about your friend.'

'You mean it's my turn to tell my story?' Byron said.

Thea nodded.

'You may want to put another bottle of wine in to chill. If you have one,' he said.

'That long or that bad?'

'A bit of both,' said Byron.

Thea got up, opened a larder cupboard and popped a bottle of the same wine they were drinking into the inside door of the refrigerator. He'd barely finished his first glass, so he could hardly blame the alcohol, but he felt something stirring inside him as he watched her. There was a grace to the way she moved and, if he was honest, a feminine sensuality that he felt himself pulled towards. Given the circumstances, it was almost surreal to be feeling what he was. Or perhaps it was another sign of a human response – complex and irrational – to a crazy situation. Maybe there was more hope for him than he wanted to believe. Too bad he was possibly facing his final few hours or days.

CHAPTER SIXTY-SIX

Although Thea was opening a second bottle of wine, he doubted that any amount of alcohol would make the unabridged version of his story seem credible. He decided to edit certain details, and stick with the parts that were easily digestible.

With what had happened, especially in New York, the authorities had been forced to create their narrative of why a man called Byron Tibor had done what he had while fleeing their grasp. Their version was full of carefully constructed lies, mostly of omission. Maybe if he followed their model and left out the parts that were hard to believe, he could come up with something that bore some resemblance to the truth.

The start was easy enough. There was no dispute about his credentials or, for that matter, what he had done for his country.

'So you were some kind of special-forces guy?' Thea asked.

She seemed entirely skeptical. He didn't blame her. Bars across the country were full of men who spun women some bullshit story about their military career. They were never cooks or engineers or infantry grunts, no, sirree, they were always special forces of some stripe. Delta Force. SEALs. Army Rangers.

'I had special-forces training but I mostly worked for the State Department. I was a troubleshooter,' Byron told her.

'Is that code for someone who kills people?' Thea asked.

'Killing people was less than zero point one per cent of the job, so it's not code. I did kill people, yes, but more often than not it was indirect. I'd call in strikes, that kind of thing.'

'And the rest of the time?'

'The *majority* of the time I was involved in building alliances, gathering intelligence, making sure that local communities got what they needed. Clean water, sanitation, schools, books. Not very exciting but probably more effective in the long run for the country's interests than drone strikes.'

She still looked skeptical, only now Byron couldn't be sure whether she didn't believe his story or whether she didn't buy that someone from the State Department could have done something positive in a foreign country.

'So when did it all go wrong?' she asked.

He did his best to explain what he called, for lack of a better term, his eventual breakdown, following the death of a young girl in Afghanistan. Perhaps it was the emotional connection he still had to those events, or how it allowed him to relate the story to Thea with something approaching real emotion. Whatever it was, she was looking him in the eye, unblinking, with a sincerity to her reaction which matched that of his telling.

When he got to the part about digging a grave for the girl and the psychologist appearing, Thea reached over the table and put her hand on his. 'I'm sorry, Byron.'

He looked down at her hand. Her touch sent a shiver through him that he struggled to suppress. She drew back but he reached out with his other hand and pulled hers back to where it had been. She let it stay there while he moved on to the facility.

He didn't mention the neuro implant or the other surgeries. He just said, 'It was a new technology they wanted to trial to see if they could help veterans with severe PTSD. It takes millions of dollars of training and years of experience to get someone to the level I was at. They didn't just want to help me, they wanted to get me to a point where I'd be able to go back out into the field. As good as new, if not better.'

'I never read about anything like that,' she said.

'You weren't supposed to,' Byron said. 'Even the name of the project was likely to spook civilians.'

'Why? What was it called?'

Byron finished his glass of wine. 'The guilt-free-soldier program.'

Thea raised her eyebrows. 'Guilt-free? Wow.' She drew back her hand from his.

He tried to be as truthful as he could about the next part. About how the technology hadn't worked. How it had made him more irrational, more violent. He left out the part about the gifts it had bestowed.

'I hurt people, Thea,' he said. 'Innocent people. Not all of them were, but hurting one innocent person was still one too many.'

'Then you ran?'

'Yes.'

'And your wife?' Thea asked.

'She was scared of me,' he said. 'I didn't blame her. She had married one man and ended up with someone else.'

'So how did you end up in Butthole, Texas?' Thea said.

'I was on my way somewhere else.'

'Well,' said Thea, 'that is regarded as a pretty serious crime around here.' She drained the last of the second bottle of wine into their glasses. She raised hers to her lips and began to laugh.

Byron looked at her. 'What's so funny?' Not that he minded her laughing, quite the opposite. He just wasn't sure they had much to laugh about.

'Well, they're going to run your details now, and when they do, they're going to shit a brick.'

Byron reached back across the table. He grabbed her hand, trying to keep his touch light and the panic out of his voice. 'They've run my details?'

She stared at him. 'Maybe not now. But they will. They're bound to after what happened today. Even if you turn round and tell the feds what's been going on, your credibility is shot to hell.'

Byron's head sank onto the table. Here he was thinking he'd been so slick with Mills, but all he'd achieved was to bring more heat on himself. The county sheriff might not be able to capture him, but he wouldn't need to.

He felt Thea's fingers running over his skull and down his neck. She stopped when she came to the long, grooved scar that was a reminder of the tracking device he'd had to cut from his own flesh with a knife. She traced it gently with the tips of her fingers. 'Byron?'

He didn't respond. Not at first.

'Byron? You're scaring me.'

'I'm sorry. I shouldn't have come here. I shouldn't have asked for your help.'

'Don't you think it's a little too late for regrets?' said Thea.

CHAPTER SIXTY-SEVEN

Like the connection they felt, their lovemaking was urgent and raw. Byron suspected that Thea was, like him, someone who had built a wall around herself. It wasn't that he lacked the physical urges of a normal man. It was more that, like the violence inside him, he was aware of what would happen if he let go. Like violence, sex for Byron could be dark and animalistic, a place of shadows and dark transgressions.

All that had been swept aside by Thea. As she touched him, stroking his neck and rubbing his back, her black hair had fallen over his face. He breathed in her perfume, savoring her own smell beneath it, and he was lost.

He turned his head and their eyes met for a lingering moment. Any pretense that had lain between them fell away. His hands moved up to cradle her face. He kissed her gently on the lips.

She returned his kiss with an urgency he hadn't expected. Her tongue pushed beyond his lips to meet his. Her breasts crushed against his muscular chest. Her hands clawed at his clothes, pulling his T-shirt up and over his head.

He helped her take it off. They looked at each other. Byron sensed that what had just happened hung in the balance. Thea might withdraw, decide that this was a bad idea. If she did, she would be right. It was a bad idea. Without question.

'It's been a while,' she said, with a smile, reaching down and starting to unbutton her blouse to reveal a lacy black brassière under which lay perfect coffee-brown breasts.

Byron reached up and helped the blouse over her shoulders. His lips fell to her neck. He took a long draw of her essence and began to kiss his way down her shoulder.

His lips kept moving, pausing occasionally to savor her perfect caramel skin.

His right hand traced a path up from the small of her back. He unclasped her bra. She leaned towards him. He pulled the straps gently over her shoulders and pulled the rest of the fabric away.

He buried his head in her breasts. Starting with small butterfly kisses around her nipples, he nuzzled and licked until, in turn, they hardened.

Her hands clasped behind his head, pulling him in closer and guiding him to where she wanted his mouth to be. She moaned softly. 'I want you inside me,' she whispered in his ear.

Reaching down she began to unbutton his pants. His hand slid down to hitch up her skirt, then ran his hand all the way up the inside of her thigh. When he reached the top he found a burning hot wetness.

He pushed her panties to one side. She let out a gasp. He moved his hand away, teasing her.

She pushed her hand into his shorts.

'Wait,' he told her.

He kicked off his pants and shorts, reached both hands under her ass and lifted her up. She wrapped her legs around his waist. Her arms rested on his broad shoulders. Slowly, she slid down onto him.

With every inch of him inside her, Thea's back arched. With his hands cupping her ass, Byron hoisted her up before lowering her again. Her nails dug into the back of his neck. He allowed her moans to set the pace as he thrust inside her.

Thea buried her face between his neck and his shoulder, as they kept moving together.

'Take me into the bedroom,' she said.

He carried her from the kitchen to the bedroom. He toed the door open and lowered her down onto the bed. She spread her legs wide and he went deep. She clung to him, her fingers running through his hair, her thighs pressing against his waist.

He kissed her, and grabbed her wrists, pinning them down on the bed. He could feel her tighten around him as he moved a little faster.

She came in a series of loud, shuddering waves, begging him not to stop. He took his time, moving more slowly, controlling himself as best he could. He let go of her wrists and they switched so that now she was atop him, her hands pinning him down. Her hair tumbled over his face. He reached up, caressing her neck. His hands ran over her shoulders and down her back. She squeezed herself around him and began to rock back and forth. Her nails dug into his shoulders and chest.

She kept moving, her rhythm steady, and they came together in a hot rush. She collapsed on top of him and he wrapped his arms around her, keeping her close. Suddenly, he tensed. He'd heard a car outside.

Beyond the window, brakes squealed. Headlights swept across the bedroom. The beams were followed by a single whoop from a patrol car. A car door slammed shut.

CHAPTER SIXTY-EIGHT

Byron stood in a darkened room off the front hallway as Thea opened the door. Through a gap in the blinds he could see the officer standing on the front porch. He was pretty sure it was one of the cops who'd arrested him. The taller one.

'Hey, Arlo, what can I do for you?' Thea asked.

'I saw your light on,' said Arlo. 'Figured I'd see if you were okay.'

'That's very considerate of you, but I'm fine. I was just going to bed.'

From his vantage-point, Byron watched as Arlo leaned in towards Thea, propping himself against the side of the door frame and resting the point of his boot between the door and the frame so that Thea would be unable to close it unless he moved.

'The guy's still out there. He's a pretty dangerous character by all accounts,' Arlo said. 'Of course he was like a lamb when I arrested him. Knew better than to try anything.'

In the half-light, Byron smiled to himself. No doubt Arlo would be dining out on having arrested someone like Byron for years to come.

'Well,' Thea said, 'if I see anything suspicious, I'll call it in.'

'You want me to take a look around before I go?' Arlo asked. 'You have that shed out back, don't you? That could be the kind of place someone like him might hole up.'

'Appreciate the offer, but it's okay. If he was hiding out nearby I'm pretty sure I would have noticed by now.'

'It'll only take a minute,' Arlo said, pushing past Thea. 'It's no trouble at all.'

Byron moved from the window and pressed himself

against the wall that backed onto the hall as he heard Arlo walk into the hallway. He could hear the tension in Thea's voice. It was a mixture of panic and annoyance at the unwarranted intrusion.

'I really do have to go to bed now, Arlo,' she was saying.

Byron saw a flash of police uniform as Arlo walked past the living-room door and down the hall towards the kitchen. That was bad news. The passion with Thea had been so sudden that cleaning up hadn't been a consideration.

Thea's footsteps hurried behind Arlo.

'Look,' she was saying, 'if there was someone else here, I think I would have noticed by now.'

Byron heard the cop push open the kitchen door. The squeak of his footsteps came to a sudden stop.

'Is that so?' said Arlo.

'This place is a mess. I haven't had the chance to clean up.'

'You career girls, not enough time in the day, huh?' Arlo said. 'Here, let me help you.'

There was the unmistakable sound of glasses clinking against each other. The two wine glasses on the table. They were still there. By the sound of it, Arlo had just picked them up.

'There's really no need,' said Thea. 'Now, I want to get some rest, so if you wouldn't mind . . . I promise that if I see anything I'll call it in.'

'You had company, Thea?'

'Excuse me?'

'These here two glasses that were on the table.'

'Oh, those,' Thea said. 'It's been a long day. I must have got distracted and forgotten I already had a glass.'

Byron edged slowly along the wall towards the living-room door. He was trying to work out if he could make the front door before Arlo had time to draw his gun and get into the hallway.

'Uh-huh,' said Arlo. 'You take off your lipstick between glasses too?'

Thea didn't say anything to that. There was nothing to say.

'Where is he?'

'I don't know what you're talking about. I didn't invite you into my home, and I'm asking you to leave.'

'It's a little too late for that,' said Arlo. 'Now you'd better tell me where he is.'

'Where who is?'

'Don't be a smartass, Thea. You know who I'm talking about.'

There was anger in Thea's voice now. 'Get the hell out of my house, Arlo.'

'You tell me where he is and I'll leave it at that. You don't and you'll be looking at time.'

Thea laughed. 'For what exactly? Having two empty wine glasses in my kitchen? Now, I won't tell you again. Get the hell out of here.'

Byron decided to stay where he was for the time being. Maybe Thea would have enough righteous indignation to get the cop out of the front door.

Byron heard the unmistakable of handcuffs being unclipped from the cop's belt. It was a sound he'd become more than familiar with over the past few weeks.

'You have got to be kidding me, Arlo,' Thea said. 'You even think about arresting me and your career is over. Y'hear me?'

'Turn around, Thea. Hands behind your back. I'm arresting you for harboring a fugitive.'

'Go fuck yourself,' Thea shouted at Arlo.

There was the sound of a scuffle.

'Turn around!'

'Get your hands off me, you asshole.'

'I'm not playing. Turn around or I'll Taser you. You hear me?'

Byron tensed at the mention of the Taser. He took a deep breath and tried to clear his head. Arlo obviously had no idea that he was as close as he was. If he did he would have called for back-up. Either he thought Byron had already fled, or he actually believed his own bluster about Byron somehow being intimidated by him when he was arrested. It was hard to believe that anyone could be that stupid but the male ego was a wonderful thing.

'You're hurting me,' Thea said.

'Well, don't struggle.'

There was the ratcheting click of the cuffs being snapped around Thea's wrists.

'See? We don't have to fight,' Arlo said.

'You patronizing asshole,' Thea shot back.

Byron snuck a peek around the doorframe. He could see a sliver of the kitchen. Thea was facing the rear window, her back to the cop.

Byron would wait until Arlo went to put Thea in his patrol car, which he would undoubtedly do before coming back in to search the house, and make a run for it through the back door. Arlo would find an empty house. He ducked back into the living room and waited.

'What the hell are you doing?' Thea said.

It was hard to catch Arlo's response. His voice was low and as quiet as a whisper.

'What the hell are you doing?' Thea repeated, this time with panic in her voice.

Byron caught what Arlo said next.

'I see the way you look at me, Thea. This whole front you put up. How you talk to me. I know what it means.'

'Take your goddamn hand away, Arlo.'

Byron stepped back into the hallway. Looking into the kitchen he saw Thea still pinned against the sink. The cop was running his hand up between her legs.

'Don't fight it, Thea,' Arlo said, his other hand reaching up, grabbing her hair and pulling it hard enough to snap her neck back and make her scream.

For a second Byron struggled to process what he was witnessing. The second passed. He started down the hallway towards the kitchen, the Glock punched out ahead of him.

CHAPTER SIXTY-NINE

Lauren's stomach churned as she climbed the steps of the Cessna Citation CJ4. The backdraft from a C-130 military transport plane taxiing down the opposite runway whipped her hair across her face. She pushed back the rogue strands and ducked into the cabin. The rest of the team were taking their seats, ready for the short flight down to Texas.

A four-man kill team sat together at the back. They had broken out a pack of playing cards and seemed completely relaxed. All four were drawn from various branches of the military and were veterans of numerous missions around the world. They had been selected not just because they were extremely capable but because they could be relied upon to take the knowledge of a mission like this to the grave with them.

Lauren settled into her seat, popped open her laptop, and reviewed the intelligence that had prompted the flight. It was frustrating beyond belief. Tibor had been in jail in Texas for weeks but for some inexplicable reason had only popped up on the official radar when he had broken out.

Nick Frinz hustled down the aisle and flopped into the seat next to her. She'd been hoping he might not make the flight.

'Finally found him, huh?' he said.

'Not yet.'

'Come on,' said Frinz. 'Where's he gonna go?'

CHAPTER SEVENTY

'Don't kill me.'

Byron had to pick out the words between Arlo's sobs. He had already taken Arlo's service weapon, Taser, and the small back-up gun that had been hidden in an ankle holster on the cop's right leg.

The Glock was pressed into the back of Arlo's neck. For good measure, and to ensure full compliance, Byron had the wrist of Arlo's right hand bent back close to fracture point. That wasn't the reason for his sobs, though. They both knew that, given what Byron had just witnessed, there was every chance that Arlo might not survive the next few moments.

Byron would feel no guilt for killing a cop who had been about to rape a woman he had just handcuffed. Byron glanced at Thea. She was sitting at the kitchen table. Her hands shook as she struggled to light a cigarette. Mascara ran down her cheeks. She hadn't offered any opinion on what Byron should do next. He wasn't about to ask her. Not because he wouldn't have gone along with what she wanted, but because she had enough trauma to process without this asshole's death or survival in her head. If she wanted to give Byron the thumbs-up or -down that was her decision to make. But right now Byron was happy to fulfill all three roles of judge, jury and, if need be, executioner.

There was no doubt in Byron's mind that Arlo would have raped Thea. For that, in Byron's opinion, he had forfeited his right to life. But there were other considerations. The cop (although it was an insult to the good men and women who did this job that Arlo had the badge and the title that went with it) could die now. Or he could die later. The only question was which would better serve Byron's chances of escape, and Thea's safety.

A cell phone rang close by. The cop tensed. Thea got up, went back into the living room and answered it. She walked back in with it held to her ear. Whatever the person at the other end was saying, she was listening intently.

'Where?' she asked.

There was a moment of silence. Byron pressed the barrel of the Glock a little harder into the back of Arlo's neck. 'Don't say a word,' he told him.

'Okay,' Thea said. 'I'll meet you there.'

She ended the call and put the cell phone on the table. 'Don't kill him,' she said.

Byron nodded, easing the pressure against Arlo's neck. Arlo let out a sigh of relief.

Thea took another deep drag on her cigarette. Some ash fell onto the floor. 'It's not that I think you should live, Arlo,' said Thea, 'because I don't.'

'So why?' Byron asked.

'Because Arlo's going to tell us why Hank Foley just called me to say that while he was out checking his ranch, helping the sheriff look for you, he found a bunch of dead women and children buried in a shallow grave. Isn't that right, Arlo?'

Arlo's head snapped round on a swivel. 'I don't know nothing about that.'

The denial was more than a little too sudden. Byron grabbed him and propelled him towards the door.

'Where are you taking him?' Thea asked.

'You want to go out to this ranch and see for yourself, don't you?' Byron said to her. 'Or have I got you all wrong?'

'I have to put some clothes on first.'

'We'll wait for you, won't we, Arlo?' Byron told the cop.

Arlo nodded. Byron sensed a fear inside the man that ran deeper than that of being at the wrong end of his weapon. A fear of discovery. Maybe the search for Byron had turned up something far more dangerous than a fugitive.

CHAPTER SEVENTY-ONE

Arlo sat in the driver's seat of his patrol car. Thea sat next to him. Byron handed her the Glock and kept Arlo's service weapon for himself.

'You know how to use one of these things?' Byron asked, as she took the gun from him.

She glanced back at him, her eyes suggesting she was surprised at the question. 'We're in Texas. Of course I know how to use a gun. My daddy took me out hunting while I was still in kindergarten. Got my first real gun when I turned twelve.'

'Hope your daddy's proud of you taking one of his officers hostage and helping an escaped killer,' Arlo piped up. 'He's had to put up with all your liberal bullshit up until now, but this, I don't know what he's gonna say.'

'Shut the hell up, Arlo,' Thea said, lowering the barrel a shade so that it was pointed at Arlo's groin.

In the back seat, Byron's head was spinning. 'Your father's Sheriff Martin?'

'Sheriff Martinez,' Thea corrected. 'He changed it to Martin as part of his drive to fit in with the good old boys around here. He's done a pretty good job of it too. Too good probably, but, hey, you don't choose your family, do you?'

There was no way Byron would have made the connection between the man he'd seen on the posters and Thea. 'No offense but you must have got your mother's good looks.'

Thea spun round, the sudden movement making Arlo swallow hard. 'Careful where you're pointing that thing.' He shuffling fractionally towards the window.

'You might want to take your own advice, Arlo,' Thea said. She turned back towards Byron. 'My mother was a beautiful woman, inside in and out. She'd have been ashamed of what's happened to people around here. Now, Arlo, you know where Hank's ranch is.'

Arlo nodded.

'Good. Then you're going to drive us out there. And if you try anything, I'll put a bullet in you. You hear me?'

Arlo grunted, put the patrol car into reverse, pulled back, and made a big, looping turn onto the street. Byron lay down on the back seat, out of view of any passing cars.

The patrol-car radio crackled with activity. According to reports called in by concerned citizens, Byron was in at least three other places. It was an ability even he hadn't realized he possessed.

A call came in for Arlo to give the dispatcher an update.

'Take it,' Byron told him.

Arlo relayed his location and left it at that. A smart move.

They continued on through the darkened trees. Occasionally they would pass another patrol car. Thea told Arlo not to slow down, but to keep moving.

As they turned a corner and saw a three-car roadblock up ahead, remaining in motion was no longer an option. Byron lowered himself into the rear foot wells, lying on his back, his gun pointed up at the rear window.

'What you want me to do?' Arlo asked.

Thea seemed panicked. Arlo had been right about one thing: she was out of her depth. Way out.

'Stop. Say hi. Tell them you've had a call from a rancher and you're going to check it out,' Byron told him.

Arlo slowed the patrol car. 'They'll want to know why I have her in my car.'

Byron racked his brain for some kind of a credible explanation. Thea got to one before he did. 'You came to check on me and I was freaked out because I was representing the escapee. I asked to stay with you but you had to go back out on patrol so I came with you,' she said, reaching down so that she was holding the gun out of sight.

Arlo leaned out to talk to one of his colleagues, a lanky beanpole of a sergeant. 'Hey, Sarge, you guys having any more luck than I am tonight?'

Byron lay in back and prayed that the sergeant or one of the other officers wouldn't take a casual peek through the rear window.

The sergeant didn't answer him. Instead he hunkered down and peered past Arlo at Thea, who was doing her best to look like the front seat of a cop car was exactly where she'd be on a night like this.

'Hey, Thea. You come out to help us catch a bad guy?' the sergeant said, sarcasm oozing from every syllable.

'Something like that, Clay,' Thea replied.

'Thea was a little spooked,' Arlo cut in. 'She asked me if I could look after her. Ain't that right, Thea?'

Thea didn't reply.

The sergeant appeared to chew over Arlo's explanation. He didn't seem to buy it, not entirely anyway. 'Same old story, I guess,' he said. 'Cops are all assholes until someone needs us.'

Byron could only imagine the effort involved for Thea not to respond to that one.

'So where you headed?' the sergeant asked Arlo, when Thea didn't take the bait.

'Out to Hank Foley's ranch. He called me about something bothering some of his cattle. Probably a coyote, but I thought I'd check it out in any case,' said Arlo. 'How about you guys? Any word on our boy?'

For a man with two guns close to him, both held by people who could shoot straight and with good reason to blow him away, Arlo was proving cooler under pressure than Byron would have suspected. Notwithstanding the fact that 'their boy' was lying in the back of the car,

Byron's interest had been piqued by the question.

'Nothing solid yet,' said the sergeant.

No kidding, thought Byron.

'But we've got some additional resources coming in,' the sergeant continued. 'Feds or something. They're been kind of cagey about it, but it seems like they've been looking for this guy for a while.'

Byron froze. He'd known this was coming. He'd been sure it would happen long before now. But it still pulled him up short. He'd hoped he'd at least be out of the county before Washington showed up.

In the front seat, Thea leaned over Arlo to talk to the sergeant. 'They say what they wanted him for?'

'I shouldn't have even told you that much.'

'Come on, Clay, I could find out easily enough,' Thea said.

'Okay, well, you didn't hear it from me, and they haven't actually used these words, but the impression I get is that this guy is some kind of terrorist or something. I mean, they won't even let the FBI office here handle it. They're flying down from Washington.'

The sergeant stood back from the window, and hitched his thumbs into his belt. 'In any case, if we don't find him, they sure as hell will.'

CHAPTER SEVENTY-TWO

Sheriff Martin put down the phone and looked at the three other men settled into wingback chairs in the main room of the Kelsen County Country Club. Apart from the four of them, the room was empty. A screen in one corner looped silently through a repeat of an old US Open golf tournament.

'This is gonna be a goddamn shit show,' said Sheriff Martin, putting his cell phone down on a small mahogany side table next to his chair. 'I already got a State Department attorney asking why that guy's alias never showed up anywhere for them. Guy sounded pissed too. Wanted to know if we dropped the ball or whether we're just a bunch of dumb rednecks.'

Across from him, Warden Castro massaged his temples with the tips of his fingers. It had been a bad few weeks and it had all started with Martin's men picking up that vagrant. Castro had known there was something about the guy as soon as he'd laid eyes on him. They should have cut him loose instead of Romero.

'Did they ask anything about how he managed to escape?' Castro asked.

'No,' said Sheriff Martin. 'But they will. Everyone's going to need to come up with some answers.'

Sheriff Martin made a point of taking in Judge Kelsen and his brother, Fidelius Kelsen. Fidelius was, in every respect that mattered, the real power in the room. They were both great-great-grandsons of the man for whom Kelsen County had been named, but Fidelius was a good old boy with an eye for a business opportunity. It was Fidelius who had come up with the idea of the prison and using the inmates as near-zero-cost labor. He'd had other ideas too, and it was those ideas that everyone in the room were concerned with now.

Detaining thousands of people who hadn't done much wrong was one thing. But what concerned Sheriff Martin was the county policy of turning a blind eye to other illegal activity in return for a share of profits. If the people from Washington started digging around Kelsen County, then everyone in the room would be going to jail for a very long time. And that was if they were lucky, and their business partners didn't decide to head off the questioning and deal with them first.

Martin, Castro and the judge were all looking at Fidelius now. He'd had all the answers in the past. When they'd hit bumps in the road he had been the one to stay calm and resolve things. Now, more than ever, they needed him to tell them what to do.

Fidelius rested his elbows on a stomach that spilled over the top of his pants. He looked like a slightly gone-to-seed college dean. 'Gentlemen,' he began, 'did you really think I wouldn't have planned for this type of eventuality?'

Sheriff Martin saw the others relax a little. He wasn't so sure, though.

'Why else have we made campaign contributions to every single politician worth a damn to come out of Texas over the past twenty years?' Fidelius continued. 'Insurance for a time such as this. We have done nothing wrong. Not morally. Sure, we may have cut some corners, if you could even call it that. But these people.' He waved a hand dismissively. 'They come across the border illegally. They aren't citizens. Does anyone think that the taxpayer, the people who actually pay these government bureaucrats' salaries, will care about any of this? Hell, no. I repeat, and I want you all to remember this, we have nothing to be ashamed of. Nothing at all.'

Martin couldn't quite believe what he was hearing. This was the emergency plan? Tell the feds to go take a running jump and call in favors from a bunch of politicians who, when it came to the crunch, would be concerned only with saving their own skins? As for the taxpayers, everyone who lived here loved the low taxes, low crime and everything else that the money paid for. But, like everyone else, they'd feign the same outrage the politicians would when they found out how it was all paid for.

The nature of the general public, as Martin had learned over his years in office, was that when things ran as people liked, they didn't want to ask any questions. It was only when it all went wrong that they discovered a sense of moral outrage. It was human nature.

Martin didn't buy what Fidelius was saying. He wasn't even sure that Fidelius believed it. He probably did have a contingency plan. Guys like him usually did. But it was more likely that it involved tossing everyone else in the room to the lions and distancing himself from them as fast as he could, his brother included.

Sheriff Martin's cell phone started vibrating, working its way towards the edge of the table. He picked it up. 'You'd better be calling me with some good news,' he said to the person at the other end of the line.

The call was brief and the opposite of good news.

'You know I said this was going to be a shit show?' Sheriff Martin said, when he'd finished.

Warden Castro had gone over to the unmanned bar to pour himself another shot of bourbon.

'Well,' said Sheriff Martin, 'that doesn't even begin to cover it.'

'Will you just tell us what the hell that phone call was?' Judge Kelsen said.

Sheriff Martin smiled as he looked at the warden. 'Remember that container with the *rotten produce* we had to dump? Well, it looks like someone just found the contents.'

Castro chugged the drink he'd just poured straight down his throat, gave up on the glass and tipped the bottle to his lips.

CHAPTER SEVENTY-THREE

A sickly stench rose from the ground in waves. The smell was accompanied by twisting cords of steam, which Byron had always associated with rotting animal dung, until he'd encountered his first mass grave.

Hank Foley, the rancher who had called Thea, was already waiting for them when they had rolled up in the patrol car. He didn't seem overly alarmed to see Arlo get out of the vehicle at gunpoint. Nor did he question Byron's presence. It was as if his own grisly discovery meant that the entire world had somehow morphed into a place where it was perfectly reasonable for the local do-gooder defense attorney to be prodding a cop with a firearm.

The three of them had followed Hank's truck to the grave. Hank parked next to a stand of live oaks. He got out and hobbled, with the help of a cane, under the trees. Arlo parked the patrol car behind the truck and they followed Hank, the smell hitting them long before they reached the grave.

Hank stopped beyond the trees and pointed with his cane. 'I had one of my guys preparing the ground here for some new planting. We usually leave this area for cattle. He came running up, screaming about how he'd found some bodies. First I thought he'd taken something, because of how he was babbling like a crazy man. I came down to take a look for myself and there they were.'

Byron walked over to the edge of the grave. He counted twenty or so dead people. Not skeletons. Bodies. Rotting. Buried perhaps a month ago, though that was only a rough estimate.

Some were face up, others face down. A few lay on their side or with limbs hanging over the person next to them. They had been dumped, thrown in and covered as quickly as possible. Probably in the middle of the night, if the rancher hadn't known anything about it.

Of course, that was assuming he was telling the truth, which was by no means a certainty. It was plenty possible that Hank had known about this shallow grave all along, heard that the feds were on their way down to Kelsen and panicked. Calling Thea wasn't a bad strategy, if you wanted to cover your ass.

Thea had already dug out her phone and was taking pictures of the grave. Byron had been surprised by her stoicism since they'd arrived. She had gagged, but that was an involuntary physical reaction to the odor. She lowered her phone and turned towards him. 'What do you think happened?'

Byron had been wondering about that. They'd need a pathologist or coroner to give them any meaningful answers. But they could likely rule out a few things. He knelt down at the edge of the freshly excavated grave. The bodies didn't show any substantial evidence of violent trauma, such as gunshots or broken bones. They were pretty much intact, apart from one body at the very end, which had likely been snagged by the digger, lifting it up and snapping the left leg in half.   'Well, whatever it was,' he said, 'it sure as hell wasn't natural causes. They all died at the same time.'

Arlo was standing alongside them, staring into the trench, his jaw slack. The horror of what they were looking at seemed to have dulled his immediate fear.

'You know anything about this, Arlo?' Thea said.

He shook his head.

'Arlo?' Byron said. 'What happened to these folks?'

Arlo's hands went to his face as it crumpled. His lower lip began to wobble. He started to sob. The rancher shot him a look of pure disgust. Men here weren't given to naked shows of emotion. Not in front of women. Or other men. Especially not if they were sober. Definitely not if they were a cop.

Thea moved next to Arlo. 'Arlo, if you know anything about this, you'll feel a lot better if you get it off your chest.'

'I didn't know,' Arlo said. 'I didn't know until it was too late.'

'Know what?' Byron and Thea said simultaneously.

'Arlo!' Hank barked. 'Shut your mouth now.'

So he did know. At least, he knew more than he was letting on. Byron raised the gun and leveled it at him. 'Let him talk,' he told the rancher.

Hank Foley glared at Byron, but didn't say any more. Byron waved him off to one side with the gun. Arlo was more likely to open up to Thea than to him. He'd leave her to play the role of confessor. That would give him the opportunity to speak with Hank.

He walked the rancher over to the furthest live oak. 'We both know that you didn't just find these people. For a start, what the hell were you about to start planting here? Dirt?' Byron said to him. 'You helped bury them, didn't you? Maybe you did a lot more than that.'

Hank didn't respond. Not that Byron had expected him to. Not at this stage anyway. He wasn't going to break down like Arlo either. He wasn't the type.

'Right now a whole bunch of federal agents is on a plane on the way down here because Thea over there has spent the last however many years gathering information for them,' said Byron.

Hank's eyes slid, for a split second, to where Thea was speaking in hushed tones to Arlo. That was all Byron needed to confirm that he'd hit a nerve. Hank might not have been buying it completely, but he was prepared to entertain the possibility.

'I heard they're here for you,' the rancher said, with a hint of a smirk.

'You think I'd be standing here now if that was true?' said Byron.

Hank looked him up and down. Yeah, thought Byron, he was made of sterner stuff than Arlo, whose guts were all in his badge.

'All I know about this is what I told Thea,' Hank said. 'One of my workers found 'em here.'

Byron dug a toe into the dirt. 'Whatever you say. If you're lying the feds'll find out. Won't be difficult either. They've had their eyes on this place for a while.' He looked up into the broad canopy of sky above them. 'You know what Google Maps is?'

The rancher shrugged. 'Of course. We're not all hicks.'

'Well then,' Byron continued, 'you must know that the government has a much sophisticated version. They can pull up a satellite image of this area of ground right here going back years. They'll be able to tell when this was dug and, if they catch a break, who was here when those bodies were getting tossed in and covered over. Never mind you helping to throw them in, if you dug this hole that'll be all they need.'

'Horseshit!'

Byron smiled. 'You do know what conspiracy means? Or would you like Thea here to explain it to you? Hell, you don't even have to dig a hole to be found guilty. Just offering the use of your land makes you as bad as the people who murdered these folks.'

'No one murdered them,' Arlo said.

'Sure they didn't,' said Byron, his voice dripping with sarcasm. 'They were probably just walking, tripped, fell in and hit their heads on the way. That what you're going to tell the jury, Arlo? Or are you going to be screaming the same old song while they're strapping you to the gurney and sticking the needle into your arm right next to your buddies?'

'It was an accident,' Arlo said.

CHAPTER SEVENTY-FOUR

'Arlo!' Hank shouted, trying to shut the cop up.

Byron turned to Hank. 'You're screwed. The feds haven't even got here yet and people are already starting to sing.'

Arlo and Hank glared at each other.

'What kind of an accident?' Thea asked Arlo. 'Byron's right. This doesn't look like an accident.'

Arlo shot the rancher a look. 'They were in a container. Ran out of air. Prison guards thought we were with the container, and we thought the guards were. It was a mix-up. An accident.'

Byron saw the muzzle flare and heard the shot before he even realized that Hank had pulled a pistol and fired a single shot into Arlo's stomach. Arlo folded over with a groan and hit the ground face first, almost tumbling forward to join the others in the open grave.

Hank squeezed off another shot. This one hit Arlo between his shoulder blades, the impact, or perhaps his body's delayed shock, pushing him forward. He flopped over the edge of the trench and down into the hole below, his legs still sprawled on the ground until gravity took effect and he tumbled right in, coming to rest on top of one of the corpses.

Byron brought his gun up as Hank spun round, aiming for him. Before Byron could get a shot off, Thea fired once, hitting the rancher in the middle of his chest. She followed up with two more rounds in quick succession. All three clustered in the center of the man's body. Hank fell forwards, his pistol dropping from his hand as he rolled onto his side, knees pushed up into his chest.

Byron walked over to him, and picked up his gun. Thea knelt down next to him. She reached over, and

247

touched Hank's neck, checking for a pulse. She glanced across at Byron. 'He didn't give me much choice.'

'No,' said Byron. 'He didn't. But it might be better if we switched weapons. There'll be plenty prepared to believe I did this.'

'Speaking of they,' she said, standing up, 'shouldn't you be getting the hell out of here before they arrive? Whoever they are.'

He was going to ask if she'd be okay on her own. He stopped himself. After what had just gone down it was fairly clear that Thea was more than capable of looking after herself. 'I should. You mind if I take Arlo's patrol car?'

Thea shook her head. She dug in her pocket, produced the keys and placed them carefully in Byron's open palm. She left her hand there for a moment as his fingers closed around them.

They looked at each other. Byron leaned in and kissed her cheek. She turned her face to kiss him on the lips. 'Good luck, Byron.'

He didn't want to leave. He would have happily stayed with Thea. Or gone where she wanted to go. But neither was an option. Not now, and probably not in the future. And if he didn't get moving soon, he likely wouldn't have a future.

'Before I go, I need to ask you for one final favor,' he said to Thea.

A mixture of hesitation and exhaustion flitted across her face. 'Well, seeing as you're prepared to take the rap for me here, how could I refuse?'

'You haven't heard what it is yet.'

He told her. As favors went it was extraordinarily simple. This time, though, her expression was one of complete and total confusion.

CHAPTER SEVENTY-FIVE

Lauren's body felt like a single knot of tension as the door of the Cessna finally lowered. Shortly after takeoff, the pilot had informed them that they couldn't land at the designated landing strip near Kelsen, and would have to reroute to nearby San Antonio. It would add only ten minutes to the flight time, but they now faced an hour-long drive from San Antonio to Kelsen.

Although she was used to these types of completely avoidable SNAFUs (Situation Normal, All Fucked Up), they still rankled. Especially since time was precious. Although the four special-forces operators on board were semi-officially designated a kill team, Lauren wanted Tibor breathing. They would learn a lot more by recovering a live specimen than a dead one.

Behind her, the others were already grabbing their gear. A bewildering array of hardware was carried down the steps and deposited in the backs of three Escalades, two black and one silver-grey. The last item loaded was a blue body bag.

CHAPTER SEVENTY-SIX

The face of the dead child stared back at Byron from the screen of Thea's phone. Big brown eyes that had glimpsed, in the last moments of her life, the full horror of the world. For a moment, Byron was no longer in Texas. He was in Afghanistan, cradling another dead little girl whose name had been Sasha.

Sasha's death had been the final straw for the old Byron. Seeing her die had triggered his descent into madness. Or, arguably, into sanity.

He had never been convinced that his previous stoicism in the face of needless death and suffering was the reaction of a sane man, but his inner turmoil after so much exposure to horror, and the behaviour it gave rise to, was the mark of a mad man.

He touched his thumb and forefinger to the screen. He pinched them together and the image zoomed out to reveal the mass grave he had left behind. In a way that made him feel ashamed: the collage of bodies was less upsetting than the close-up view of the little girl. He couldn't explain why that was so. It just was.

Byron tucked Thea's phone into his pocket, and sounded the horn of the patrol car one more time. He gave it a long blast, counted off ten seconds, and hit it again.

It was parked facing the building's front door. The headlights were on full beam so that anyone looking out would only see someone sitting in the driver's seat.

Finally, after two more blasts, the front reception door opened and a woman emerged. Her hair was tousled and she looked like she hadn't long woken up. Byron knew who she was. She wasn't the person he had expected to see. Not that it mattered.

The same rules would apply. She would have to follow his instructions. If she didn't, she would face the consequences.

It was too bad. She was pretty much an innocent in all of this. Just a woman who had taken a job to pay her bills. It wouldn't be fair if this proved to be her last night on earth. But when had the world been fair?

Byron checked the Glock as the woman stepped uncertainly through the glass door. She left it wedged open behind her. Byron laid off the horn and waited.

She was hesitant. Nervous. She couldn't understand why the police officer in the driver's seat wasn't getting out. She tried to peer through the front windshield. Byron slumped down in the seat. His head flopped to one side. He reached over with his free hand, the other holding the Glock, and hit the button to lower the window.

'Help me,' Byron said. 'I need help. I was just shot. I can't feel my legs.'

That got her moving. A cop who couldn't exit his vehicle because he'd been shot offered sudden rationality to the situation.

He listened as her heels clicked smartly across the parking lot. 'Oh, my God,' she said.

She stopped suddenly and began to turn back towards the building. 'I'll call for help.'

'No,' Byron shouted after her. 'I already did that. I need someone to put pressure on the wound before I bleed out.'

Her worry about what to do next assuaged, she started back towards the patrol car. As she came level with the open window, Byron raised the Glock and pointed it at her. 'Don't move until I tell you,' he said.

She started to speak but the words got choked at the back of her throat. Her eyes were wide with fear. She didn't move. Finally, she blinked, as if she was trying to clear her head from a nightmare. Byron swung the door open, and got out. He took the woman's hand and turned her round. 'What's your name?' he asked her.

'Jacqueline,' she managed, after a few stuttered attempts.

'Okay, Jacqueline, here's what you're going to do for me. Are you listening?'

'Yes.'

'You're going to walk me inside. When we get inside you're going to get them to open every door I need to be opened. If they hesitate or don't co-operate, you're going to tell them that if they don't do what I tell them I'm going to kill you. Did you get all that, Jacqueline?'

'Yes, I think so.'

'That's good. You're doing real well. Okay, so let's start walking. I'm going to be right behind you every step.'

She started to move back towards the door. She was shaking, her footsteps uncertain. At the door, she stopped. 'Can I ask you something?'

'Sure.'

'I don't understand this. Why do you want to get inside? It doesn't make any sense.'

'It does to me,' Byron said.

She half turned and looked at him. He stared back at her. He was praying she wasn't about to do something stupid, like reach for the gun and try to run back out into the parking lot.

'Are you out of your mind?' she said.

In the glass-fronted reception area he could see two prison guards staring at him, jaws slack, presumably asking themselves the same question. 'Something like that,' he said, pivoting around and shooting out the glass partition.

CHAPTER SEVENTY-SEVEN

Byron guided Jacqueline, one of the jail's civilian administration workers, through the open door. He used the Glock to back the two guards against the far wall. He ordered them to turn round and face the wall.

Thankfully, they both complied. He asked them to unhook their belts, and let them drop to the floor. When they'd done that, he told them to turn round and kick the belts over to him.

Jacqueline picked them up and, following Byron's instructions, removed the Tasers, batons and pepper-spray canisters and kicked the belts back to the guards.

'Okay, you can put them back on.'

The guards did as they were told, shooting quick glances between each other and then at Byron. The older of them, whom Byron recognized as one of the guards who hadn't seemed to take any great pleasure in the job, certainly not in the way Mills had, was the first to speak.

'Look, Davis,' he said, 'we never did anything to you. We're just doing our jobs. You have a bone to pick, then go find Castro.'

'No bones to pick,' Byron told him. 'Just do what I say when I say it and you can all go home when I'm done here. Disobey me, though, and I'll kill you.'

'You got it,' said the older guard. 'What do you want us to do?'

'Take me back inside,' Byron told him.

CHAPTER SEVENTY-EIGHT

'Hit the lights,' Byron instructed the guard.

Sleepy-eyed inmates sat up, or rolled out of their bunks as the lights flickered into life. They rubbed their eyes, and coughed. One began to head straight for the bathroom to take a piss before he realized what was going on. Soon, all eyes were on Byron.

If the guards had been surprised at seeing him back in the Kelsen County Jail, it was nothing to the inmates' collective reaction. This bunkhouse was almost all Mexicans and Hispanic. That was why Byron had chosen it. The one word that seemed to hang in the air needed no great translation skills.

Loco.

What else could you call someone who had escaped only to break back inside less than twenty-four hours later? Byron scanned the men until he found who he was looking for. Cesar was a Mexican in his late twenties who had been close to Romero.

Byron motioned for the man to come over to him. He dug into his pocket, and handed him Thea's smart phone. 'You recognize any of these people?'

The man swiped through the images. His face darkened. Other inmates joined him, peering over his shoulder. One said something in Spanish that Byron didn't catch and began to break down.

The man looked at Byron. 'Miguel does. One of them is his wife.'

Byron took the phone back, swiped to the picture that included the little girl and handed it back to the inmates. 'Anyone know who she is?'

The phone was passed from hand to hand. There were gasps, tears and heated discussion. There were also murderous glances towards the guards.

Finally, the inmate Byron had spoken to first asked, 'Explain this. Where did you find these people?'

Byron explained, slowly and patiently, waiting for his words to be translated to the others. Behind him, the two guards studied the floor. The older one said, 'I didn't know nothing about this.'

One of the inmates walked over and, without saying anything, drew back his fist and struck the guard in the face, a powerful blow that sent him to the floor.

CHAPTER SEVENTY-NINE

The three Escalades pulled up outside the Kelsen County Sheriff's headquarters. Next to Lauren, Nick Frinz voiced what everyone else in the convoy must have been thinking.

'How much money d'you think it cost to build something like that?' he said.

Lauren reached for the door handle and got out. While she and Nick went to speak to the sheriff with an agent from the FBI's San Antonio field office, the rest of the team stayed put. No one, Lauren included, wanted any of the locals to see a four-man special-forces kill team wandering down the main street in Kelsen, armed to the teeth.

In any case, the plan was not to have to use them. Lauren was hoping that they could flush Tibor into open country where a drone could do the job with minimum fuss. Technically the use of an armed drone on US soil to kill a US citizen was illegal. But since Lauren had begun to climb the ladder within the agency she had discovered that lots of things technically never happened. At least, not officially. Tibor himself was one of those things.

The FBI liaison explained who they were. They were told to take a seat as sheriff's deputies ran in every direction. Out in the street, patrol cars sped past, sirens wailing. Lauren wondered if this was a show they were putting on for the big boys from Washington to prove how seriously they were taking the search for Tibor. If it was, they needn't have bothered. They'd had him in jail and hadn't even realized who he was. When this was done and dusted, people were going to be called to account, and it wasn't going to be pretty.

When five minutes had passed and Sheriff Martin hadn't appeared, Lauren got to her feet. She grabbed a passing deputy. 'Sheriff Martin? Go get him for me. Now,' she said.

'Pardon me, ma'am, but we're kind of busy right at the moment. If you'd like to take a seat someone will be with you shortly.'

Lauren took a step back. 'Listen up, shit for brains, we're the United States government. Now, go tell Martin to get his fat ass down here or he's going to be facing federal obstruction charges quicker than you can spell federal, which, admittedly, may not be that fast. But you get the picture, don't you?'

The deputy stared at her. 'I'll let him know.'

'Get him,' Lauren repeated, letting him go and watching him head through a door still shaking his head at her rudeness.

Ten minutes later, the deputy was back. He walked slowly over to Lauren. 'Ma'am, Sheriff Martin sends his apologies but he's running late.'

'Where the hell is he?'

'No idea, ma'am.'

'Then go find out.'

CHAPTER EIGHTY

Sheriff Martin pulled up next to the ranch house. He could tell by the faces of the deputies who were already there that something very bad had happened. It wasn't just their expressions. Not one of them would meet his eye.

He noticed Judge Billy Kelsen's car, a black Lexus, parked nearby. Next to it was a Mercedes Benz S-Series that belonged to Fidelius. The most expensive car in town for the richest man in town. Their presence explained why the deputies weren't looking at him. The Kelsen brothers let him handle stuff like this. They didn't dirty their hands with the details.

The men who worked for him probably saw their presence as bad news for the sheriff. A show of no confidence. Sheriff Martin already knew about Hank calling Thea to tell her about the grave site. Dumb asshole. Already covering his back before there was any need, and in the process making life more difficult for everyone.

Hank was up to his neck in all this. He'd been the one who'd suggested they could use his ranch to hide the bodies. Of course he'd wanted free labor from the county jail in return. Like everyone around here, he only helped out if there was something in it for him.

Sheriff Martin tipped back his hat as he saw Fidelius emerge from the Benz and walk towards him. God, he was sick of this place. All of these people had been happy when times were good, but were running around like headless chickens now there was a problem.

Fidelius reached him, and put a hand on his shoulder. It was a gesture that set him on edge. Beyond a congratulatory handshake every time he'd been elected, Sheriff Martin couldn't remember Fidelius ever touching him. He just wasn't that kind of guy.

'I'm sorry, John,' Fidelius said, squeezing his

shoulder. 'I really am. It should never have come to this.'

'Sure,' said Sheriff Martin.

Fidelius must have been talking about Arlo. A fellow officer struck down while doing his duty.

'I'll walk you down, John,' said Fidelius.

Together they started along the track to where they had buried a container full of illegals. Not that Fidelius had been present. He'd left everyone else to deal with that.

Billy Kelsen fell in beside them. He patted Sheriff Martin on the back and offered his condolences. Weird, he thought. He usually wasn't much more emotional than his brother. Jesus, maybe they were planning on throwing him in with the bodies and burying him too. The thought made him laugh. The two Kelsen men traded a look.

'Sorry,' said Sheriff Martin. 'I just don't know if this whole situation can get any more messed up than it already is.'

Neither Kelsen brother said anything. They kept walking until they reached the stand of trees and stopped.

It was all coming back now. Taking the bodies out of the containers. The little girl still clutching the pink rabbit. That had got to Sheriff Martin more than anything else. He'd tried to tell himself it was an accident. A mistake. Wires had been crossed and they'd been left too long in the heat with too little air and no water. It wasn't as if they'd been killed deliberately. It had been a tragedy. A terrible tragedy.

Sheriff Martin had thought about returning them to their families back home. But that wasn't possible. There would have been too many questions. Questions with answers that no one wanted to give. Someone dying in the jail or being injured in the factory was one thing. A whole bunch of people dead was something else. There was nothing else to be done but bury them and make sure it didn't happen again.

They cleared the live oaks. Fidelius put his hand back

on Sheriff Martin's shoulder. 'I know this must be hard, John.'

It was like Fidelius was talking in riddles.

'It's okay,' Sheriff Martin said. 'We can get some quicklime. John McGarry can make the arrangements for Hank and Arlo.'

McGarry was the town undertaker.

'And what about Thea?' said Fidelius. 'Would you like McGarry to make the arrangements for her as well?'

'What do you mean? What are you talking about, Fidelius?'

'No one's told you?' Fidelius said, with a look of horror. 'None of your men told you?'

'Told me what?' said Sheriff Martin.

'She's over there,' said Fidelius. 'That lunatic must have shot her straight after he murdered Arlo and Hank.'

Sheriff John Martin looked to where Fidelius was staring. There was a white sheet lying on the ground. A body under it. A puddle of black hair spilling out from one end.

In a daze, Martin walked over to the sheet. He knelt down, pulled back the corner. He struggled to take in what he was seeing. Thea. His only child. The person he loved more than anyone in the world. Beautiful, proud Thea.

It was a trick. It had to be. She was sleeping. Playing dead. He reached over and shook her shoulder. His hand came away wet with blood.

In that moment, the world imploded. He reached down again, picking her up and cradling her in his arms.

No. It wasn't possible. He rocked her back and forth, as he had done when she was a little girl.

Over by the oaks, the Kelsen brothers stood and watched Sheriff Martin break down, cradling Thea in his arms.

'Hell of a business,' said Fidelius.

His brother sighed. 'She was never one to keep her

mouth shut.'

Fidelius stared ahead over the flat, open country beyond the oak trees. 'A damn shame.'

CHAPTER EIGHTY-ONE

Byron stood in the middle of the exercise yard and watched the flames lick up the outside wall of the bunkhouse. A group of four prisoners wandered past him wearing guard uniforms they'd raided from stores.

Over by the fence two actual guards were being pushed around by another group of prisoners. Byron marched over to where the two terrified men were cowering as they were spat on, kicked and punched by men still enraged by what they had seen only minutes before.

News of the grim discovery, as well as the story of what had happened to Romero, had spread rapidly through the facility. Half a dozen guards had made a half-hearted attempt to quell the initial disorder. It hadn't worked. They had quickly given up when faced with hundreds of enraged inmates.

For his part, Byron had brokered an agreement with Cesar, the leader of the Latino inmates: the guards were to be released alive. Unharmed had quickly proven too much of a stretch, given the level of simmering resentment that had boiled over into cold, unrelenting rage. At least some of the guards, the ones who had dished out their own brand of justice, would catch a beating. Byron just didn't want any more graves being dug that didn't absolutely have to be.

As the blows raining down on the two hapless guards intensified, Byron shouldered his way through another crowd of prisoners, who were busy assembling a bonfire in the middle of the yard, and made for the fence.

He pulled a couple of inmates out of the way. One rounded on him, caught up in the collective madness, and ready to swing. He saw who it was. He saw the Glock held down by Byron's side, pointing into the dirt. He put up his hands and went to join the bonfire assemblers.

Byron kept at it, peeling off assailants from the edge until there were only two men left, spitting threats in Spanish, their eyes full of murder. One aimed a kick at the head of a guard who had slumped, close to unconscious, with his back against the fence. Byron grabbed the kicker by his collar and dragged him back. He lost balance and fell. Scrambling to his feet, he raised his fists. Byron brought the Glock up hard and fast. 'Back off.'

He grabbed his buddy and sloped off into the shadows, no doubt hoping to catch more fresh meat.

Cesar joined Byron. He was soaked in sweat. Organizing a prison riot while making sure that no one got killed must have been hard work.

'Help me with these two,' Byron said to him.

Between them he and Cesar managed to get the two beaten guards onto their feet. They helped them towards the mess hall where a half-dozen of the Mexicans who were prepared to take orders from Cesar were protecting the other jail personnel. Byron and Cesar found the two guards seats at a table with some of the others.

'Is that all your men accounted for now?' Byron asked the older guard he'd met near the entrance.

'Everyone apart from one. Officer Strand. Young guy. Big. Blond crew-cut. Just came out of the army. Only started here this year.'

Byron had a vague memory of a guard who fitted the description. He hadn't been notable for much, apart from being overly concerned with following procedure. He and Cesar traded a look. With the riot at fever pitch a guard on his own was bad news. They started for the door at the same time.

They hadn't got back out into the yard when they heard the first crack of live gunfire. Byron broke into a run. As he pushed through the door and out into the yard he saw the group of inmates carrying bedding out to the bonfire scatter in a dozen different directions.

Another shot was fired. This time he was close enough to see where it had come from. Hunkering down, and staying close to the building, he saw a fresh muzzle flash from the watchtower and a prisoner fall to the ground.

CHAPTER EIGHTY-TWO

'I want him dead. Do you understand me?'

As if the order needed any reinforcement, Sheriff Martin slammed both hands down on the hood of the patrol car that was parked just short of the stand of oak trees. The heart-breaking shock of seeing his daughter lying in the dirt had given way to a thirst for vengeance. Thea had always seen the good in people, and now her naivety had exacted the ultimate price. He had warned her over and over, but she wouldn't listen, and now this.

There were whispers among his deputies that it had been worse than murder. That before she'd died, she'd been violated by that animal. They wouldn't know for sure until the coroner did his work. Even the suspicion that she had been raped before she was murdered was almost too much for him to take.

Part of him wanted to throw himself into the grave, then dig himself into the ground until his mouth and nostrils filled with dirt and he stopped breathing. His rage, his need for revenge, was his lifeline. A reason to keep going. A reason to live.

He would find Davis, or Tibor or whatever the hell the guy was called. When he found him, he would kill him. After that? He had no idea what he would do. He would likely be staring back into the abyss. Maybe he would drink a bottle of whisky and eat a gun. Join in that great cop tradition.

Now he had a job to do. Find the man who had killed his daughter and take his life.

'Sheriff?'

He looked up to see one of the younger troopers standing on the other side of the car. Most of the others had drifted off. 'Yes, son. What is it?'

'We need to know what you want us to do about the

jail. We just had another call from one of the guards. He said they need us down there and fast.'

'Didn't we already send two patrols?' Sheriff Martin asked.

'Yes, sir, we did. But the prisoners have the entrance barricaded and they're saying they won't release the guards until our men fall back.'

'Okay. Tell Deputy Cross that he's to take command down there but we can't spare any more men until we find that son of a bitch Tibor.'

'Yes, sir.'

The young deputy didn't move. Just stood there.

'Is there something else?' Sheriff Martin asked.

'The people from Washington are here. They said they need to talk to you immediately.'

Two SUVs were rolling down the slope towards the trees, headlights on full. Sheriff Martin had to shield his eyes with a hand to avoid being blinded.

'That's them,' said the young deputy.

'Okay, son. I'll handle this. You go tell Cross that he has operational command at the jail until I can get down there.'

Sheriff Martin started towards the two black SUVs as they rolled towards him and stopped. A young woman got out of the lead vehicle. Some preppy-looking kid in a suit and tie, who looked like he could barely pee standing up, never mind chase down a cold-blooded killer, stood behind her.

The woman thrust out her hand. 'Sheriff Martin, I'm Lauren Stanley from the Central Intelligence Agency. This is Nick Frinz from the State Department.'

Sheriff Martin shook their hands. He couldn't help but stare a second too long at Frinz's shoes. Penny loafers. What kind of people were these? No wonder the country was going to hell in a handcart.

'I'm sorry for your loss,' said Lauren. 'We heard the

news about your daughter as we were driving over here.'

Sheriff Martin eyed her. 'Who told you?'

'We hear everything, Sheriff.'

Mother of God, thought Sheriff Martin. This little girl was totally delusional. 'That so? Because I swear I heard that you've been looking for this Tibor guy for over a year now and it took us to find him for you.'

'It might have helped if you hadn't kept him off law-enforcement radar when you arrested him.' Lauren looked past him to the trench and the three sheets that lay near the edge. 'Maybe all this might have been avoided.'

Sheriff Martin had never struck a woman. Not in anger anyway. He was damn close to it now. His hand bunched up and he drew it back.

Lauren stared him down. 'If you want to spend the next twenty years in a federal prison, go right ahead and hit me.'

He looked down at his clenched fist as if it had somehow taken on a life of its own. He dropped it back to the butt of his gun.

'Now, can we stop screwing around here and get down to finding Tibor? My patience with your department ran out about an hour ago,' Lauren continued.

'I don't need your help,' Sheriff Martin told her.

Lauren took in the carnage behind him with a sweep of her eyes. 'Is that a grave?'

CHAPTER EIGHTY-THREE

Correctional Officer Strand slowed his breathing, waited for his heart rate to fall away, and squeezed the trigger. Down below on the yard, his bullet caught the prisoner in the shoulder. The prisoner spun, lost his balance and fell forward. Other men scattered in every direction.

Strand got ready to fire another round. He had the span of the fallen prisoner's back caught flush in the crosshairs. He took another deep breath.

The fallen prisoner began to wriggle forward. The movement threw Strand off for a second. He lowered his rifle, knowing he couldn't take the shot. He couldn't kill an injured man who was crawling for his life. He didn't have it in him. He'd thought he had. He had been mistaken.

He brought the rifle back up to his shoulder and quickly panned across the rest of the yard, first using his eyes, then narrowing down possible targets with the scope. He stopped abruptly as he caught sight of one of the guards, blood pouring down his face from a nasty gash across his forehead. The man was being held up by two of the prisoners. One was the rabble-rouser, Cesar. The other was a Mexican, whose name eluded him. He was holding a kitchen knife to the guard's throat.

Cesar waved his arms, calling for the prisoners to quieten down as thick black smoke blew across the exercise yard and spiraled into the sky.

Strand shouldered his rifle. 'Touch that guard and I'll blow your head off, Cesar.'

'Throw down that rifle and I won't need to,' Cesar shouted back. 'No one will touch you or him. You have my word on that, but you have to come down.'

Strand wasn't buying it. 'Why should I believe you?'

'Because you don't have any other choice,' Cesar

replied, with a nod towards half a dozen inmates who had breached the fence and were busy carrying pieces of wood, blankets and a green metal can of gasoline towards the bottom of the watchtower.

Screw it, thought Strand. If they were happy to burn him to death they sure as hell weren't going to let him get out of there in one piece after he'd shot at least three of them. He'd rather take his chances up there until he ran out of ammunition and he was a long way away from that happening. In any case, the sheriff had to be sending help to the jail soon. Hell, for all Strand knew, they could be about to mount a raid and he'd be surrendering for nothing.

'Go to hell,' he shouted down to Cesar. 'You cut his throat, that's on you.'

From nowhere, cold metal parted the hair at the back of Strand's neck and pressed into the flesh. Fingers closed around his throat and squeezed in a vice-like grip.

A voice whispered in his ear, 'Put the gun down. This place doesn't need any more heroes.'

Strand slowly lowered the rifle to the deck of the watchtower. The man behind him pulled him backwards, sweeping his feet out from under him with his leg. He turned Strand over, so he was lying face down, grabbed his hands and cuffed him.

Byron Tibor hauled Strand to his feet and led him towards the spiral steps that led down towards the yard. At the bottom, he unlocked the door. A couple of inmates moved to swarm Strand. Byron backed them up with the Glock, gun-facing them hard, his finger on the trigger and a look that said he was itching to go the last half-inch. They got the message, and retreated back into the shadows.

Cesar was waiting for him in the middle of the yard. The smoke was billowing in every direction, making breathing difficult. Byron pushed Strand towards him.

'Present for you.'

Cesar caught the guard before he could fall. 'Just what I always wanted,' he said.

'If this is going to work you can't hurt any of these people any more than you absolutely have to,' Byron said to Cesar. 'And preferably not at all.'

Cesar nodded. 'I don't want to hurt them any more than you do.'

'That's not saying much. You know what I mean, though, right?' Byron said.

'I do.'

'Okay, get everyone ready,' said Byron.

CHAPTER EIGHTY-FOUR

Byron stood next to Cesar and took in the teeming mass of inmates gathered in the corridors near the main entrance to the administration building. There must have been several hundred men, women and children. Cesar had sent a party of armed prisoners to the neighboring women's facility to free the occupants. The guards there hadn't bothered to offer so much as token resistance as soon as they'd seen a few dozen armed inmates.

Byron peered through office blinds at the two patrol cars sitting in the parking lot, doors open, sheriff's deputies standing behind them, guns trained on the entrance.

'You think this will work?' Cesar asked Byron.

Byron didn't know for sure. The cops could get freaked and start firing. He very much doubted that, but it was a possibility. The question was whether it was a risk he was prepared to ask innocent people to take.

He dug into his pocket, pulled out Thea's phone, tapped on her contact list and scrolled down until he reached the name he was looking for. The name it was listed under was a painful reminder that almost everyone was more than one person. Sheriff Martin was, as far as Byron could see, a petty tyrant corrupted by power. But here, on his daughter's phone, he was simply 'Dad'.

Byron hit the phone icon and waited for the call to connect.

CHAPTER EIGHTY-FIVE

Sheriff Martin looked in disbelief at the name flashing up on his cell phone. He blinked, wishing it away. The four letters placed side by side hit him harder than a punch in the stomach.

THEA.

Frinz, the kid from the State Department, was wandering back from the grave, his fancy leather loafers coated with dirt. 'Sheriff? Are you going to answer that?'

Martin glared at him. The little punk. Here they were, not twenty feet from his dead daughter, and this kid was ordering him around.

Thea. Dead.

Sheriff Martin looked around for his guys. He spotted one poring over a paper map of the area with the girl from the CIA and the FBI liaison agent who'd been the only one smart enough not to try to make this a pissing contest. Martin had told his men to give the feds whatever they asked for. If they found Tibor that was all well and good. If they thought he was being co-operative, they might let their guard slip and he would have the chance to kill the sorry sack of shit before they realized what was going on. The girl from the CIA had already made it plain that she wanted Tibor alive. Sheriff Martin didn't, but he wasn't going to get anywhere by admitting that now.

'Hey, JD, do we know if Thea had her cell phone on her?' Sheriff Martin asked his deputy.

The deputy glanced up from the map. So did the others. 'Wasn't on the body – I mean on her. You want us to start looking for it, Sheriff? I can get a patrol to run by her house, see if it's there.'

'No, that's okay,' he said.

Her name was still flashing on the screen.

'Son of a bitch,' he muttered, under his breath.

Frinz and the others were still staring at him. He walked back towards the live oaks, ducking under the canopy as he hit the green button to accept the call.

'Hello.'

Finally, thought Byron, as his call was answered. 'Sheriff Martin, it's Tibor.'

There was silence at the other end of the line. For a moment he thought the call had dropped or that he'd lost the connection.

'Sheriff Martin?'

'I'm here. Can you hear me?' the sheriff asked.

'Yes.'

Martin checked over his shoulder to see Frinz moving along the line of trees behind him, trying to eavesdrop. So much for the government's famed powers of surveillance. Sheriff Martin turned round and angrily waved him away.

He pressed the phone closer to his ear. 'Good. Because I don't want you to miss any of this. I'm going to find you, and I'm going to kill you, Tibor. Just like you killed my daughter, you piece of shit. You hear me?'

Byron took a step back from the window, the blind snapping shut as he let it go.

'What are you talking about?' he asked. 'Thea's dead?'

The denial only served to enrage Sheriff Martin. 'Like you didn't know. You killed her. Her and Arlo and Hank.'

'No, Sheriff, I didn't. She was alive when I left her. Hank shot Arlo and Thea shot Hank before he could shoot her too.' Byron's mind was racing. 'Listen, do you have any idea who might have arrived at the ranch after? Who told you she was dead?'

'Cut the act, Tibor,' said Sheriff Martin. 'You killed her. You know you did. Now you'd better keep running.

But know this, I will catch up with you.'

Byron held the phone to his chest, trying to compose himself. He counted slowly to three and put it back to his ear. He looked at the people crowded behind him. To Cesar, who was waiting for his help to help get them out of there. He raised the phone back to his ear.

'You won't have to chase me, Sheriff,' Byron said. 'I'll meet you.'

'Bullshit. You don't have the stones for that.'

'The Fashion Square mall. Front entrance on Main Street. Thirty minutes. Before you do what you promised, you're going to need to listen to me. I didn't kill Thea, but you probably know who did.'

'I'll see you there,' said Sheriff Martin.

The call finished, Byron stared down at Thea's cell phone for a moment.

'You okay?' Cesar asked him.

'They killed Thea Martinez.'

'That the lawyer lady?' Cesar asked.

'They think I did it.'

Cesar reached past Byron, pulled down one of the slats and peered out. Two of the cops got back into their patrol car, closed the doors, gunned the engine and peeled out of the parking lot.

'They're leaving,' said Cesar.

'They think I'm back in town. Probably figure they're going to need to all the fire power they can muster,' said Byron, as he opened Thea's phone with a paperclip, took out the SIM card, and ground it to dust under his heavy work boot.

'Kind of says it all,' said Cesar, his eyes still on the parking lot.

'What does?' Byron asked him.

'Well, even in the middle of this shit show, one bad-ass American still counts for more than a thousand

Mexicans about to make a break for it.'

Byron turned back to where the assembled prisoners were waiting for his signal. 'Be grateful for that,' Byron told Cesar. 'At least this one time.'

CHAPTER EIGHTY-SIX

Sheriff Martin turned back to the feds, who had assembled at the ranch house, ready to deploy to the jail. Four men in tactical gear were standing beside a silver-grey SUV, talking in low whispers while they ran through a final weapons check. Lauren Stanley was hunched over some kind of computer tablet, staring at the screen in a way that suggested it held an ancient secret.

Sheriff Martin marched over to her. 'Shouldn't we be moving out?'

He was already pissed that, even though they had traced Thea's cell phone to the jail, Lauren and Frinz had told him not to send any men over there unless they gave him the all-clear. They were hunting the man who had killed his daughter, and they wanted to push him out.

Lauren looked from the tablet. 'There's no "we" here, Sheriff. Leave this to us.'

'The hell I will,' said Martin. 'This is my county. I have jurisdiction.'

Frinz joined them. He stood, hands in his pants pockets. 'This is a very dangerous individual, Sheriff. We have the resources to deal with him. You don't. It's as simple as that. There's no offense or disrespect intended.'

When he had mentioned resources, Frinz had made a point of shooting a glance towards the four heavily armed men who were now clambering back into the SUV.

'He killed my daughter,' Martin protested.

'Precisely,' said Lauren. 'That's what he does. He kills people. Without hesitation or remorse. That's why this is better left to us.'

She turned her back to him, the conversation over, at least as far as she was concerned. Martin stood there, knowing she was right. He couldn't risk issuing any of his men with orders that would place them in harm's way. Arlo was already dead. Mills had come close to being killed.

Lauren walked over to the black Escalade with Nick Frinz. 'You ready to do this?' Frinz asked her.

She was.

They climbed into the back seat. Frinz leaned over to take a peek at the images on the tablet computer. In a few minutes they would be running live, everything they did. The entire operation would be relayed back to a situation room in DC. Drones were in the skies. Their heat-sensing capabilities meant that anyone moving in a thirty-mile radius outside the jail would be picked up and tracked. They would also pick up any vehicle movements. The border patrol had been drafted in to establish roadblocks at five-mile intervals on the three roads that ran into and out of Kelsen. So far only half a dozen vehicles were out there and three of those were County Sheriff patrol units that had now been ordered to return to headquarters until further notice.

The last location they had for Thea Martinez's cell phone had been logged just under seven minutes previously. That was the call Tibor had made to Martin from the jail. Unless Tibor had developed the ability to fly, which they had covered anyway via air traffic control, he would have been picked up by now. Even though the cell phone was dead, he was in the jail with no place to go.

The only question that remained for Lauren was just how Tibor planned on making his extraction. Would he conceal himself among the other prisoners and make them drag him out, or would he surrender to the inevitable?

He had nowhere to go. If he did try to leave the jail, they had more than enough fire power in the skies to kill him. They wouldn't even need the kill team on the ground. It could be done by the press of a button from a T-shirt-clad operator in the drone control facility outside Vegas.

Tibor wouldn't know anything about it until it was already too late for him to take evasive action.

CHAPTER EIGHTY-SEVEN

Cesar gave the signal to a group of two dozen prisoners, made up of men, women and a couple of children, and they darted out into the darkness. With enough food and water for two days, this group wanted to return across the border. They would head east before tacking south.

Other groups had decided to press north and take their chances there. Some were heading west before moving south. Their route had been left up to them. A few were staying.

Byron looked to the heavens and said a silent prayer. He figured it couldn't hurt. It wasn't a prayer for him. It was for the others. He knew that the people he had once worked for, once killed for, were out there. He knew what they were capable of.

Cesar and some of the others were busy helping the next group prepare. He handed out clothes, water and food that had been requisitioned from the jail's kitchen to each person who passed.

Byron shuffled along at the back of the line. This was his group, at least for the first part of the journey. He planned on staying with them only as long as was necessary. His presence among them would bring extra danger to an already hazardous situation. He collected extra water and food as he reached Cesar. He figured that the least he could do was be a water-carrier. And he had the Glock.

Cesar put out his hand. 'Good luck.'

'You too,' said Byron.

Cesar was leaving with the final group. They would attempt to head north and west, to continue the journey that had been interrupted in Kelsen County. The irony hadn't escaped Byron. He was heading south into Mexico to escape America while Cesar, a Mexican, was trying to escape the land of his birth and settle in America.

Byron took one last look at Kelsen County Jail and followed the others outside. Minutes later they were swallowed by the vast, black emptiness of the desert at night.

A woman in her early twenties with a little boy of about four, called Hector, was bringing up the rear of Byron's group. They hadn't gone three hundred yards before the little boy was struggling to keep up with his mother. They would fall further and further back until they were separated from the others.

Byron paused next to them. He put down the supplies he was carrying, scooped the little boy up in his arms, hoisted him onto his shoulders, picked up his supplies and kept moving. Hector squealed with delight. His mother hushed him.

Byron covered the ground with long strides until they were nearer the front and he could lead the way for the others. High above them he could hear the signature whine of a drone. He said one final silent prayer, and kept walking with little Hector on his shoulders.

CHAPTER EIGHTY-EIGHT

The silver-grey Escalade screamed to a halt in the parking lot. The doors sprang open, the Escalade's engine still running, and the four-man kill team got out, rushing towards the jail entrance in a tight deployment pattern, rifles raised, fingers on triggers.

A few moments later, the two black SUVs arrived. Lauren climbed out with Frinz and waited for the all-clear signal from the kill team before rushing towards the administration building entrance. She pushed through the door and went inside.

It was empty.

Her cell phone chimed with an incoming message. She pulled it out of her jacket pocket, read the message and swore under her breath.

'What is it?' Frinz asked her.

She pulled the tablet computer from the bag slung over her shoulder, pulled up the live feed from the surveillance drones and tapped the screen so that Frinz could see a map of the area around the prison. Tiny clusters of green dots moved out from the prison in every direction. Each dot denoted a person. Lauren counted at least thirty clusters before she stopped counting.

She didn't have to explain to Frinz. He got it.

As she studied the screen, one cluster split, about two miles from where Lauren and Frinz were standing. One section, maybe six people, went west, the other east.

She and Frinz stood, transfixed. It was like watching cells divide under a microscope. Every few minutes a group would split into two. Every split made their task harder.

One of the kill team marched back down the corridor towards them. He was pushing a white man with red hair ahead of him.

'This guy says he has some intel on Tibor,' said the

kill-team member.

'Let's hear it,' said Frinz.

'I want to know what's in it for me,' said the red-headed inmate, who was sporting a couple of nasty bruises.

The kill-team member pressed the hit end of his rifle into the man's back. 'How about I don't blow your head off? How's that sound, Red?'

The inmate began to babble. His words rushed out in a semi-coherent torrent that gave no clue as to where Tibor was or might be.

Lauren's eyes fell back to the tablet screen as the green clusters moved further and further away in every direction, pushing the search area into a wider circle.

'We're going to need help,' she said to Frinz, who had already walked away from the inmate and was on a call, his cell phone pressed to his ear.

CHAPTER EIGHTY-NINE

The little boy on Byron's shoulders squealed in delight and jabbed a chubby little finger up at the sky. Byron didn't want to look. Certain air-to-land missiles left a blazing trail of light that a child might easily mistake for something magical and benign.

The others in the group slowed and stared up, grateful to take a break from walking, if only for a few seconds. Although Byron was carrying the slowest among them, he had set a blistering early pace that some of the older people had struggled to maintain.

They were two hours out from the jail and, by his crude estimate, they had covered half of the distance to the border. The rumble of the drones had fallen away only to return. He hadn't heard one in the past twenty minutes, but that wasn't to say they wouldn't be back.

Reluctantly, Byron stopped and scanned the sky where the others were looking. A falling star faded to a dim ember. Little Hector clapped his hands. Byron signaled for the others to take a drink and rest for a minute. They were due a break.

Ahead of them lay the same carpet of junipers and sequoia cactus that had accompanied them since they had left the jail. They moved, but the landscape stayed the same. It was an easy place to get lost. If you didn't have a direction and the ability to navigate, the desert would swallow you.

Byron was about ready to start everyone moving again when he saw the headlights. They started out as two pinpricks to the north and slowly grew bigger. He lifted the little boy from his shoulders, handed him to his mother and stepped away from the others. Signaling for them to stay where they were, he walked slowly towards the headlights, tacking right in a big loop so that he approached the vehicle side on, cutting out the glare of the lights and taking the others out of the potential line of fire. As he walked, he plucked the Glock from where he had shoved it into his belt.

Byron found himself looking at a double-cab, red pickup truck. Two men sat up front. Both were white, decked out in hunting gear, and looked to be in their fifties. The nearside passenger had his window down and was pointing a rifle at Byron's chest.

Despite the gun pointing at him, Byron felt an overwhelming sense of relief. If it had been a Border Patrol vehicle, he would have faced a dilemma. They would have wanted to take everyone into custody. Trying to explain that the party he was leading was heading south, into Mexico, wouldn't have cut any ice. Byron wouldn't walk into government custody voluntarily. By the same token he had no appetite for killing two Border Patrol agents. Despite his sympathy for the people he was with, he believed in the right of a nation to protect its territory and control those who entered as it saw fit.

These guys weren't Border Patrol. Their truck had no markings. They were almost certainly members of some unofficial local militia.

'Keep your hands in view,' the passenger barked at Byron.

Byron brought his hand round from behind his back, leaving his Glock where it was for now. He raised his hands, palms open and facing the truck. Normally he would have stayed silent, let them show their hand first, but under the circumstances, he figured that an American accent would carry more weight than anything else with these two guys.

'I'm taking them back over the border,' he said, with a nod.

The driver leaned over the steering-wheel and let out a cackle. 'Sure you are.'

Byron hadn't expected them to believe him. He sure as hell wouldn't have. In all likelihood they probably had him down as a *coyotaje* or *pollero*, someone who was paid by human traffickers to escort illegals across the border into the US. Just as no one had expected Byron to break back into the Kelsen County Jail, no one would reasonably expect people to be risking their lives to get back into Mexico from Texas.

'Tell you what,' said Byron, 'if you don't believe me, why don't you drive us to the border yourselves?'

It would be a squeeze but Byron reckoned that between the truck bed and the rear cab, they might just be able to squeeze everyone on.

The passenger turned to the guy behind the wheel. 'What you think, JD?'

The driver sucked air through his teeth. 'Only problem with that is that a few weeks later we'll be picking them up again. Illegals are like cockroaches. Doesn't matter how many you squish, they just keep coming.'

Byron took a step towards the truck. 'These folks aren't coming back. You have my word on that.'

'Your word?' The passenger snickered. 'What's that worth exactly?'

'I have five hundred bucks. You can have it all if you drive us down to the border,' said Byron, testing the waters to see if they'd be amenable to a bribe. He knew from past experience that even a slight hesitation would provide him with a valuable insight into what kind of people he was dealing with.

'Five hundred bucks?' the passenger said. 'Fuck you, asshole. You think we come out here every night, risking our lives, with the cartels and the illegals wanting to kill us, for money?'

Byron guessed not.

The passenger lowered the rifle and started to get out. 'The worst thing about this bullshit here is that you sound like you're a goddamn American,' he said, as Byron reached behind him, pulled the Glock, aimed it and fired.

CHAPTER NINETY

Byron's shot hit the passenger in the shoulder. The rifle wobbled in his hands, but he kept hold of it. The angle of the truck door meant he didn't have a clear shot.

Byron fired again, catching the passenger in the same place, high up on his shoulder. He didn't want to kill him, just get him to drop his weapon.

The driver was a different matter. He came up with a handgun, punched it out past his buddy and fired. The shot went wide. Byron didn't wait for him to squeeze off another round. He ran six feet so that he was level with the back of the truck, giving the driver no angle.

The passenger pushed out of the vehicle, barely able to raise the rifle. Byron hurtling towards him, catching him in a low tackle and taking him to the ground. Before the man could anything, Byron punched him hard in his already bloodied shoulder and followed up with two quick jabs to the face. This time he dropped the rifle. Byron reached over and picked it up.

The driver scrambled over to the passenger side. As he grabbed the edge of the door, gun in hand, Byron brought the passenger's rifle up, aiming it square at the driver's head.

The driver's and Byron's eyes met. A second passed. The driver would have to raise his gun before he pulled the trigger. By the time he did that Byron could have fired the rifle. Unless the rifle jammed, it wouldn't be much of a contest. The narrowest of margins was all Byron required.

Another second passed.

'Just take us to the border. That's all I want,' said Byron.

'What about him?' the driver said, with a nod to his wounded buddy.

'He'll keep until you can find a doctor. Now drop the

gun,' said Byron.

He could only pray that the driver would trust him. If he didn't, if he raised the gun, Byron would have to kill him. He didn't want to do that.

The driver let the gun drop onto the seat. Byron called to one of the men in the group. He came across and picked up the handgun. Byron escorted the driver out of the truck, the Glock never leaving him. When both men were clear, Byron searched the vehicle, coming up with two more rifles and another handgun. He kept one of the handguns and one of the rifles and tossed the rest into the brush where they couldn't do any harm.

There was a medical kit in the back of the cab. He staunched the worst of the bleeding from the man's shoulder wound and patched him up. A morphine lollipop usually carried by combat troops would give him some pain relief and keep him mentally checked out. He could ride in the rear cab with one of the Mexicans as a companion in case he got squirrely.

Byron's instructions were simple: 'If he gives you any trouble, punch him in the shoulder. But only if you have to.' The passenger shot Byron a dirty look and went back to sucking his morphine lollipop.

Byron helped the others onto the back of the truck. The night sky had cleared of clouds as he climbed into the cab next to the driver.

'Where to?' the driver asked Byron.

'I already told you.'

CHAPTER NINETY-ONE

Green dots pulsed slowly across Lauren's screen. A number in the centre of each dot tallied the people in that particular group of escapees. A sprinkling of red dots signified the teams of law-enforcement personnel deployed to intercept the escapees. The teams were a mix of Border Patrol, Texas Rangers, FBI, Kelsen County Sheriff, and Homeland Security.

A single black dot signified the kill team. They were moving between the various search teams as and when someone suspected that Tibor might be in the group they were chasing down.

As the green and red dots converged, signifying that a search team had caught up with a group of escapees, the dot turned brown, and Lauren awaited news of whether Tibor was among it or not. If he wasn't found the dot was removed from the screen, and they could focus their efforts on the other clusters of escapees who remained at large.

The current tally was seven. Seven groups of escapees, each consisting of between six and fifteen individuals. Three of the groups were moving south, two north-west, and two north-east.

The same live feed was being relayed to Washington. Nick leaned over to watch Lauren's screen. She angled it towards him so that he could get a better view.

'Looking good,' he said.

'You think?' said Lauren, unable to share his optimism.

'Every group we find that doesn't have Tibor in it reduces our odds. We started out with . . . what? A couple dozen groups. We're down to seven,' he said.

'But three of them are closing on the border,' said Lauren. 'Or maybe Tibor isn't with them. Maybe he found another way out.'

Nick studied her for a second. 'Chill.'

She shot him a withering look. 'How long have you been involved in this? A couple of months?'

Nick pointed at the screen as two more green and red dots converged. Lauren tapped a button on her headset, patching into the direct comms line for that search team.

'Only six to go. Unless they found him,' said Nick.

Lauren glared at him. 'They didn't. It's all women. One man, and he's five foot four.'

'So, the odds just improved even more.'

Lauren ignored him, switching her attention back to the screen.

'You want to know my theory?' said Nick.

'Sure,' said Lauren, knowing that he was going to share it anyway.

'I don't think you really want to find Tibor.'

'That's absurd.'

'Face it. The chase is way more fun than the kill,' said Nick.

He might have had a point. The Tibor mission had absorbed her far more than any other task she'd been given. Not only was he a worthy adversary for anyone, the more she had gotten to know about him, the more interesting he had become.

Tibor was, or had been, in many ways the operative Lauren could only dream of becoming. But she sure as hell wasn't going to concede any of that to Nick Frinz. Or anyone else for that matter. 'That's absurd,' she shot back, a little too tetchy to be convincing.

'Is it?'

Back on screen, another search team was closing in on one of the groups heading towards the border. Lauren watched the red dot pulse a little faster as it closed on its quarry. It matched her increasing heartbeat.

Nick was right. The chase did offer more than the kill.

CHAPTER NINETY-TWO

The red pickup truck bumped past a narrow slot canyon that was obscured by a ridge of rock, ready to snare the unwary. The last few miles, Byron had noticed the driver hunch up over the steering-wheel, peering as far he could towards the end of the headlights' reach.

'Don't usually come this far south,' the driver said. 'Too dangerous.'

'Cartels?' Byron wondered.

'Pretty much,' said the driver.

'Mind if I ask you something?'

The driver shot him a wry look. 'You're the one holding the gun.'

'How come you do this, risking your life?'

'If we don't do it, who will? Government sure as hell isn't that interested in protecting the border.'

Byron didn't argue. The man was telling the truth. The government managed the border. They didn't protect or guard it.

'So what's your story?' the driver said.

'I'm taking these people home.'

The driver shook his head. 'I got that part. What I'm asking is why.'

'Maybe the promised land wasn't everything they thought it would be,' said Byron.

'Shit. You kidding me?'

Byron thought about explaining conditions inside Kelsen County Jail, then thought better of it. 'You want to make up your mind?' he asked instead.

'What you mean?'

'Well, you don't want these people crossing over, but you get all pissy when they want to go home.'

'It's not the same thing,' said the driver.

Something caught Byron's attention. A sudden flicker of light in the night sky. He narrowed his eyes.

'Kill the headlights,' he ordered the driver.

'You miss that canyon I had to drive round back there? You fall into one of those things, you ain't getting back out.'

Byron hadn't missed it. But he still needed the headlights off so he could confirm that he was right about what he thought he'd just seen.

'Kill them,' he said, raising the barrel of the Glock a fraction and dropping his finger to the trigger.

The driver reached down, twisted the stalk. The lights died.

'Shit,' Byron muttered.

'What is it?'

'Nothing,' said Byron. 'You can put the lights back on.'

'What was it?' the driver asked.

'Let's just say that our number-one problem right now isn't any cartel foot soldiers.'

'*Our* problem?'

Byron stared at him. What he'd just seen in the sky above them wasn't about to discriminate between him, an illegal immigrant, a militia man or anyone else. It would kill everyone in the truck. Instantly. There would be nothing left but a pile of blackened ash.

CHAPTER NINETY-THREE

The black Escalade raced down the highway, dash-mounted blue lights clearing out any forward traffic. Lauren was tucked into the back seat, next to Nick Frinz, her eyes glued to a live feed from a Harop 'suicide' drone that had located a red pickup truck heading across open ground about three miles shy of the border. A smaller surveillance drone, with better visual capability, also circled the area, as they tried to gather a positive ID.

All the other groups of escapees had been apprehended. If this wasn't Tibor, he'd evaded them.

Lauren tapped on an incoming email from the NSA and opened an enhanced screen grab from the surveillance feed. It showed the man in the front passenger seat of the truck. She could hear an NSA data analyst on the conference call, updating everyone on the images he was sending through.

'Front passenger is Tibor,' said the analyst.

'How sure are we?' The question came from someone sitting in a conference room near Georgetown.

'Facial analysis gives us a hundred per cent match. Or as close as we can get to a hundred per cent.'

A hundred per cent match. No margin of error. It was Tibor.

A positive ID and the Harop drone in the sky above, all ready to go, meant only one outcome. Lauren tapped the screen again and checked the satellite map. The red pickup was just under two miles from the border.

Two miles, Lauren thought. It was the very definition of a day late, and a dollar short. Tibor would know that, with the current political sensitivity about the area, the US government was unlikely to deploy a drone above Mexican soil. It carried way too much political risk.

If he got into Mexico they would try to keep tabs on him and use a lower-tech method. A single shot to the back of his head while he was wandering down a street in Tijuana could have been anyone. A kamikaze drone containing a warhead with fifteen kilograms of high explosive was an option open only to a government. Not even the cartels had access to that kind of hardware.

A lone assassin was deniable. People got shot for no special reason all the time, especially somewhere like Mexico. Mistaken identity. A mugging gone wrong. Someone with mental-health issues. A drug deal that had soured. There could be any number of explanations. A suicide drone didn't offer any beyond the obvious one. Someone wanted Tibor dead so bad they were prepared to spend several million dollars and kill a dozen civilians in the process. Not even the cartels were prepared to risk that kind of exposure or spend that kind of money to take out one man.

A suicide drone used over US soil was still one hell of a risk. It would need to remain covert. But that could be achieved only if you had jurisdiction over the area where it was dropped.

'Do we know who the driver is?' Lauren asked the analyst.

Silence followed. Next to her, Frinz shot her a look of sheer disbelief. It was a question that had been avoided for a reason. If the drone was deployed and they killed someone they shouldn't, they could claim ignorance. It would look sloppy, but sloppy held up better than knowingly taking out an innocent American civilian as part of the overall collateral damage.

The next person to speak was from the operational command room. 'Clock's ticking here. Another few minutes and we have a new set of protocols to navigate. We don't have executive authorization to conduct this particular operation once Tibor moves beyond our territory.'

'Do you want me to go ahead with an identification? I have the name of the person the vehicle is licensed to in front of me now,' said the analyst.

Nick threw up his hands in a what-the-hell gesture directed at Lauren. Now they had to get the name. Otherwise the question would be why no one had asked for the likely identity of the driver when it was at their fingertips.

'Go ahead,' came the instruction from the command room.

'Owner of the vehicle is a Mr Harris Troy. That name shows as the leader of a local militia who patrol the border.'

For a few seconds no one said anything. Finally, a voice from the command room said, 'Do we have any non-UAV termination options?'

'UAV' was shorthand for a drone.

Nick keyed the mic on his headset so he could speak to the command center. 'The original kill team is heading for the location now.'

CHAPTER NINETY-FOUR

The pickup truck came to a stop. Through the gloom Byron could see a ragged chain-link fence and beyond that the river, silver-black in the moonlight.

The driver pointed towards a section of the fence about fifty yards to the west of where he had stopped the truck. 'There's a hole just there. We noticed it last week. Soon as it gets repaired, the traffickers send a crew out to open it up again.'

'Thanks for the ride,' said Byron.

'Like I had a choice.'

Byron opened the passenger door and got out. He walked to the back of the pickup truck and began to help people down. They stood for a moment, shaking the cramp out of their limbs. As soon as everyone was off the vehicle, Byron banged on the side with his hand.

The pickup reversed, turned in a wide loop and was gone. A few seconds later the only trace left of it was the plume of dust kicked up by its tires as the driver sped away, eager to get his injured buddy to a hospital.

Byron began to hustle the others towards the gap in the fence. He grabbed the part where it had been cut and peeled it back so that they could climb through without snagging their clothing. The last person was climbing through when he heard an engine behind them. He turned.

Headlights swept across the fence, catching him in their glare. He held up his hand, trying to shield his eyes. He could make out the outline of a large silver-grey SUV.

All four of the SUV's doors popped open. Two men spilled from the rear, immediately peeling off in opposite directions. They ran in a low crouch, rifles held across their chests, and disappearing into the shadows, flanking him on either side.

The driver and passenger got out, crouching low behind the doors, guns drawn. The last thing Byron saw was the muzzle flash from the driver as he dove headlong through the gap in the fence.

All around him, people screamed in the dark as more rounds flew overhead. Byron belly-crawled forward on his elbows and knees. Ahead was a thick grove of cottonwood trees.

Cottonwoods could mean only one thing.

A river.

CHAPTER NINETY-FIVE

Lauren pressed two fingers against her earpiece, straining to hear what they were saying over the staccato beat of gunfire. A split-screen showed four live feeds from the body cameras clipped onto the vests of the four kill-team members as they deployed from their vehicle.

The leader was seeking permission to go beyond the fence. He wasn't getting an immediate answer and his growing frustration was evident as he let loose a torrent of invective over his headset. 'Do we have permission to continue pursuit or not?'

Byron made the grove of cottonwood trees, and pushed up onto his feet. The gunfire had stopped, bathing the area in an uneasy silence. He blinked, forcing his eyes to adjust to the gloom. He could hear the rush of the river behind him, the noise signaling a fast-moving current.

Byron cursed his own stupidity. Dropping them at this crossing point, where the river was high, and the current powerful had been the pickup driver's act of petty revenge.

To his left, he could hear someone trying to quieten a child's cries. It sounded like the little boy he had carried on his back.

The gunfire could start again at any moment. Byron didn't want to see a child, or anyone else, shot because he was hiding with them.

There was only one thing for it. He stepped out from behind the trunk of the cottonwood tree he'd been standing behind and took off, sprinting a hundred yards as fast as he could. Gasping for breath, he took cover behind another cottonwood.

He filled his lungs, and made another sprint, staying parallel to the fence. When he was confident he was clear of the others hiding in the grove, he pulled his Glock and fired a single shot back towards the SUV, which was still parked, headlights on, on the other side of the fence.

Lauren heard the single gunshot echo from the other side of the fence as the Escalade she and Frinz were traveling in came to a standstill five hundred yards from where the kill-team vehicle had stopped. The team leader was shouting into his mic, seeking fresh permission to keep going. Now he had a trump card.

'We just took fire.'

That was all operational command back in DC needed to hear. The word came down a few seconds later.

'Permission granted to continue pursuit.'

A second later a fresh barrage of gunfire poured towards the fence in the direction of the single shot that had been fired from the Mexican side, and the four-man kill team were on the move, taking turns to low-run towards the fence in pairs. One man ran while his buddy provided covering fire and then they switched.

Byron pushed deeper into the grove of cottonwoods, moving away from the others, trying to get as much distance from them as he could. It would be very easy for a round to go astray and hit one of them if he stayed too close.

He scrambled through dense riverbank undergrowth. Branches whipped across his chest and face. The toe of his right boot caught on a root. He lost his balance and fell forward, banging his knee on the ground. He took a second to catch his breath, then got back to his feet.

A round slammed into a tree trunk a few feet to his

left. He ran forward, towards the sound of the river. More rounds poured in behind him, tearing up the ground. He felt one punch just past his ear, close enough that he felt the slipstream.

Byron kept his head down and his legs pumping. He pushed through a final thicket of branches and there ahead of him was the bank that led down to the Rio Grande.

The kill-team leader reached down to his chest and keyed the radio clipped to his vest. 'I lost him.'

He waited for the others to come back with better news. None of them did. He ordered one man to retreat towards the fence in case Tibor doubled back. He and the other two would push out in either direction down the river and wait for a location from the UAVs that were still in the sky. Between them they would form a triangle that they could gradually narrow until Tibor had nowhere to go but the river.

This time a river wasn't going to save him. Not like it had back in New York. If he tried to cross this one, they would pick him off with ease.

CHAPTER NINETY-SIX

Terrified by the sound of gunfire, Hector closed his eyes and clung to his mother as tightly as he could. She sang softly to him and stroked his hair. When the loud bangs stopped, he opened them again to see a river. Some of the others were already scrambling down the bank and into the water. One of them, a man, stood waist-deep in it, and beckoned Hector and his mother towards him.

Hector didn't want to go into the water. It scared him. But the loud bangs coming from the trees behind them seemed to be scaring the others even more. The man standing in the river waded slowly back towards the bank, and put out his hand as Hector's mother struggled down with him still clinging to her.

His mother sang a lullaby to him as she stepped down into the cold water. She told him to keep hold of her, no matter what happened. Not to let go, no matter what. He closed his eyes and shivered as the water rose around them.

Byron watched from behind a cottonwood tree as one of the four men who had breached the fence picked his way slowly through the grove towards him. Slowly he raised the Glock. His finger fell to the trigger as he took aim, the hunted turned hunter.

From the river, Byron heard a woman screaming. Reflex caused him to turn his head a fraction. The man in his sights dove for the ground. Byron dropped. He punched the Glock out, took aim and fired a warning shot above the man's head.

Before the man tracking him could return fire, Byron

stood up again, pivoted and ran back towards the river as the woman's screams grew louder and more persistent. A three-round burst of gunfire sprayed overhead as he cleared the trees and scanned the surface of the water.

The woman's screams were louder. He could see people in the water. Some were wading. Others had fallen, pushed over by the rushing current, and were being carried downstream into deeper water.

The air around Byron lit up with fresh fire. Tracer rounds swept in from behind him and off to one side. He hunkered down, taking cover as best he could. As the moonlight slashed across the blue-black water, he could see the screaming woman. She was flailing wildly with one arm. The other was folded around a child. She disappeared under the surface only to reappear a moment later as the river threatened to tear the child from her. She tried to strike out with her free arm, to swim towards the bank, but it was a futile effort. There were no more screams as she went under again.

Nick Frinz grabbed Lauren's sleeve as she opened the door of the Escalade. She wrenched herself away, and ran towards the fence. He called after her. She kept running. She found the gap Byron and the others had used, peeled back the wire, cutting the palm of her hand on a jagged edge, and dove through, landing face first on the ground. She got to her feet and ran towards the sound of the gunfire. Through her earpiece she could hear someone at the command center ordering her to stop and return to the vehicle. Reaching up, she tore out her earpiece, snapping the wire, and threw it away.

The Glock lay abandoned on the riverbank. Byron

powered through the water, arms tearing ahead of him, driving him forward, legs scissoring frantically, as he struck out for the spot where the little boy and his mother had got into difficulties. He choked as he caught a mouthful of river water. He spat out what he could and looked around, treading water as he caught his breath.

On the far bank he could see the people who had made it. He shouted to them, 'Where are they? You see them?'

When he didn't get a reply, he struck out again on his own, moving with the current, heading downriver. Every twenty yards he would stop and scan the surface. Still no sign of them.

Every second that ticked by felt like an hour. He could no longer see anyone on either bank. As far as he knew, there was only him and the Rio Grande.

He pushed the water with one hand, turning slowly a full 360 degrees. He caught a glimpse of yellow.

Yellow? What could be that color and floating on the surface?

The answer came to him.

He could see a small shape floating about fifty yards downstream. The flash of yellow was something only Byron could see. Yellow equalled fear.

Byron reached Hector with a series of powerful strokes. He grabbed him, turned onto his back and, with his hand under the child's chin, kicked towards the far bank. The little boy's eyes were shut. His face was blue with cold, his body limp and seemingly lifeless.

Pushing away any thought that he might already be dead, Byron focused on reaching the bank. There was no sign of the boy's mother. Byron already feared the worst. She wouldn't have left her son to fend for himself in the river.

Finally, Byron made the riverbank on the Mexican side. He hauled Hector out of the water, carried him up the muddy slope and laid him on the ground. 'Stay with me,' he said, opening the little mouth and checking for an obstruction.

Lauren stood with two members of the kill team on the opposite side of the river. Using one of the team's night scopes, she watched Tibor, bent over the little boy. The boy's legs kicked out suddenly. He was alive. Tibor had spent the past two minutes administering the kiss of life, at first, it had seemed, with no results. But he had kept at it regardless.

She watched as he helped the child sit up. Next to Lauren, the leader of the kill team spoke. 'Well?' he asked.

He was asking whether he should take the shot or not. Lauren no longer knew what the answer should be. Tibor was supposed to be a killing machine, a creature devoid of feeling whose only concern was his own survival. She watched through the scope as Tibor picked up the child, slung him over his shoulder and began to walk away from the river.

Next to her, the kill-team leader lowered his rifle. 'He has the kid. It's too close. I had him too.'

Byron could almost feel the guns trained on his back as he kept walking. From the shadows of the grove the other men, women and children joined him. In less than five hundred yards they would reach a road used by the Mexican authorities to patrol their side.

There was already a Mexican federal authority chopper overhead. Its spotlight slashed the ground in front of them before circling back to catch them in a pool of light.

Next to his ear, Byron heard Hector ask for his mother. Byron held him a little tighter. 'It's gonna be okay,' he told him.

EPILOGUE

Seven months later

Fidelius Kelsen pulled his Mercedes S-Series into a spot at the back of the country club. For these late-night meetings, they had taken to using an entrance that led through the kitchen and out into the main members' dining room. His brother Billy's Lexus was already there, which surprised him. Billy was rarely the first person at any event. Among the family, he was notorious for being late. Fidelius had always figured it was a passive-aggressive show of power from his being a judge that had carried over into his regular life. He usually kept people waiting for no other reason than that he could.

Getting out of his car, Fidelius took a moment to reflect on how far they had come. Even with a small battalion of high-priced lawyers, and a lot of even higher-priced favors called in, it was a minor miracle that he was a free man. There were plenty of civil lawsuits to come, but the threat of criminal conviction and jail time seemed to have receded. It had been the fight of his life, but he had come through it, as he always did. Survival gave him no small measure of satisfaction.

He stepped past a metal dumpster full of kitchen waste and pulled open the side door. He walked down a narrow service corridor and emerged into the club's kitchen. When called upon, the club's chef could produce a six-course meal for over five hundred guests and the kitchen's size reflected that. Fidelius skirted a wheeled laundry basket full of staff uniforms, his head down, his mind on what needed to be arranged at this meeting. There were so many seemingly minor details to contend with that it was hard to keep track and they avoided writing anything down, even a simple note on the back of a cocktail napkin.

Looking up, he stopped dead in his tracks. It took him a second to process what was ahead of him. Billy was lying on top of one of the large kitchen ranges. His hands and feet were bound and, apart from a pair of white briefs, he was naked. His hair was soaking wet.

A cooking pan rattled and a man stepped out of from behind a metal storage shelf. He had a white kitchen towel in one hand and a bucket of water in the other.

Fidelius recognized him immediately. It was Tibor.

Tibor ignored Fidelius. He walked to where he had staked out Judge William Kelsen on the range, and placed the soaking wet towel over his mouth and nose. He lifted the bucket of water. Billy thrashed around as Tibor slowly poured the water onto the towel.

Billy gagged and choked, screamed and pleaded for Tibor to stop. He twisted his neck from one side to the other, but there was no escaping the water. Tibor made sure of that.

Finally, Tibor stopped. He placed the bucket on the floor and turned towards Fidelius. 'Your brother has already spilled his guts,' said Tibor. 'This last bucket was just for demonstration purposes. To give you a little insight into what the next few hours might hold for you.'

Fidelius took a step to one side. There was a wooden knife block on a counter next to him. He could easily grab one of the knives before Tibor could stop him. He placed his hand on the counter. 'Why did you come back?' he asked.

'Unfinished business,' said Tibor.

Fidelius inched his hand along the counter towards the knives. Tibor didn't seem to notice.

'You and Billy killed Thea.'

Fidelius wasn't about to admit it. Not now. Not ever. 'I think you're mistaken,' he said to Tibor. 'And if my brother said we did, it's hardly a surprise.'

'It doesn't really matter what I do or don't believe,' Tibor replied.

Billy was gurgling and groaning. He twisted his neck, staring wild-eyed at his brother. He was trying to say something, but Fidelius couldn't make out the words through all the coughing and choking. He took a step along the counter so that his hand was behind his back. His fingers felt for the handle of the biggest knife. His hand closed around it. He eased it gently from the block.

A hand grasped his wrist and twisted it. The knife clattered onto the tiled floor. Fidelius spun round. Sheriff Martin was standing on the other side of the counter, still holding Fidelius's wrist. He let go without saying anything. He didn't need to speak. The way he was staring at Fidelius told its own story.

'You don't believe this crank, John, do you?' Fidelius said to him, with a nod towards Tibor.

Sheriff Martin plucked one of the smaller knives from the same block. He tested its sharpness with his thumb. 'I didn't. Not at first. But why would a man come back here to tell me he didn't kill my daughter if he'd done it?'

Fidelius made a lunge for one of the knives. Sheriff Martin was faster. He leaned over, raised his arm and stabbed the smaller knife through Fidelius's hand, skewering it and pinning it to the wooden block. Fidelius screamed.

'Billy's told us everything already,' said Sheriff Martin. 'He had details that only someone who was there when Thea died would know.'

'Bath time's over, Billy,' said Tibor.

Fidelius watched as Tibor began to free Billy from the kitchen range. He helped him back to his feet.

Sheriff Martin grabbed the knife handle and yanked the blade. Fidelius yelped. He clutched his hand as blood poured from the wound. Billy was bundled into a ball on the floor, his knees up at his chest.

Tibor walked towards Fidelius, who backed away, only to run into Sheriff Martin. He struggled as they dragged him towards the kitchen range, kicking and screaming.

His screams grew louder as, between them, Tibor and the sheriff lifted him onto the range, still fully clothed, and staked him out on top of it.

'John!' Fidelius screamed. 'Don't do this. Please. I'll give you anything.'

Fidelius heard the click of the gas burners being turned on.

As the first ignited, Sheriff Martin asked, 'Can you give me my daughter back?'

There was another click. The second burner caught. The pain was beyond anything Fidelius had ever experienced. He kept screaming and pleading as, one after another, the burners ignited and his clothes began to melt into his skin.

Byron walked across the parking lot. The sickly sweet smell of burning flesh still hung in the air. He had no idea how Sheriff Martin was going to explain what had happened to the Kelsen brothers. They hadn't discussed it.

The answer came as Byron reached the car Sheriff Martin had given him. It was one of many confiscated over the past few years by the Sheriff's Department. What Sheriff Martin did next took the form of a single gunshot that was followed by silence. Byron started to turn back, then decided against it. He already knew what he'd find.

Without his daughter, Sheriff Martin didn't want to go on. He had already told Byron as much. But before he departed the earth, he had wanted the Kelsen brothers to experience a little of his torment. With that done, he had made good on the final part of his plan and taken his own life.

Byron climbed into the driver's seat, turned on the engine, and pulled out of the parking lot. Fifteen minutes later, he reached the outskirts of Kelsen County. Glancing in his rearview mirror, he saw a sign welcoming visitors. He stepped a little harder on the gas. The car lurched forward. A few seconds later the road sign was nothing but a dot as the road opened up in front of him.

Made in the USA
San Bernardino, CA
29 September 2017